A Man Made of Smoke

For
HARRY
my brother

STANLEY MIDDLETON

A Man
Made of Smoke

HUTCHINSON OF LONDON

HUTCHINSON & CO (*Publishers*) **LTD**
3 Fitzroy Square, London W1

London Melbourne Sydney Auckland
Wellington Johannesburg Cape Town
and agencies throughout the world

First published May 1973
Second impression June 1973

© Stanley Middleton 1973

Printed in Great Britain by litho on antique wove paper
by Stellar Press, Hatfield, Herts. and bound
by Wm. Brendon, Tiptree, Essex

ISBN 0 09 115060 4 (cased)
0 09 115061 2 (paper)

I

'It's not far now.'

The two men, stepping from the bus, shouldered a way into the street. The younger, nearly six inches taller, walked deferentially behind, making no reply to his companion's remark. Above them the sky was dabbed with pink clouds, and the February weather seemed exceptionally mild.

They turned right off the main road, uphill, where a group of children scattered to make room for them.

'Home.'

Again the older man spoke, as he held back the iron gate to the four yards of front garden, dwarfed by an ash tree tall as the three-storeyed terrace. They climbed two red steps and into the passage.

'By,' said the young man, 'it's warm in here.'

They moved into the scullery where the older man switched a light on for the first time. He tapped a white central-heating boiler.

'That's the fellow,' he said, 'that's responsible.'

The room was large, with its unplastered bricks painted pale green. Two shelves ran the length of the wall away from the window. The glass-fronted cupboards, the sink unit, the washing-machine all shone, squared up, immaculately straight.

'First job, the boiler.' The host had removed his coat and trilby hat, hung them on the other side of the cellar door. 'Take one of those stools out, and sit yourself down.'

The young man, smiling nervously, poked fingers into

5

his rough bob of hair before he pulled out one of two scarlet-topped stools from under a matching table, and squatted without removing his anorak.

'Nice place here,' he said, when the other returned with a hod of coke. His companion did not answer as he emptied the ash-can, re-stoked, washed his hands, and filled the kettle.

'Nice place, Jack,' the other said again almost aggressively.

'I look after it.'

Jack Riley smoothed the streaks of hair over his bald head. At forty-five his young face contradicted the hairless scalp and its greying fringe, while his shoulders were held stiffly back, as if years with F.S.M.O. had permanently braced them to attention. Skilfully he lowered the drying-rack, removed washing which he stacked neatly outside at the foot of the stairs.

'Never leave that up when we fry,' he said.

There was nothing military about the voice, which issued softly, like the sound of tissue paper and comb.

'Can I do anything?' the younger asked.

'Get your coat off, and lay the table. Knives and forks in the drawer above your knees.'

The two worked. Suddenly Riley said to the youngster, 'Read the headlines.' He pointed at the evening paper he'd picked up in the passage.

' "Murder Hunt in City".' The youth fumbled in embarrassment at the unaccustomed chore. Frozen chips into the pan.

'Couldn't hear you,' Riley said. 'Try again.'

' "Murder Hunt in City". Shall I read any more?'

'Please yourself.'

Stumbling, the boy read into the first column, while the other stood at the stove.

'Somewhere up your way, isn't it, Frank?'

'Not too far.'

'Don't know 'em, d'you?'

6

'No. But it in't very likely. There's flats an' all sorts. You don't know who lives there.'

Francis Oxford was nineteen, but certain enough of himself. He had no compunction about allowing the older man to cook the meal while he sat with the newspaper in front of him, reading indiscriminately, 'Australia Declare in Test', or 'Local Mother's Once-in-a-Lifetime Meeting'. He had no notion whether Riley listened.

They set about their food, did not talk.

At the end, Riley, wiping his plate with a piece of bread, began to issue instructions.

'You'll have to make your mind up,' he said, softly.

'I've done that.'

'Undo it, then. You've had a row with your parents, but that's not the end of the world.'

'They wouldn't care if I'd strangled the Queen.'

'So you think.'

Oxford shrugged, or shuddered.

He and Riley worked in the same office, and though they were, with the rest, on Christian-name terms, hardly knew each other. At the same table in the canteen during the lunch hour by chance, Riley had made some jocular allusion to the youngster's down-in-the mouth air.

'Crossed in love again?'

They were alone together so that it was easy for Oxford to spill his tale. They were not overheard. But why he had begun to a man twenty-odd, thirty years his senior eluded him yet. If their plates had been in different places on the table, or another number on the radio, or one of the typists grinning at or ignoring him, he'd have said nothing.

Riley listened, concentrating on his plate.

It appeared that the boy and his old man had quarrelled the evening before. While his father had noisily scoffed his tea, Francis and his mother had burst out laughing at some anecdote. This was unusual. The television set was off, and Mrs. Oxford had precious little skill or practice as a raconteuse. But as the pair of them giggled, the father, one hand plying his fork, the other crushing his *Evening Post* in front of him, had ordered them to make less noise. This, in itself, was almost habit.

'Why should we?' Francis had asked.

'Because I bloody well tell you to.' Neither fork nor newspaper was abandoned; mastication continued.

'I shall laugh if I like.'

'Not in my house you wain't.'

Mrs. Oxford hurried from the room, the trouble.

'Who says so?' Frank.

'I do.' Both stood, perhaps three, four yards apart. Father approached. 'If you don't like it, you can clear out.'

'I will, then.'

They stood, nose to nose, the son taller, his head large with its busby of hair. Describing it, then, the boy saw it as comical. He felt fear, he'd not forgotten his father's hidings, but he had not moved, had defied, challenged the old man. It had not lasted long. Father had resumed his place at the table, shaken his newspaper into upright submission and pronounced, without heat:

'And you can't go soon enough for me.'

Riley had drummed with his stubby fingers, pulled his lips in thin before he'd inquired:

'What are you going to do, then?'

The lad's face wrinkled in a tiny passion of dismay.

'I shall have to creep back. Nowhere else to go. But I wish there was. I'd like to show that loud mouth.'

'You don't like your father?'

'Does anybody?' The ambiguous question was delivered again with a pout of disgust, more suitable to a schoolgirl. 'You haven't got a spare room, have you?'

'I might.'

That answer spoke caution, promised nothing, opened negotiation.

They had separated, but at three o'clock, when Riley was suddenly, happily busy, Oxford put a cup of tea on his desk, and said:

8

'Can I come home with you tonight, then?'

'If you want.'

Riley had no wish to protract the conversation, but looked up for a minute from the pile of labels he was addressing. The room was large, too high, unplastered with a smooth-wet mustard paint on the bricks, disfigured by wedge-shaped patches of dirt over the radiators. It reminded one of a prison or a barracks. The other clerks were smiling as they sipped their saucerless cups of tea, working on, all content, it appeared, with this elementary comfort and five o'clock in sight. At the far end, Addison, the chief cashier, stood at the door of his glass-paned cubby-hole and waved to Riley, a movement of the hand that finished in a quasi-military salute.

Riley covered his typewriter at the end of the afternoon, clocked out with the rest, and had nearly forgotten Oxford until he presented himself in his shabby anorak with its fur-trimmed hood.

'All right?' the lad said.

'As long as you let your mother know.'

'You're not on the phone?'

'No. You'll have to trot round.'

They walked away, neither pleased.

The boy knew that he'd cast up a mountain, that his father had probably forgotten their exchange, that his bedroom at home was comfortable, with its record-player and his painting-by-numbers sets. He'd barely said a hundred words to Riley since he started at Erskine and Willetson's twelve months back. This old, brown-faced, bald, saturnine chap had spoken pleasantly, even offered a tip or two, but was regarded, it soon appeared, with suspicion by the younger men.

'What's his trouble?' Oxford asked Smedley, a fellow-clerk.

'Bum.'

'Eh?'

'He's a queer.'

'I tell you this,' Oxford said. 'He's been married. Saw his records.'

'So had Oscar Wilde.'

'He don't look it,' Oxford argued. The subject intrigued.

'Well, don't bend down to tie your shoe-lace when he's about,' Smedley grimaced. 'Or else it'll be too late to save your virtue.'

The others laughed, straining, grimacing.

'I wear casuals,' he said. The rest stopped the row as if he'd spoken out of turn.

On the bus they'd hardly budged, and now they sat in this warm kitchen, with the shining scissors, sieves, cooking utensils on the wall, staring at one another. Riley's face, which seemed so smooth at a distance, had a heavy growth of beard; the lines by his mouth were deep, his jowl slightly flabby. He appeared older, less solid, more human than at work, and more cunning.

'We'll wash up, then.'

They did so.

'Into the dining room.'

Riley pulled the curtains, took down a magazine, manhandled his chair closer to the modern gas fire.

'One of the drawbacks of this place,' he waved Oxford towards couch or twin-chair, 'is that there's no telly.'

'Never look at it.'

'I doubt that.'

The sentence dropped almost spectacularly; flat denial in unusual mode, so that the youth looked scared out of his wits, as at a guarded offer of perversion. Squinting, blowing, he sat down, jamming his back into the cushions, to defend himself perhaps.

'They won't be worrying at home?'

'My mother will. She'll ha' cooked something up, and she hates waste. That's the only thing that makes her get on at my dad.'

'She'll be doing just that?'

Oxford consulted his ostentatious wrist watch.

'I expect so. She'll natter at him. And he'll chunter and swear until he gets washed and changed for the pub.'

As they talked, Oxford became uneasier. His companion probed, like a boss, as if it mattered what the mother would think or say. Riley had now lit a pipe with a silver band at the stem's end, to fill the room with slowly shredding smoke. Between puffs his slow catechism continued. Soon he'd want to see a birth certificate or know dates of inoculations or vaccination. The room was not well lighted, but two pink shells glowed over the mantelpiece, like advertisements for petrol. The boy wriggled uncomfortably, observed from the other's heavy-lidded eyes, looked about for reading-matter, tried to hear the radio which muttered stock-exchange prices.

In the end, Riley knocked his pipe out into an ashtray in the hearth, drew his shoulders back to pronounce.

'You've had a meal here. And welcome. You've had a bit of your own back. If I was you, I'd wait until his lordship's gone out, then nip back and make it up with your mam.'

'I don't know.' Oxford didn't want to give in so easily.

'You wouldn't fancy it here. I live like an old maid.'

'They reckon you're an old soldier.'

'That's that lippy sod Smedley; he's been talking. And other things. I know him. He's told you I'm a queer, hasn't he?'

'Not exactly.'

'One day that young fellow's going to find himself dangling out of the window by his braces.' The voice sounded flat, flatulent; no jokes about.

2

Jack Riley dusted his furniture.

Half an hour earlier he'd despatched young Oxford to talk to his mother, to stay at home or not as he liked. The lanky boy, six foot two, had hesitated and stuttered so that the older man had practically to push him into his coat and out of the door.

'You can come back if you want. As long as you see your mam first.'

Now, on his own, tired, he began on the slow work he loved, polishing wood until it shone darkly with a heavy warm sheen, reflecting book-jackets, bibelots, black ash-trays.

Eighteen months ago Riley had retired from the army with the rank of sergeant after twenty-five years' service. He and his wife had decided that they'd live in Beechnall, his birth-town, where one of his former officers had offered him a place in the family firm. The Rileys had bought two terraced houses, large, late Victorian homes, and his wife had settled in nearly a year before his discharge. She collected the rent from one, and thoroughly decorated her own. Whenever he was off-duty her husband had driven back, given her a hand, put up shelves, built-in cupboards, re-pointed the front of the house, and re-painted the outside after he'd replaced all the guttering. He did not entirely trust his wife. She was capable, clean, energetic, but eccentric. For example, she'd struck up a friendship with the next-door neighbour, a Mrs. Scotten, a slut if he'd ever seen one. The women went to the cinema together, leaving the Scotten brats to look after themselves, and in the end they'd taken jobs together in a nearby factory.

'There's no need for it,' he'd argued that week-end. His wife never wrote when she could give the message orally inside the next six months.

'I know that.' She had money of her own. 'It's the company.'

'That Scotten woman.'

'You've nothing against her, Jack, and you know it.'

Both enjoyed the mild argument, seemed in agreement about the neighbour's dubious character, but they were certain enough of their own moral probity to think themselves safe from contamination.

Eight months later while he was on his final leave his wife died. They were walking about the shops in town when she'd collapsed. Rushed to hospital, she'd begun to recover, when a sudden relapse widowed him after only a few hours. He had not realised that Rachael had been under medical treatment for her heart; she had said nothing. Her death seemed typically wayward; this mousy unassertive woman could be relied on to surprise him two or three times a year. Now, he was lost, staring at the spick-and-span house where he'd expected the pair of them to enjoy the next three decades together. Tributes poured in from the factory, the street; Rachael's few relatives appeared, and the funeral was decent.

He'd pushed a note through Mrs. Scotten's letter box, explaining that he wanted to get rid of his wife's clothes and shoes. The neighbour appeared, a buxom woman, still in her twenties, with dyed hair, uncertain how to hold her face before the bereaved husband. No, the clothes wouldn't fit her, but the shoes would. Missis had lent her a pair once before. She could get rid of the rest for him. Didn't want money? That wasn't right.

As they talked, she'd gripped his arm unexpectedly.

She stood powerful, but womanly, in a mild smell of

sweat. His arm circled her waist and they kissed with a flat-faced violence. The action surprised him, as her strength did, her insouciance. When she stepped back, her big mouth loose, her hair bushily comical, she shoved her hands up her skirts to snatch off her laddered tights before she'd dragged him down to the sofa.

Dazed and delighted, he mounted her, lay exhausted across her white legs.

At a call from the yard that he'd not heard, she ordered him off, stood, smoothing her ruffled skirt, slipping tide-marked feet into disgraceful shoes. She screwed the tights together in one hand.

'It's our Alison,' she said. 'The baker's come, or summat.'

She left, not looking behind, while he stood abandoned, hoisting his trousers. The whole business, discussion and all, had not taken more than a quarter of an hour. He had the impression that to her the episode had been to her as casual as an unexpected packet of chips. He did not know her Christian name, had spoken only twice to her husband, and here he lay convalescing from her sex. Even now he could hear her calling outside, warning some child to get off that bleddy wall or she'd murder him. Riley, groping out to the kitchen for the teapot, felt murdered himself.

His wife's death had tricked him, removed stability, and now this white-thighed Venus had upended him on his own hearthrug. A cautious man, he clawed at ambiguities. He hated what he'd let himself in for by that ten-minute adultery, and he feared as he shook with pleasure. The woman would come pushing back, his mistress, filthing his house with her raucous voice and her warm body and her discarded underclothes. Riley trembled at the sink.

It did not happen.

Mrs. Scotten appeared modestly the next evening with her husband, a thin, confident man who kept his hands bunched in the bulging pockets of his cardigan. In a reedy voice he'd outlined his plan for selling the clothes and had

14

told Riley not to act daft when he said he did not want money.

'Nobody's got too much o' that these days,' he pronounced.

'You have it, then. You're going to all this trouble.'

'That's not trouble.'

Riley looked at Mrs. Scotten's solidity beside her husband's pale, husk-fed energy. She stood with those white legs slightly parted, her blue dress shaping dark between her thighs, eyes darkly slight, her expression neutral, unconcerned.

'You're doing me a favour.'

Scotten tugged at his sagging cardigan as if he'd pull it in shreds from his shoulders.

'I don't know what we s'll do wi' 'im, Alma. Do you?'

Alma.

A creamy sound. Was it a battle? Alma Barracks? The black eyes sorted him out, dismissed him as southern-soft, while he reached back into regimental history.

'I'll leave it to you, Mr. Scotten.'

'You do right, an' all. Me an' Alma know a thing or two.' Scotten's rat's eyes flashed with water. 'We'll see you come out on top.'

Riley invited them to sit while he put the kettle on, and was vaguely disturbed to see Scotten lounging on the sofa where his wife had demanded her seduction. Neither was uneasy, the man tapping his fingers soundlessly awkward on the cushions as if he were unravelling some tricky question while she sat bolt upright, her hands clasped deep between her knees.

'Terrible thing,' Scotten said, stirring his tea.

'I beg your pardon?'

'Terrible. When the wife goes. Sudden. Like that.' Words splashed like raindrops into a bucket, heavily single.

'Yes.'

'I don't know what I sh'd do.' His expression changed,

from foxy wrinkled mud to diamonds of mischief. 'Put the flags out.'

'I'll put your flags out for yo', you cheeky 'aporth.'

Both smiled; they had done their best.

For the next quarter of an hour Scotten described life in a scrap-yard run by a friend. The pavements were worn hollow with little men with ten thousand pounds' worth of lead 'up the allotments' or who'd have the machinery out of any factory you'd name in between the nightwatchman's rounds on a Sunday. He talked with a dry enjoyment, as if every word were gospel, but seemed to pay attention neither to his wife, who did not interrupt, nor his host. In the end, he put his cup on the floor, delicately stirred the leavings, returning sucked spoon to saucer, and instructed his wife to stir her bum off that chair because they had to get on. She complied, smiling, all white flesh, a goddess to his temple monkey. Upstairs they stripped the wardrobes, returned the coat-hangers, sent in two boys for the remainder.

When Riley for the second time refused payment, Scotten scratched his pate.

'It'll go to my favourite charity, then.'

'What's that?'

'Scotten's Beer Fund.'

They'd both laughed, and Riley had fetched a quart bottle of nut-brown from his pantry. He felt neighbourly to this man, able to patronise without shame. Oddly he felt no guilt about Alma, but he'd little idea how to treat her. She would always stop with a pleasant word, for though she worked energetically she was a confirmed yakker at street corners, but she made no further attempt on his sex. It was as if she'd conducted some sort of test, but like a busy G.P. had forgotten to pass on the unimportant result. And yet he did not recall the occasion as clinical; she had been all warmth and kindness with her frock rucked up from the broad whiteness of thighs and belly. Once, she'd been in to borrow a box of matches, she was punctilious about repayments, she'd briefly stroked the back of his head.

'I like you.'

He'd put a hand to her breast, as she smiled.

'But I think you're a dirty old man.'

'Is that good?' he'd asked.

'How should I know?' Laughing, she trotted out, but she shouted back, 'Ask her next door.'

He'd known that his tenants, the O'Brien family, were at enmity with the Scottens, but judged it none of his business. According to his wife, she'd had no difficulty with the O'Briens' rent; they paid on the nail, even if they complained. They were perhaps fifty years old, dark, of face, of suit, and of room behind heavy brocade, lace curtains and linen blinds. He worked with the Electricity Board; she stayed at home to spy on the street. Mrs. Riley had reported this to him flatly because she clearly made nothing of the pair. They'd lived there for thirty years, had no children in the four bedrooms, but had endeared themselves nowhere. What had they been like as a young married couple, anxious and enthusiastic in their new home? It was impossible to envisage. The wrinkles and sagging outlines of the two sallow faces seemed permanent.

'He was a bit of a dancer,' the old dear in the corner shop said. 'That was before he had to go in the army. That was war-time.'

Riley wondered what the street had been like then, when bombs had burnt the roof of the factory in the next street, and windows were blacked out. He'd been a boy, and had walked one Saturday morning to 'see the damage', for bombs were rare on this city. Perhaps, he didn't remember, he'd actually passed this house, and seen Mrs. O'Brien, a munitions girl or a bus conductress, aged twenty, glowering from her front-door steps, or scrubbing in preparation for Charles's leave. Ay, one could stand there and look up where Victorian houses on the main road stood still unaltered into shops and imagine one's self, but for the cars, old and large, back not in the forties but in the early nineteen-hundreds.

'Is your husband Irish?' he'd asked, pleasant on collection day.

'No.'

'Thought he might be, with that name. Like mine.'

'Well, he isn't. Not for a long way back, any road.'

She spoke as against an insult, but glumly. When his wife had died, she had not sent flowers, nor called, but had pushed a letter through the front door, signed by both, one underneath the other, ladies first, expressing sympathy. There had been no mention of religion or comfort, even. They were sorry; they said so. Mrs. Riley was a good woman. They all knew it. On the other hand, the Scottens had appeared themselves, in black, with an ostentatious wreath. Mrs. Scotten had wept a little, and was the cynosure of the dull gathering at three o'clock for ham sandwiches and cups of tea.

'Has sour-belly been in?' she'd asked him then.

'Who?'

'Vinegar-mouth?'

Now, John Riley, duster flying as he waited for young Oxford's return, listened to the noises from the houses on either side. Muted television and from the Scottens' a series of thumps as the children leapt and threw. He liked these sounds which were not too obtrusive to distract; he'd be round sharp enough if they'd started up with a thrashing record-player or an electronic guitar. But they had not.

He slaved puzzled, mouth puckered in.

Last night he'd suffered a recurring nightmare. The setting was always the same, a back-yard rather like his own, with a grating under the kitchen window leading down to a cellar at double or treble depth. At the outset he knew that the dream had some connection with hell, but he was granted, or assumed, a stoical obstinacy. 'I know you'll hurt me, disgrace me, but I'll struggle to put up with it.' And that moment, always, his fortitude, his bravado, disappeared, and he stood in the cellar where broad-shouldered, legless figures ranged. These were blind, deaf, dumb, with only enough consciousness to recognise their own deficiencies and despair, and he made one of them, utterly comfortless, leaden-sick with grief. His neighbouring dwarf looked at him, and he knew the man, Mr. Macmillan, the former Prime Minister, whom he'd always admired with his Edwardian face and his pragmatic cleverness. But as they'd stared, nothing could shift the despair, the helpless shiver of total deprivation.

His dream unmanned him.

Worst was the sense of opposition he felt at the beginning when he squared his shoulders, threatened to take 'them' on. The gesture was hollow, made no difference; soon he'd squat in the sewer, no, that was too good a word, recalling humankind and its cleanliness, with man's sense to know humanity had gone.

He worked, bustling, putting Satan behind. Breathing a little heavily, he lugged the vacuum-cleaner upstairs. Friday night meant back bedroom this week. When his wife died, women from her factory, walking in, had convinced him he needed a cleaning female and he'd complied. But not for long. Careless tin lids or floor-cloths left about; dust on his radio set though the dials were retuned; windows grey in the corners or by the catches annoyed him until he'd paid the last cleaner off. Now he had a scheme, which he modified according to reason, but which laid down daily or week-end tasks. And he enjoyed nothing better. That he'd sooner kneel polishing a chair than sit in the cinema staring at the naked beauty of film actresses intrigued him. He ought to know better. Perhaps he did not want to waste money. Keep the pence jinking in his pocket. Or life.

A knock at the back door.

There, under the outside lamp, stood Oxford with his mother, both stiff as pokers, like children playing at statues. He invited them in.

Mrs. Oxford inspected his kitchen as he looked her over. A pretty woman, forty perhaps, with spectacles and curling thick hair, attractively greying.

'I don't know what to do,' she said.

Riley led them into the lounge, lit the gas fire again.

'He says he's left home. I don't think that's right.' The voice nasally pinched created a poor impression, of deprivation, complaints behind the back, dissatisfactions.

He waved the two to sit down, and the mother to speak. When she begun she strung sentences together inconsequentially, not as if she lacked argument but conviction. As long as she made noises of grumbling that seemed enough. The boy was young. She didn't know Riley. His dad wouldn't like it.

After she'd finished, stopped rather without conclusion, he said:

'I insisted that he consulted you.' The vocabulary appeared choice.

'Is that right, Frank?'

'Yes.'

The woman shrugged, wriggled, fingered the chair-arm.

'I don't know what to say, then.'

'What's he decided to do?' Though he spoke to her, the lad answered.

'I don't know.'

From next door a burst of energetic music preluded a news bulletin.

'Then I'll tell you. Take him back home with you.'

Her eyes shone with tears.

'I'm not standin' for . . .'

'He's your father, Frank, when all's said and done.'

'And I've had about as much of him as I can stick.'

Both voices whined, fretful animals.

'That's it, then.' Riley stood, and Mrs. Oxford followed, fingers fluttering about her coat, as if her clothes had dissolved from her and she was left with two small palms to cover her nakedness.

'Good night.'

Mother and son had spent ten minutes here, wasting time. Riley remembered as he closed the front door the legless figure of Macmillan with him in despair, a wire fixed to his head as to the rest of the hell-puppets, but unused, conducting no signals, jerking in no obedience, merely a symbol of slavery. Clicking his teeth he went back to the bedroom to complete his schedule.

3

On Saturday morning Riley did his round of the shops, finishing at the public library. As he dragged his two heavy bags away, Francis Oxford waved at him from the other side of the road.

'You might have given me a bit of support,' the boy said, crossing.

'Not my job to make your mind up for you.'

'The old man played hanover. You could hear him all over the street. He's coming round to sort you out.'

Oxford smirked.

'Aren't you big enough to clobber him yet?' Riley asked testily.

The boy shook his hair round his shoulders, muttering: 'I shall one of these days.'

Immediately Riley pitied the beanpole, with his jeans and scuffed shoes. At six foot two and nineteen one should take the world on.

Back in Stoney Street, he trundled his groceries and books down the entry to fumble at his back door. O'Brien, his neighbour, emerged. Deliberately.

'Been shopping, then?'

'I have.' He dumped the bags inside.

'Have you got time for a cup of tea?'

If this was an invitation, it was unique. Though Riley called in weekly to collect the rent, he did not stay for conversation. Again he locked his back door.

O'Brien led him into the parlour, which was cold, ignorant of the sun on the far side of the street. The room was polished, but bare, without character. Nothing showed on the mantelpiece, not even a speck of dust. They had hung neither pictures nor pot ducks on the nondescript wallpaper. Riley sat in one of the two plush armchairs, studied his feet, the carpet, the wooden fender, the green tiles of the hearth. O'Brien appeared almost immediately with man-sized china mugs into which he shovelled sugar.

'Drop o' sergeant-major's,' he said. A muddy-faced man with greased hair and small eyes, he stroked a non-existent waxed moustache.

'Very nice.'

'I like to get a taste. Cups is no good.'

Riley complimented his host, waited for an explanation. Perhaps the tenants were about to leave, or ask for permission to sublet the third floor, or press him to replace this perfectly acceptable, unused fireplace with a small modern grate. The delay was soon over.

O'Brien stood from his chair, replaced his mug on the tray, took a key from his pocket, unlocked the bureau drawer and took out a packet.

'I've got some'at to show you.'

He stood by Riley's chair, opened his envelope and took out a piece of card.

'How do you like that, then?'

It was a photograph of a nude girl, wearing a top hat and high-heeled shoes, with a silver-knobbed cane held rifle-wise over one shoulder. Apart from the bush of pubic hair, such a photograph might have been in a dozen magazines hanging in the newsagents. Riley sipped his tea.

'Very nice,' he said. The girl was not pretty, even, and her hair-style shone old-fashioned.

'Got that off an American soldier,' O'Brien said. 'In India.' He shuffled again. He produced more naked girls, smiling inanely, their thighs slim, their biceps glistening. These pictures would be nearly thirty years old, and the models themselves now in their fifties, sixty, probably dead. Riley turned one over to find the name of the firm who had pro-

23

duced these innocent distractions for veterans, but there was nothing. The back was a plain khaki cardboard, like the bottom of a Christmas-cracker box.

'Very nice.'

For twenty-odd years this queer sod had kept these locked in the cupboard from his wife's eyes. And when he died, first for sure, she'd find them and before she burnt them in the dustbin, she'd blush and wonder, as Riley did now, what sort of man or maniac she'd slept with all those years.

But why fetch them out now? One old soldier to another?

O'Brien shuffled again and laid on the top of the pile a piece of paper, a cutting from *Picture Post*, showing factory girls on a roundabout in a seaside funfair. They were shrieking like maniacs and their skirts ballooning handsomely up to their necks revealed stockings, suspenders, knickers. The photograph had at one time been folded, in a wallet, and was criss-crossed by a grid of creases. Certainly it had a more aphrodisiac quality than the cold, shiny bellies and neatly hairy mounts of Venus, underneath. These young women screamed, seemed lusty, lively, would have kissed your mouth, let the hair grow long in their armpits.

'D'you know any of them?'

O'Brien looked affronted.

'No. It's a picture. Cut it out, I reckon.'

He laid his envelope aside to stand and pour a second mug of tea for his guest. Then he resumed his first pose, hands on his knees. Riley, pleased to clutter his hands with cup and saucer, admitted his shock; a pile of photographs face downwards, topped by the folded news picture; three feet away, more to come. And there, the owner, solid, sensible, half-friendly as usual, making a gesture presumably. It was childish; one expected the card splashed with masturbator's sperm and yet O'Brien did not seem excited. He might have been showing off some set of postage stamps, cigarette cards that he collected in his youth and had now

24

become valuable. More photographs changed hands; girls at leap-frog, in languor, at nothing particular, all naked.

'No men?' Riley said.

'Who wants to see them?'

Finally, from the large envelope O'Brien took a smaller which he waved fan-like as he pursed his lips. Making up his mind, he opened it, extracted a postcard which he still held away from Riley, who, embarrassed, picked up his cup and saucer.

'Look at this now.'

'Right.' Men together.

'Finish your cup of tea first.'

Two middle-aged boys in a front parlour. Riley felt the situation both ridiculous but frightening. If a man could act as wildly out of character as O'Brien did now, he could run to murder. And yet the man played himself, was not unusual, in no way different seemingly from the humdrum workman who paid his rent on the nail or shut the back door five mornings a week as his clock struck seven-thirty.

He passed a postcard over.

This time it was amateur work, but clear, well focussed and developed. A young woman lay, odalisque fashion, left hand to face, elbow to ground. Her hair shone in wide permanent waves, and she lay, as he expected, stark naked. Her legs were chastely together so that the pubic triangle seemed slightly diminished, and the breasts, smallish but firm, were squashed lop-sided on account of her position. Riley studied the face. The girl was tense, might have been biting her lip or willing the photographer to get his distasteful task over and done. Her features were not without prettiness, and seemed somehow familiar. Miss Any-Body, 1942.

'Do you know who that is?'

Riley looked again. Taken indoors. One could make out a stretch of skirting-board, a pattern of wallpaper.

'No, I don't.'

O'Brien coughed gruffly.

'That's the wife.'

Riley blushed; his body fiercely shrivelled. The world tippled unstable. He wished he could see this as a joke, an aberration to be talked out in the pub, but it gravelled him, seriously. Nobody could be sane. Nobody wise.

'You took it?'

'Who else d'you think? In this room. Here. Before I went abroad. July, 1942.

'How old were you then?' As if it mattered.

'Twenty-four.' He backed again. 'Married three year.'

'She didn't mind?'

'Why should she?'

'Suppose somebody else found it? Or she thought other men had seen it?'

'Why should she think that?' O'Brien demanded.

'You've shown it to me, Mr. O'Brien.'

'So I have. So I have.' Mischief twisted his face. He leered.

'Have you shown it to others?'

O'Brien put his face on his hands, sullen now, solemn.

'Only one. A mate I had in the army. "Let's have a look at your missis, Chas," he'd say when we were on our own. "Does me good." And he'd have a look, and give it me back, and never say a word to nobody. "When I get back to England, Chas," he used to say, "I want to come and say how-do to your lass. And I shall think, 'She kept me going out there.' She's a beauty, she is." He never did see in. Died in transit camp on the way back. Heart-failure. Older than me. He was about forty. Seemed a big age, then.'

'Wasn't he married?'

'Wife had left him. You'd be surprised. Never seemed to hear of anybody's wife runnin' off up here, but in the army very near every second bloke's had. Nice chap, though. Alec Bell. "Let's have a look, Chas," he'd say, and I'd know what he meant. But didn't shout his mouth off, like some of 'em. Never said a word to nobody else.'

'Yes.' Sadness settled. O'Brien packed his treasures away.

'He didn't like these others.' He flicked the envelope with his fingernails. ' "I don't want to see them dirty whores," he said. "A real woman, not them pox-ridden bags." '

'Did you ever tell your wife about it?'

'Alec?'

'That's right.'

'No. I thought about it sometimes. But you never know with women. And we never had children. Makes a difference. To a woman. Might have gone flying off the 'andle.'

'I see.'

'I don't think you do, mister.' O'Brien chuckled, phlegmily. 'I know what she thinks about many things, but not about all.'

He stood, unlocked his bureau, replaced and covered his envelope.

'Does she ever mention it?' Riley asked.

'What?'

'The photograph.'

O'Brien locked the drawer, sat, tucked his feet awkwardly in by his chair.

'You're a nosy sort of sod,' he said. No aggression.

'Forget it.'

'She's not said a word. Not one. You'd think she would. Wouldn't you?'

'It's a long time.'

'You think she's forgot. Not her. She kept calling out, "I'm all goose pimples." She was ashamed. When I think back now, I don't blame her. It come as a shock. But I was wild in them days. You never see nobody in the army wi' a photo of his wife stripped nude, did you?'

'No.'

'Nor me. Just me. I made her. She didn't want. Didn't want to look at it. Wouldn't.' O'Brien took a match from his jacket pocket, thumbnailed it, then began to poke at his teeth. 'I did wrong, if you ask me,' he said. 'Now. But I was going abroad. I wanted some'at. Not that it kept me straight. Well, you couldn't expect it.'

'Why did you show it me, Mr. O'Brien?'

'It were like this.' He stroked his chin, a caricature. 'There you was. Wife gone. You looked a bit lost. So I thought, "I'll show him them." '

'Thank you.'

Riley wondered if that were the truth. The Christian act. Yet the man was naive enough. The back door rattled and Mrs. O'Brien appeared, still holding a bag in her left hand.

'Pull your arms out o' their sockets,' she said, by way of greeting, untwisting the handle. 'And the prices of things. Shocking.'

She was ugly, no doubt, with her cracked lips and lined, puffy eyes. Naked or not, she lolled, shapeless, drop at nose end, shoes split, rag-bag hat skew-wiff on her grey hair.

' 'Mornin', Mr. Riley.' She dragged her crocheted hat loose. 'Never offers me a cup o' tea, you see. Been havin' a talk, have you?'

'About women,' her husband said.

'What sort of women?'

'Nude women.'

'I can never get a sensible answer out of him at the week-end. Comes Sat'day an' his brain addles.' She was unperturbed, and grinned sourly as she went from the room.

Riley made his excuses, was not stopped, but as he closed the yard gate he heard the woman chide her husband.

'Fancy sayin' that to him, Charles. What will he think of us?'

'What?'

'About nudes.'

4

John Riley moved into the office, softly.

The manager's secretary smiled at him, adjusted the pretty clustered lace at her throat and thrust a leg from the slit of her maxi-skirt.

'Mr. Bowles won't be a minute. Please sit down, Mr. Riley. He's expecting you.'

He should be; he'd sent for him. Addison, the cashier, had nobbled him as soon as he'd arrived, three minutes to nine.

'Manager wants to see you, Mr. Riley. Ten-thirty.'

'What for?'

'Don't know. Phone call down, first thing, from Pretty Polly. Suppose he left a message with her last night.'

'Why didn't she send it, then, straight off?'

'You have me there. Didn't want you losing your beauty sleep.'

'It isn't the sack?'

'I don't know. I'd tell you if I did. Bowlesy wants you ten-thirty, spick and span, flies done up, hair brushed flat.'

Riley did not trust Addison with his patter. He capered, yammering as if his trivial chirp of words registered something: friendliness, perhaps, bogus concern. A tic. A display of counter-chat acquired when he'd been promoted and felt bound to show fraternity with the underlings. His Clark Gable moustache scarred a monkey-face. All middle-aged men are ugly, wizening or growing soft like slack-bellied women.

Riley was shown into the boss's presence, made to wait

while Bowles wrote, rang, issued orders to the queen secretary.

'Now, Riley. Draw a chair up.' The correct chair was indicated. 'We've been watching you. We're pleased with you. Mr. Robert praised you.' Mr. Robert was Major Erskine, his old company commander. 'You've given satisfaction.' Bowles nodded, smiled, lifted his glasses up, poked his moustache and his subordinate pondered where his master's superiority rested. They were of an age, but Bowles was podgier, with sausage-shaped sideburns, executive's glasses; he boasted shortness of temper, sucked tablets kept in the dove-grey waistcoat pocket, could make his mind up, disliked and distrusted his underlings. If Addison was a fake, so was Bowles; both would be useless when Fylingdales gave the four-minute warning of eternity, but both achieved success here, earned heavily, spent readily. Bowles now flicked a hand over the polished wood of the desk, with exactly the same movement that he used to flick the ash from his cigarette into the tray of his cherry-red Rover 2000.

'Are you satisfied with us, though?' Bowles whimsical.

'Yes, sir.'

'Would you like a move?'

'Depends where, sir.'

Riley rapped his answers back; they meant nothing. They gave the appearance of close attention, alacrity, prompt decision.

Bowles began to expand. Of course, Riley realised that the cartons they used, not merely at this place, but over at the two big hosiery factories, were made by Messrs. Carnell and Bloom, in Crocus Street. Riley did. Good. That concern had now been acquired. Old family firm. Bloom giving up. Favourable terms. Chance of expansion. Riley allowed the boss to belch on.

'Now,' Bowles said, 'here is the proposition. There are twenty people employed in that place at present. With more economical use of space we'd double that.' Off again.

It sounded vaguely like sense. In their way these cartons a quality product. Need for expansion. Hands flicked, tongue gabbled. 'We come to the nub. We want you to go as manager.'

Riley clicked his teeth together, got ready to acquiesce.

'Don't say anything yet, Riley. What question comes to your mind?'

'Haven't they got a manager now?'

'Yes. He's retiring with Mr. Bloom. Worked there all his life.'

'And there's nobody to step into his shoes.'

'Good questions, Riley. Oddly enough, not. It appears. The employees are mostly women. Make any difference?'

'No, sir.'

'You'll take the promotion.'

'Yes, sir.'

Bowles breasted into verbiage again. The salary would be discussed. The training. The snags. For the present he wanted Riley to go away, get on with his day's humdrum work, but at three-thirty he was to return, his mind made up for good, and ask his questions, flash his ideas. Good man. Three. See you, then.

Riley trailed back, but remembered to smile at Pretty Polly and to shake a circle of thumb and middle finger in a delicacy of success at Addison. The others asked nothing, not even Frank Oxford carrying a late cup of tea. At twelve-thirty the cashier insisted on escorting him to the canteen, and half-way, in the urinals, Riley broke the news.

'He never said a word to me.' Addison. 'He can be close if he wants. You'd think he'd ask.'

Riley thought no such thing. Bowlesy played his own little games. Hail-fellow-well-met at nine; bastard, king-size, at half past. He listened to the shop stewards on his works committee, never lectured them, but issued 'Bowles's bumf', cyclostyled sheets with the men's demands on one side, and the directors' putative offers on the other. Whether the manager consulted his superiors, his guesses were never

ludicrous and his suggestions invariably worth considera-
tion. Nobody liked his manner, but they could not beat
him on his knowledge; they claimed that he knew the wage
of every worker in the town's equivalent factories to within
a penny. He wasn't averse to accepting demands, there on
the spot. When he dug his heels in he issued the men a
balance sheet to tell them how much it would cost them when
they went out on strike. The unions would have employed
him, he said, if they'd had the money. He continued to
meet them and bargain in the large committee room down
the passage from his office. In his favour, he drank com-
munal tea from a large mug while they negotiated. No fool.
Exactly on top of his job.

Addison mused over his stew.

He had not been asked, but now he considered it, did
not want that promotion. His subordinate would soon be
making as much, more, than he was, but without security
of tenure. The factory was perhaps alive with reds or
nymphomaniacs, seeking gaffers to devour. Addison pep-
pered his peas.

At three-twenty-eight Riley disturbed Pretty Polly, who,
serious mien now, invited him to sit, announced him tight-
jawed. After the expected wait, Bowles himself came to the
dividing door to usher the new man to his seat.

'Now, young fellow-me-lad. Yes or no.'

'Yes, sir.'

'That's it, then.' He poured out two cups of tea; deli-
cate small china here. 'Any questions?'

'Hundreds.'

Bowles smiled; he liked surprises. They got on with it.
Salary, surprisingly small, rises dependent on success.
Training. Two weeks away. Hard work. Ignorance useless.
He'd find that soon enough.

This took perhaps a quarter of an hour, a second cup,
when Bowles held his hand up. That was sufficient now.
Information deteriorated into chitter-chat.

'There's one thing, Riley, and then you can go back to

pen-pushing. Nobody loves managers. Your head needs to be screwed on. If you make a hash you'll be out on your arse. But it's a great opportunity.'

'Thank you, sir.' Riley used the neutral politeness of private to officer.

'Thank yourself.' I'm an old soldier.

Dismissed, the manager-elect knew excitement, in his shoulder-blades, his fingers, his chin. He called in the lavatory, stroked down his thin hair.

'Yes?' asked Addison, sepulchral.

'In at the deep end.'

They shook hands, in sight of the goggling wage-earners. At tea-time, the rest gathered for information. He announced his departure, and they nodded sadly, held a hand out. Then, not before, he seemed to love them, in their suits. Oxford appeared specially moved, eyes bright. That jarred; to spread the treacle of the office Christmas on this spring day was inappropriate. And yet, the boy, with his long hair, his fancy cuffs, his scruffy fingernails, played no games. This move meant something. Soon this man he called John now would be in the boss-class with his own office, secretary. Careful men, mostly young, stood nodding for the moment old before their time at a promotion they had not expected, that seemed perhaps undeserved. Santa Claus in February.

At home, John Riley sat, hands between knees, in his parlour. He could not bring himself to cook. He wished he knew how to pray, not for guidance, he didn't need that yet, but in thankfulness. But his prayer would rise to the capitalist system, not to the unknown god, and his casually cocked ear at church parades had warned him off that. No great god, Bowles. He leaped up, fingered a glass swan by the neck, struck an attitude, and finally compromised by saluting a long photograph of an N.C.O.s' course in Aldershot. Plenty of spit and polish there, jutting chins, and a few leather-hafted swagger-sticks. He bounced down again, removed his shoes.

Without thought, he cut a sandwich and this frightened him because he'd abandoned habit. Why should he, a man with a steady job and a bit of a property, poke into management. He fidgeted like a budgerigar in its cage, but he had no song.

5

Time moved tediously towards Riley's promotion day.

Dressed in a suit he spent two days at the factory, listening to the present manager, a grey-haired man with yellow teeth. He asked questions, not because he wanted to know, but to create an impression; as he walked round the machines he hardly said a word to the women. The place was larger than he expected, airier, and with up-to-date light and warmth. His office seemed small, the one prison, shut away even from the filing cabinets and the typewriters.

Next he spent two days at the manufacturers', learning the plant. Fortunately he found no difficulty, even though he sat at night in his hotel, reading pamphlets and making notes. When a few days later he spent ten days at two larger factories he was quickly bored. What concern was the actual process? He might, at a push, have a shot at a temporary repair. Certainly, he'd have a good idea whether or not the maintenance engineer did a respectable job. But that was not managerial training.

He framed hypothetical questions.

Suppose, he demanded of a factory manager, it was decided to treble the output of this particular carton, what course would he suggest? Institute a shift system? Try to persuade his employers to buy two similar machines, second-hand? Or scrap the old and purchase largely, a new, multi-purpose machine?

The manager answered drily, sensibly, explaining why

shifts wouldn't do here, at this moment. As for the rest, he muttered, rolled his clenched fists in his trouser pockets.

'I don't know what your employers are like. They may be different. Mine would ask my advice, expect me to say something reasonable. But they wouldn't play a blind bit of attention. The accountants'll decide. I'm not responsible for policy.'

'My boss talked about expansion.'

The manager blew his cheeks out. A young man, twenty-five or six, with a colour-supplement suit and magnificently polished fingernails which he examined for flaws as he thought, he exactly portrayed the rising executive, but now he wrinkled his forehead.

'I send reports in regularly. I append notes on improvement, efficiency, increase in production, cost economy. They read them, I hope. It shows them that they haven't put the village idiot in charge. But that's about all. They pay less attention than I do to the suggestion box.'

'Isn't there anything . . . ?'

'Yes. But, minor, minor. About canteen queues or trolley wheels. Worth a fiver or two in bonus. And in goodwill, for that matter. We give it publicity in the *Works Gazette*. But I've not read anything that'll revolutionise the place. It's not likely.'

'It's happened.'

'Yes, when you'd got fellows at the bench who should have been at the university. We've a shifting population. Young women who get restless or in pod. Not surprising.' He indicated a girl who leaning over a trolley flaunted slim buttocks, panties, tights under her mini-skirt. 'But the high command. 'Morning, Sharon.' To the now upright girl, who blinked silver-daubed eyes at him. 'They don't want to hear from you. They want an efficient unit, so that a fiver invested here makes ten. But if they want a thousand they go elsewhere. Even for cardboard boxes.'

'Uh.'

They pushed back into the manager's office.

'Will you stay here?' Riley asked.

'I hope not. I hope to God not.'

'A directorship?'

'Just on. Here or somewhere else.'

This young jockey, Riley thought, looked on him as a yokel. Foreman type, at forty-odd in charge of twenty. The man's skin was clear by his bushy sideboards, his hair just beginning to thin. He smoked too many cigarettes, was nobody's fool. But what had he got over Riley? Youth. An educated accent. A university degree. A pretty wife. A line of chat. But when it came to argument with the men? This jack-in-office wouldn't admit it, but it was officer-class. Nobody like jumped-up rankers. Riley had difficulty not calling the man 'sir'.

When he returned from instruction he went back to his clerk's desk until his superiors were ready. He spent the last week of the retiring manager's tenure at the factory. Morley bared his yellow teeth, grinning.

'This'll annoy your gaffers. Paying two to do one man's job.'

The old chap did not say much, was glad to be off, had been taking it easy now for months. If pressed, he would explain procedures, in a dry uninterested voice. Sometimes his large grey eyebrows would rise at Riley's questions.

'Trouble-makers? There aren't any. You get across one or the other now and again. You don't like them equally. But they're men, and women, earning pay. They don't kill themselves, and why should they?'

On Thursday Riley drew up pay-slips in preparation for Friday. Morley, inspecting these, sighed, said:

'Not much of a job, is it? But it got me down, when I first come. I used to go to church, but I gave it up.'

'On this account.'

'I guess so.'

The thick bush of hair over the thin face, the pale blue eyes, suggested authority, wisdom, control. Instead, here was a confession of sickly boredom. And this job, which had killed his religion, he'd abandon to somebody else the next week, to go home and skulk.

'What'll you do all day at home?'

'Garden. Drink. Television.'

'Bingo?' Riley's sarcasm.

'A woman's game.'

From his desk, Riley could see the factory floor where two women were arguing while the maintenance man made some slight adjustments to their machines. An air of lassitude revealed itself at this early hour of the morning; one pair had sewing patterns on the desk which both poked at, shuffled idly. Morley tapped his teeth with a pencil.

'Don't let 'em see you watching from up here.' He yawned. 'And don't fret yourself. Today's output'll be up to normal.'

At lunch-time, there was no canteen, a woman presented herself.

'I've got to take my lad to the children's hospital tomorrow morning,' she told Morley.

'Right, Mrs. Gibson.'

'I'll be back as soon as I can.'

'I'm sure you will. What's wrong with the boy?'

'It's his feet. I've been taking him to the clinic.' She thrust with her account. The manager nodded. Riley had already considered the drill which operated when one person was absent, and pondered improvements. He could think of none. In the stuffy office the three of them occupied space. A not unattractive woman became garrulous; Morley listened for the kettle next door which would signal the imminence of his cups of tea; Riley, unable to improve the *status quo*, stared depressed at Mrs. Gibson's legs. She thanked them both; Riley was flattered at his inclusion, and stepped off just as the kettle boiled.

'Attractive woman.'

Morley took out his silver pencil to tap his teeth.

'Yes. I suppose she is. You fancy a few, do you? I've never had the nerve, and I'll say this: they've never made

38

any motions towards me, if you know what I mean. But it's there, if you want it, I imagine. Too dangerous for me, by half. What would I do if I was caught out?'

'You've got a family?'

'Ay. Grandchildren an' all.'

Riley would be glad when this scarecrow had gone. There was nothing to the man but pottering and indigestion tablets. Once he got this crud-bucket off his back, he could start.

On Friday afternoon the old proprietor, who wore a gold-watch chain, appeared with Bowles and presented Morley with a dining-room clock and fruit bowl. Dry speeches were coughed through, ghostly applause before the hands returned embarrassed to their work. Bowles walked the length of the place, once. The old man took Morley off in a Mercedes and Riley signed the letters, in charge. His secretary, a middle-aged charmer, smirked at him when he told her that he depended on her. At five the women clocked out and the maintenance man began a casual round.

'I s'll be in tomorrow morning,' he told Riley. 'That's when I get everything in order for next week.'

'I'll come down.'

'No need. Mester Morley didn't.'

'He knew his way about. You've got to teach me.'

'You was in the army, wasn't you?'

'A regular. Why?'

'You've got that look about you.' The man pushed his cap back. 'I don't like bullshit.' No rancour. Not even argumentative.

'What do you like, friend?'

'People to get on with their own wo'k, and leave me to mine.'

Riley nodded, looked the man in the eye, saying nothing. An old trick. The other stared truculently back, then dropped his eyes, while his boss waited. Not to speak. Not to give oneself away. To hold the whip-hand soundlessly. He stared again straight into the man's face.

'I shall be down at ten, Mr. Dyson,' he said, at length,

and waited until the other moved. When he walked upstairs to lock his office, he found he was trembling.

Back at home he cooked his tea coolly, washed up, before he sat down to a thorough perusal of the evening paper. The front page did not detain him long, and soon he considered the property advertisements. None of the fancy 'Sale by private treaty', but the bread-and-butter 'three bedrooms, new developments, over £7000'. The figures, the jargon, 'secluded garden, full gas c.h., storm-porch, garage-space', excited him, like a game over which he had control. He suspected dry-rot here, laughed at the estate agents' simplicities of omission, marvelled that people would pay hundreds of pounds to live in one street rather than another.

An unexpected knock on his back door annoyed him as he cleaned his dining room.

At five past eight on Friday his time was his own. He'd ignore the caller. A second tapping. Somebody selling him car sponges or *The Watchtower*. He opened the door.

In the darkish yard, he peered at a woman.

'Yes?'

'Mr. Riley? It's me. Mrs. Oxford. Frank's mother, you know.'

'Yes?' Grudging.

'I wonder if I could have a word with you.'

That meant lighting, heating the lounge. They sat either side of the gas fire, but he had not bothered to put his jacket on. Oddly, she had dressed for the occasion in a summery blue coat and a hat with large artificial primulas; the colours set off her slim prettiness.

'They've come to blows,' she said. Another woman with neat legs explaining her domestic difficulties. He did not answer, from his sour unsympathy. On a Friday he allotted his time to his own problems as he dusted and polished.

'You don't work with Frank now, do you?' He shook his head. 'You've been made a manager. He told me.' She sketched mild variations on these three themes, and added a coda on his wisdom. ' "Why don't you talk to Mr. Riley?" I said. "Don't work with me." "Well, that's no matter," I said. "You know where he lives as well as I do." ' Mrs. Oxford repeated these, while he wondered whether she suspected him of stupidity or merely had acquired the habit of spinning banalities out.

She had been there for ten minutes before she returned to her subject.

On Tuesday last it was parky all day, her husband had been a bit off, caught a cold, grumbled at his tea. This wasn't usual; he'd a hearty appetite, but he couldn't well, y'know. He'd snapped at Frank to stop whistling. The lad did so, but, a bit later, not thinking, y'know how it is, had started again. When Mr. Oxford ordered him to have done, Frank told him to shut his trap.

'What did he say?'

'Belt up.' The father rose, inquired in a soft voice:

'Say that again, my man.'

'Belt up.'

Oxford hit his son across the cheek with his flat hand, and immediately the boy lashed out straight into his father's face. The old man tippled on to the table, knocked his plate and dinner to the floor where it shattered, arrows of china in a mess of mince. Then his nose began to bleed. Perhaps it was the cold, but it poured, they couldn't stop it, key down back, an' all. Frank stood white as a ghost, and there was his dad, blood splashing all over the tablecloth. In the end, when they staunched the flow, and plugged a nostril, Frank, who'd cleaned the floor up, went over to his father and apologised. Oxford, shirt-front stained, bloody handkerchief at the ready, had ordered his son out of the room. With a second, 'I'm sorry, Dad', he'd gone. Oxford had nursed the fire all the evening and when his wife had spoken had told her to shut her face.

Next day he'd refused to speak to his son and had gone to bed early, surprising behaviour in spite of his snuffle.

41

Beer was his usual medicine. Frank had seemed sorry, quiet and sorry, upset, but now he was as awkward as the old man, making a war of it. When she'd said, at breakfast, in desperation that she'd go to see Mr. Riley about it, he answered:

'You can go and see Jesus Christ for all I bother.'

She looked across at Riley, her glasses magnifying the pretty blue eyes, now awash with tears. As she talked, she had fiddled at, spun her wedding ring with her right hand as if to emphasise the giddiness of her home. Now she began again, explaining how unlike Frank this was. A courteous boy and so quiet. Did Mr. Riley know he wrote poetry? He did. No end. And he had a little typewriter upstairs in his bedroom, and he was always sending them away, to magazines, to radio programmes. He spent hours up there, by himself, playing his record-player, and scribbling away, little notebooks full. And some of them. Some was nice, but, well.

Finding this tedious, he asked brusquely how he could help her.

'What would you do?' she said, biting her lip.

'If I were in Frank's place, I'd apologise again. I'd tell him I was wrong, offer to shake hands and try to mean it.' As he spoke he suddenly realised that he acted the manager, little father to his people.

'I've begged him.'

'Beg him again, then.' Fool woman. 'Your husband will be down-in-the-mouth. Knocked about in his own house. All his authority's disappeared. But the boy won't be any better off. He's beaten his father, and nobody wants that. He's a bit proud, is he? He's unsure. Has he written a poem about it?' Gabble, gabble.

'I don't know.'

'You haven't looked, then?'

'No.'

Her eyes opened wide and helplessly. She fingered the flowered hat. Riley, who'd been barking out his sentences without expectation of success, from pique, suddenly, unaccountably to himself, felt sorry for the woman.

'It isn't going to be easy,' he said. 'For you especially. You've got to keep the peace.'

'Will you talk to him? Frank.'

'If you like. If he'll come here.'

She thanked him at last, in breathless bursts.

'Does he know you're here?' he asked. She nodded, smiling as if she remembered a miracle. 'And your husband?' That wiped her face glum. 'What did he say?' Malice narrowed her eyes. He pressed.

'I couldn't repeat.'

'I'm trying to help.'

'He thinks, you know, he thinks you, er, ah, fancy boys.' She blushed scarlet, crushed one thigh on to the other.

Riley, watching her antics, flared in anger. That summed the visit. Dull rigmarole which culminated in insult.

'I see.'

She finished squirming and said:

'You're mad, now, aren't you?' Her voice reeked of the local accent.

'What d'you expect.'

She began to weep. He pushed his fingers into his trousers, spanned his back and waited for the end. Taking her glasses off, she dabbed her eyes, looking blindly, bluely outwards. Restored, she stood. He joined her.

'I'll go, then.'

'My offer still stands. I'll see him if he comes.'

The long parade of thanks halted when he took her by the arm, not at the elbow, but high, along the muscle, running his hand up to her armpit. He felt the flesh under her coat, and indulged himself. There was something sexual in his caress, as if at a breast, a thigh, for he felt her womanhood, hidden under the cloth, but tempting him. His fingers moved still as she looked up and back. Her hand crossed her body to touch, not to prevent, his at its joy. She leaned

43

on him, lightly. Now he gripped that bicep tighter, hurting. Her mouth opened; her ridiculous hat slewed.

'That's nice,' she said. Her hand left his, touched his cheek, guided his face round to hers.

He kissed her quickly, but drew back, like a suspicious animal. Her eyes were closed, her pretty grey hair hardly mussed. She might have been playing in some Victorian skit; peace after pain.

'What are we doing?' he asked. She murmured, a thin groan of pleasure as she turned her cheek to his shoulder. Without much confidence he stroked her breast. Without much pleasure, either, she was too well strapped up. He closed his own eyes, but not for long. Seizing her by the shoulders he marched her back to her chair and sat her down. She deigned to open her eyes.

'If we go on like that, things'll happen to you.'

'What things?'

'If you don't know, I'm not going to tell you.'

That's the way he'd talked at fourteen, pawing some miss in a dark shop doorway. Mrs. Oxford smiled, distantly, as she smoothed her coat.

'You don't get on with your husband, do you?'

She shook her head.

'Do you want to leave him?'

'How can I?'

'But you want to get your own back on him? Is that it?' She made no answer. 'Hasn't Frank done that for you?'

'I don't want him hitting his dad. It's not right.'

'No.' He chewed his thumbnail while she pulled at her gloves. 'I don't know what to say to you. Send him here. Do that. That's the best.'

'All right.'

'If you come, I shan't be able to keep my hands off you.' She bit her lip. 'You see that.'

'I won't, then.'

'I'm not telling you not to. That's up to you. I'm just say-

44

ing what'll . . .' He broke off, in anger. Was he trying to answer her husband's taunt? Sexually roused, he shrank from involvement. If only she'd slipped under him like that tart next door, out of sympathy, or mischief, or fancy. This woman was subtle, devious. She'd break into his life, sob every minute out of it if she could. And why not? She'd kept herself cooped up in that semi-detached, bolstering her pride with her grammar-school son, rejecting her husband's invitations to the lounge bar. He'd have been proud to see her, in her blue coat, wide eyes alert, at a polished table behind a gently sipped glass of lager, with the other wives, but a cut above them, not raucous, clean-minded, genteel. He'd be a somebody would Ron Oxford, then, living up to his income. He earned good money at the car-components place, wasn't afraid of overtime, tipped his screw up regularly, didn't, for all she said, drink a lot compared with some of the others. But she wouldn't come, not even very often on a Sunday, would milady.

Riley saw this, sourly. Her adultery would have its price, he thought. And that inflated.

'I'll get you a cup of coffee,' he said.

'That would be lovely.' She stood, mistress of the situation, if not of man, to look in the mirror, realign her hat. They drank in silence. Riley had no idea what to say, and, therefore had the sense to keep his mouth shut. He was cautious, now, squinting snags. The barrack-room Lothario had accepted women as tribute to his youth, his charm. Nobody gave free gifts to anybody of his age these days. Nobody. He stirred his drink, clinking the spoon. She had beautiful ankles, perfect.

'I'm sure it'll do Frank good to see you,' she said, smiling socially. Riley crouched in his redoubt. She continued to chatter, brightly, without meaning, at a distance, while he wished he could laugh at her. In the end when she'd put down her coffee-cup, and said she must go, she stood close to him, tauntingly, but said, whispered:

'You've set me up, Mr. Riley.'

45

'I don't know your Christian name.' Why had he said that?

'Joan Madge. I don't like them much.'

'It's a tomboy sort of name,' he said, in idiocy. She held a gloved hand which he took between both of his and they stood, not quite uncertainly, but in promise, before she made for the door, was clipping down the path.

He washed the coffee-cups, returned to his dusters and polish-rags, trembling, a middle-aged man on his knees.

6

The first few weeks as manager passed trouble-free.

He'd turned in on Saturday morning, said good morning to the surly maintenance man, refreshed his memory of the week's duty, opened the unimportant letters, and then called down to his subordinate below to come up for a cup of tea. The man grunted, but was pleased. Riley didn't say much, asked about football, but discovered that Dyson's interest was in brass bands. When he learnt that Riley had been in the same mess as Stanley Straker, once regimental bandmaster, now adjudicator and B.B.C. conductor, his interest sharpened, and he began to talk. Contests, state of instruments, near-professionalism of the big bands, lack of interest among youngsters; the man mumbled eloquently. Riley listened, poured out second cups, but at the end of twenty minutes gently cut off the flow. Dyson, he noticed, had kept his cap on through the interview. How old was the man? he wondered. In his forties? He consulted the file. Sixty. The man below him bent over a machine, singing to himself. Riley washed the cups, dusted his desk top, straightened the pencil tray, the phone, the jotters, made sure the weekly schedule he'd forced out of his predecessor was at the top of the top right-hand drawer, and withdrew. Dyson lifted his head from some oily chore to answer his good-bye.

Work started sluggishly on Monday. He was there at eight-twenty-five, and though the majority clocked in on time, they seemed more bent on conversation than production. However, he resisted the hankering to walk round, and sat in a quiet despair until nine when Miss Rogers the secretary arrived. She brought the mail up, but spent her first ten minutes in the lavatory or at the mirror and not until she had prepared herself did she bring him his letters. Only one was not routine, and that, surprisingly, was from Bowles, wishing him success and telling him not to do anything out of the ordinary for a fortnight, and not to initiate anything inside the first month, and certainly not to talk except by way of polite greeting. 'This is not the army,' Bowles ended. 'I wish to God sometimes it was.' He pocketed that so that the Rogers would not read it.

He watched the hours of the rest of the day as if every shelf were about to collapse, every phone call an announcement of catastrophe, every woman who looked up from her work about to give birth or deny him. The two orders due out that day left on time, and in perfect condition. When the radio blared below and the afternoon tea trolley was on its rounds, he was almost frightened at his own unease, as though it invited trouble.

By the time he reached home, he was exhausted. He remembered his grandfather, an old railwayman, explaining how he'd looked forward to his first full day as a driver, after the swaying labour with the shovel. 'And d'you know, Jack, I was licked. Jiggered. I'd driven plenty of times before. The drivers always let you try your hand. But that first time I was in charge on the footplate I couldn't believe it, I was so tired. The responsibility. That's what it was. That train ran on time because of me.' The old man's wet eyes stared firewards, but even in winter he'd potter off to the allotment. Now his grandson stood in charge; unlike the army, he could not pass the buck anywhere he could see. A sergeant has a platoon officer, a company commander; there's an adjutant, a C.O. about. One sees them, knows them, is instructed by them. Here at Carnell & Bloom's work continued or declined by kind permission of the commanding officer, Lt.-Col. J. R. Riley. He did not like it.

He spent his week learning routine, what had been done,

so that when Bowles or someone in a higher echelon dropped on him with a fancy demand he could comply, or at least go through the motions. He bombarded Miss Rogers with questions, which, by and large, she could answer. A decent woman, she'd worked here for eighteen years and knew exactly where every box of tin-tacks was stored, but his inquisition, he began to notice, scared her. She could not believe, obviously, that he merely wished to repair his ignorance; he'd wring her dry, and then start the alterations. The effect was that she began to offer information, and he'd listen until she repeated herself or worked over ground familiar to him when he'd stop her, send her packing. This established his superiority, though she seemed to resent it.

With the men and women at the benches he was quiet. He made two tours of inspection morning and afternoon, and often had to walk downstairs to check the stores or issue some new instruction. When there was a flap on, the hands buckled to it. Only once did he have to intervene. The two lads loading a lorry seemed in no hurry to start. He watched them, and could not exactly claim they were dodging, for they combined their present job with preparations for the next two or three, but they were casual, chatting, shouting to the women, once dribbling a broken box along the floor to the waste-bin. He went down.

'Is the lorry outside?' he asked.

'Yes.'

'Will you get it loaded, then. Weldon's'll be here for the next lot at four. Doesn't give you long.'

'They're never here on time,' the lad said.

'Shall we work on the assumption that today they will be?' Riley spoke very quietly, but noted the flint of contemptuous amusement that lit their faces at the long word. They did as they were told; the load was out of the yard at five to four.

He descended again.

'Thanks, lads,' he said. 'You never know.'

Weldon's lorry arrived at four-twenty, and he asked the

driver where he'd been. After a vague answer, he left and was hardly ten yards away when he heard:

'And who the bloody 'ell's that?'

'The new manager.'

'New broom, eh?'

'He's not so bad. O'd army man.

'Oh, Ah'll sling the bogger a salute up next time, then. Hup, two, three . . .'

Riley wasn't displeased, smiled, but decided against taking his afternoon tea with the secretary.

On Friday he did the pay in the 'small office', a large storeroom, downstairs and pleased himself by receiving no complaints. His own salary was now paid into a bank. Back safely upstairs, he realised that Miss Rogers had done all the administrative work for the last year at least, had carried the retiring manager, and that it wasn't likely she'd let him slip up. He could hear her trotting about next door, see her through the frosted glass.

Straightening his pencils, he asked himself why the hell the administrators did not make her manager. She'd include her present typing and filing and shorthand as a bonus for a salary smaller than his. Why didn't they save themselves money? Custom? Fear of shop-floor reaction? The men wouldn't wear a woman up top, and the girls, they'd soon bitch her out of it. Riley chewed a pencil, as Miss Rogers knocked, came in.

She was a good-looking thirty-five, forty perhaps, with jutting breasts, accentuated by a thin fawn sweater. Her hair, scraped back from her forehead into a bun low in the nape of her neck, challenged the bosom's display. No rings spoilt her small hands, while her nails were delicately filed.

'Finished with your cup, Mr. Riley?'

Her smile was slight, formally introduced.

Returning the crockery as he stood, he asked:

'Is there anything else, Miss Rogers?'

'Letters. I'll bring them in in a few minutes for signature.'

He liked her face, which should have been pretty, but lacked the balance. Her eyes seemed just too small, her nose too prominent, her mouth too thin. Were her legs slightly short? He knew nothing of her.

They hadn't made her manager, but he'd been employed at cut-rate himself. They might pay his salary into a bank, but he was no more than a glorified foreman. He'd get no higher. He was nowhere near the class of that young chap whose factory he'd been attached to, either in money or prospect. A pound to a penny he drew less than old Morley had here; he hadn't dared ask. Their experts had decreed that he was the cheapest they could safely employ.

Miss Rogers still stood. He looked upwards.

'I wanted to ask you something, Mr. Riley. A favour really.'

'Yes.'

'Can I leave half an hour earlier tonight?'

He did not answer, did not fiddle with the pencil-tray, merely locked his fingers and gently laid his hands on the desk.

'I've made an appointment to have my hair done. They'll just get it in if I go off early. This is the night they work late. It's difficult to fix on Saturdays.'

He looked at the straight hair, helmet-hard.

'I should think we could manage that,' he said.

'It would mean you'd have to . . .'

'Let me tell you.' He did so, she correcting him, and that on nomenclature, only once.

'If you don't mind,' she said, flushed. 'I think I should tell you that Mr. Morley never allowed it. "Once you and I start to skive off, Miss Rogers, they'd be on to it, too." ' She pointed downstairs. ' "So if we sit here for the last hour twiddling our thumbs," he said, "it's time well wasted." ' Instant Wit for Idle Moments.

'I'm not Mr. Morley,' he said.

'No, sir.' The first time she'd called him that.

'As far as they're concerned,' he pointed below again,

'you're away on company business. They're not to know. Why should they? You do a good job up here. That's what counts with me.'

He opened the door for her.

As soon as she'd gone, doubts nailed him. She'd been put up to this by Bowles or some such, and as soon as she'd left the place, an inquisitional phone would demand to speak to her, or next week he'd receive a sharp letter reporting that she'd been seen walking the streets in office hours. Frightened again, he swore out loud at the establishment and walked downstairs to the store- and packing-rooms.

That relieved him.

There one could see the finished product, nicely packaged in the firm's own containers. Once he'd learnt his way about, and that hadn't taken him long, he could, inside ten minutes, with invoices and common wits, work out exactly how the day's work progressed. He loved these lightning tallies, and wasn't above bullying the old fellow in charge. When, as sometimes happened, he was caught out and the man produced some fact he'd been ignorant of or neglected, he'd purse his lips and congratulate his subordinate by running himself down.

'Too smart by half,' he'd say, 'some of 'em.'

The old chap never smiled, merely shook his head hopelessly, as if the whole operation, mistake and all, had been planned to nonplus him.

'We've had some extra orders this week, Tom,' Riley said. 'Is that usual at this time of the year?'

'I don't know.' Neither surly nor obsequious. Riley had the answer already; he'd checked previous years and had issued orders to make up stock again for the next three weeks. Probably Tom knew it as well, but considered it no part of his work either to instruct the gaffer or kowtow to him.

Next week there were extra tasks, but arrangements had been made, and Riley had decided what he'd do in the case of an absence or two. His work-people had shown willingness to earn extra, out of duty, it seemed. The world of the machines next door, and the quiet piles of made-up or flat containers in the storeroom, suddenly became beautiful, almost religious, as if somebody had said a prayer. Some Victorian worthy had built a chapel into his factory not far off. There was no need; the floor itself. He remembered a text on his grandmother's bedroom wall. 'Surely the Lord is in this place.' Sunlight daubed the dusty windows, as he progressed upstairs.

Miss Rogers waited with the letters. She stood at his shoulder as if she would be called on to show him where to sign. He enjoyed her presence, but when she left, the mail in her hand, for her appointment, he shrank inside himself, unemployed until work finished and he padlocked the main gates.

7

I t was still light when he arrived home.

The Scotten children seethed in his yard, watching firemen dout the pother of smoke from the O'Briens' chimney. As soon as they saw him arrive, their mother made a great show of shooing them away. To give credit, they obeyed her.

Riley called the O'Briens in for comfort, but both refused. The pair gaped incredulous at the bustle, and Mrs. O'Brien muttered a chorus:

'It's no time since I had it swep'.'

Riley ate his own meal, and went back where his neighbours stood aghast before the mess. In fact, the firemen had been remarkably careful, but lumps of burning soot had fallen and exploded. The carpets had been rolled back, and the grate looked worse for wear, but he noticed no permanent damage. O'Brien glared.

'You can bear witness, can't you?' Aggression thrust his teeth in prominence.

'Witness?'

'That we had that sweep. Just before Christmas. Couldn't have done a damn' thing.'

Mrs. O'Brien dabbed here, there, with a wet cloth as if she concentrated on cleansing the odd square inch. The whole job might occupy him two hours at the outside, Riley judged, but this woman scrabbled trivially to no end. The visitor offered to do the hearth, but she turned on him, told him she didn't trust no man, with such ferocity that her husband put a comforting hand on Riley's sleeve. Whenever the males made any move, she snapped; this cross she'd bear alone.

'Leave it to me,' she shouted, 'then it'll be done as I want.'

They carried buckets of hot water for her, but she screeched ungratefully, nagging them to admit they thought her incapable. O'Brien's embarrassment showed easily, but what worried Riley was her complete inefficiency. Only this week he'd learnt from the factory that methods varied; that the apparently chaotic could be cleared by a system that seemed non-existent to the complacent observer. But she scrubbed not only perfunctorily but uselessly, in that she'd repeat the same routine minutes after she'd completed its last round. He could not understand it. Sleeves rolled back, wet hands red, she flew at, mauled her task, achieving little. Each time they intervened, she squealed at them to clear off. In the end, the men took themselves away next door where they drank tea. When they carried the pot to Mrs. O'Brien she had the carpet in place, but soapy stains disfigured the hearth, and the furniture, hitherto untarnished, was now smeared with fingermarks as if she had been round printing her displeasure over the polished surfaces.

Something had twisted awry. O'Brien stared out of his window, quietly, crazily enraged because he might have to pay for the fire brigade's labour; his wife slaved like a dervish to emphasise the extent of her inadequacies.

On Sunday morning, when he called in, order was restored, but Mrs. O'Brien was unwell in bed, and as her husband paused from preparing breakfast he blackguarded the sweep again. A sad house. Riley wished he had some miracle. 'Let's have a look, Chas.' If he could call out like Dvr. Alec Bell, then the naked photograph would be produced, and stared at, appreciated, fingered, and the battered woman would rise from her bed and work. Daily bread. Charles. Riley imagined Bell, a sallow, hatchet-faced man in steel-rimmed army-issue spectacles, his lips tight, as he was privileged to eye that body. Did he ever turn up after the war to see the reality he'd gloated over, to shake

55

hands, think his filthiness, blame the ignorance of politicians who'd pitchforked him into the ignominy of having to ask to see a few square inches of cardboard to keep him sane? Had he forgotten? A quaint memory? Perhaps he was dead. He'd died out east. O'Brien said so. Heart-failure. Chaos hovered over this Sunday room, while outside a cold spring glittered, forsythia shone, daffodils jumped, touched Riley on the raw. If he could master it, barge upstairs with a word of power, sweeten the morning for them, it would be something. But he stood, listening to the frying pan and lugubrious hymns on the radio and knew his uselessness, mourned it.

He heard no more of his neighbours until Wednesday.

The women at Carnell's had needled him, singing at the tops of their voices, doing anything but get on. There were two extra loads to pack up and despatch, and a special call from Pretty Polly in Bowles's office first thing had made it clear that these were to be on their way down the M1 for the Luton factory before three-thirty. He was determined not to panic, but had issued precise orders that the loads were to be packed by three at the latest. The drivers came at one, exactly on schedule, but parked and locked their wagons and went off to lunch. By the time they were back and work could begin Riley fretted, sourly anxious.

'What time's this?' he asked.

'We've got t'hev us dinners.'

'Why lock your lorries, then?'

'Look, I'm not leaving that standing about unlocked for you nor nob'dy else. It's my responsibility.'

'Why didn't you report in, then? Instead of sloping off?'

'At one o'clock? It's my dinner hour.'

'You know damn' well these lorries have to be ready and off by three.'

'If I'd to'd you, your lot couldn't have loaded up in their break. They want their dinner same as anybody else.'

'That's for me to decide, not you.'

56

'When they hev their snap? D'you 'av to get permission to eat here, then?' The drivers pulled faces at each other, and at Riley's returning subordinates.

'I threaten nobody,' he said, quietly. 'But if these aren't off on time, you'll know.'

'We shall, shall we?'

He said no more, handed the order of packing to his own men. Though the placing of the cartons was complicated, involved fetching and carrying, the whole operation was over in less than half an hour. He checked the loading himself, commented, but when he found it perfect, congratulated the storekeepers.

'Storm in a teacup.' The insolent driver pushed his sleeve magnificently back to consult his watch. 'You don't mind if we join 'em in a mugful as you've brewed.'

'I call it mashed,' Riley said, and they laughed, good-naturedly. And at five to three they were up in their cabs before your 'C.O. comes round'.

'Bye, 'bye, Bundook's,' one shouted, revving.

'What's he say?' Riley asked. The youth blushed, muttered:

'It's what they call you?'

'What?'

' "Bundook".'

'What's that mean?'

'I don't know. It's a bit of a name, like. T'drivers, y'know. . . .'

Riley tapped the top button on the boy's overall.

'It's the Indian word for a rifle,' he said. 'Banduq.'

'Is it?' No interest.

'It's what we called rifles in the army.'

The youth shrugged, almost unpleasantly. Riley moved away, both chuffed and narked. A nickname was good. But he should not have interfered. The lorry would have left at three without his meddling. And yet he recognised, with a sudden burst of confidence, that the bolshy driver had addressed him in the hostile, badly enunciated tone men

57

reserved for their masters. His managerial status had been recognised. Sentences from his address to the rookie squads: 'It's not the man you're saluting. It's the Queen's commission. So sling one up, and smartish.'

He had no sooner returned home from these encounters than Mrs. Scotten banged his back door. Without waiting for an invitation, she pushed her way in, to stand in a nearly obscene mini-skirt by his scullery sink.

'Have you heard?'

'No.'

'About Missis. Missis Next-Door. They've took her away.'

She was invited to sit, to start again. Her tights were laddered and holed almost to extinction.

'Mrs. O'Brien,' she said. Excitement both quietened, quickened her speech. 'They've took 'er away. To St. Anne's. To the 'sylum.'

'When?'

'This morning. The mester didn't go to work. And the doctor come. An' some others. And then the ambulance come.'

'How do you know?' She might have been one of his workwomen.

'After he come back he went to the shop. And Mrs. Warsop, y'know what she is, asked him straight out. And he to'd her.'

Riley put no more questions as she chattered until finally she swished her skirt-ends, stood, said she delayed him. He did not deny it. When his meal was finished he called next door, but the house stood locked. At eight-thirty he heard O'Brien clank up the entry, and went out to meet him.

'How did you find her then?' he called. The other turned on his step.

'Not too bad.' O'Brien sighed, shoved the sticking door open, and invited his neighbour in. 'They'd got her under sedation. But she knew me.' The jargon already.

'Come into my place.'

'No. I'm not going nowhere. Except bed. You come on in wi' me.'

O'Brien shuffled to his kitchen, trundled kettle to stove, and flatly, so that the visitor had to move close to hear, he whispered how she'd gone mad with crying fits all Sunday, how he'd fetched the doctor on Monday. She'd swallowed her tablets after a fight, but grew worse, howling, squealing, rolling out of bed. When he'd spoken sharply to her, she'd cried, not like a woman, but in a child's tantrum. Even though he'd managed to calm her, she'd sobbed on for more than an hour, mechanically, with gulping, with slopping tears.

He hadn't been to work. How could he? But by Wednesday the doctor had fetched some specialist in, a little German fellow, who'd asked her, and him, a lot of questions and who'd ended:

'Vould you spendt a few days in der hosbital vit' us?'

The imitation was ludicrous, but even when one's wife ran mad one mocked foreigners. Riley felt a surge of sympathy; the man was continuing to live, to follow habit.

'What did she say?'

'She couldn't answer. She looked at him. And then at me. And her eyes suddenly flooded with tears. As if her whole head was full of water. But she never said nothing, nor made no sound.'

'Did he tell you what caused it?'

'He said anxiety, and a lot of other long words. He was talking to the doctor, not me. And he told me that nowadays they used drugs. An arsenal of drugs, he said. They'd try until they found one as suited her, and she'd be as good as new. "Ah," I thought. "Until the next time." But there he wa', this little Jerry wi' his bow-tie.'

'Has she been like it before?'

'She's been under treatment for depression for months now. Our man said he could cure her. Seemed like it for a bit, an' all. But she got just as bad again.'

Riley, standing uncomfortably by the table, listened. All

the time this had been happening next door, he'd blundered on with his life, fretting about his factory or rubbing polish round the furniture. A few inches of brick separated him from madness, and he'd been ignorant. He shook his head.

'We've just got to hope,' he said.

'Ay.' O'Brien's face was lugubriously ironical.

'They can do wonders nowadays.'

They kept this conversation up for a minute or two; one had to face facts, and Riley at its flagging said O'Brien must ask for help. He would. He would. They paused, breathing deeply, until it appeared to Riley that both, though stationary, circled the table like wrestlers.

'I'm grateful to you,' he said gruffly. 'You did me good when I was down in the mouth. When you showed me your pictures.'

'Pictures?' He'd wasted the lie.

'Your photographs. Nudes, y'know.'

'Oh, them.'

'I felt like your mate in the army. Man who said, "Let's have a look." Did me good.'

'Would you like to see 'em again?'

'I don't want to bother you.'

'You sit yourself down.'

Though O'Brien produced the photographs without enthusiasm, and in an order different from that of the previous occasion, he kept his wife's picture again until the last. He packed the rest away with such deliberation that Riley thought he was not going to show the final print. When he did so, taking it from the small envelope, he looked hard at it himself. At the same time he did not give the impression of deep interest in the subject-matter of the photograph, merely a dullish wonder as to what he was about. It was as if he was troubled with a headache he was too worried to cure. Finally the card was passed to Riley.

Not unattractive, but diffident. Wanting to scrabble back into her clothes. The face, his imagination perhaps?, seemed tight-lipped, a young woman's expression, not smiling,

60

meeting for the first time what she considered shouldn't exist. Her soldier-husband had surprised her.

'Very nice,' Riley said, passing it back. O'Brien studied it afresh.

'Now she's come to this. It don't seem possible.' Was he about to accuse himself of initiating her frenzy all those years back? 'She was a lovely girl.'

'How old would she be?'

'Twenty-one, two. Don't seem possible.'

'You took it? Yourself?'

'D'you think I'd let other people . . . ?' He stopped, considering his dilemma. 'Seeing the photograph's different from the real thing. An' only you and Alec Bell and me have seen this. I didn't flash it about. I don't know why I showed it Belly in the first place. Shook him a bit. He was a quiet lad. Wesleyan.'

'And me?'

'It done you good. You said so yourself.'

'Yes.'

'She didn't want to. Not at first. I don't know. I'm glad I done it. I wasn't much good at indoor stuff. Developed it myself.'

'Yes. Does she ever mention it?'

'Not from that day to this. Funny, isn't it? Never even asked to see it. Seemed to go against her grain, like. An' yet it was my own wife.'

He packed the photographs away, returned the envelope to the next room.

'Now, is there anything I can do?' Riley asked.

'No. Thank you very much. I don't think there is.'

'If you want me to go up with you. To the hospital.'

'We'll see.'

They shook hands, making something of it, before Riley returned home to his housework. Down in the mouth, he did not cook the meal he had bought, but made a sandwich. He'd done an hour's polishing when the back door was hammered again. Mrs. Scotten with her skirt, or lack of it. She saw his eyes on it, lifted it brazenly away from her crotch.

'All covered and decent,' she said. 'One of our Sandra's. I like 'em.' She followed him in.

'Have you . . . have you been?' She hooked a thumb towards the O'Briens'.

'I have.'

'How is she, then?'

'Under sedation.'

'She would be.' Mrs. Scotten sat, exposing her legs. She seemed at a glance near-naked up to the waist. But she talked sensibly, rather quietly, knowing something. Apparently one of her friends had been in the same hospital, and she had visited twice a week.

'They never done her much good. I couldn't make her out. But she'd never do as she was told, with the tablets and medicines. She was odd at school. We used to make fun of her, and she fly off into such a paddy. She worked wi' me at the bleaching factory, and one day she sets goin' on the screamin' ab-dabs. Not the first time, mind you. But she was in for two years. She's discharged now. Can't do much. Goes round doin' a bit o' private cleanin'. Yet she was ever so nice when she wanted to be.'

He was on his knees at his chores, and she remarked on it, saying she couldn't be bothered, that it wasn't worth it with kids about. When she spoke her accent was by no means uncouth, and she made no attempt to light a cigarette. He wondered why she tried to impress him. As he completed the lounge, he announced his intention of starting on the dining room.

'I'm hindering you,' she said.

In truth, she was not; he enjoyed her chatter, the legs, pants, tights, her ease.

'Sit yourself down in here,' he said. 'Or make yourself a cup of tea.'

'Will you have one?'

'No, thanks. Not for me.'

62

'Then I won't.'

'Light your fag, then.'

'I'm trying to stop.' She sat in a chair, held her legs straight out, then deftly tugged her tights neater. 'I'm all right in here. But as soon as I get back, first thing I s'll do is push one straight in my mouth.'

'Why? What's the difference?'

'I'm a soft bogger, that's the long and short.'

'But you're not, in here?' He laughed.

'I swear to God I'm not. When I come, and see it all spick and span, so you could eat your dinner off the floor, I'm not the same woman as lives in that muck-heap.'

She sounded so genuinely aggrieved that he laughed again.

'It's all right for yo'. Yuh think I'm a slattern, don't you? I'm not. When I come in here and see it all so clean, I think, "A man's done that".'

'You don't get on very well with 'em, next door, do you?'

'They're not so bad. They complained about the kids. The noise and running wild, she said. She's a bit of a sour mouth. I had to tell her. I said, "Look here, if yo' expect 'em to come tiptoeing up the entry, you're goin' to be sucked in. They're kids," I said, "no older than their years." She just stood there. Miserable Mona. Looked a hundred. I feel sorry for her.'

As she chattered, she moved from chair to chair dodging his duster.

'You think I'm idle, don't you? Sitting on my backside watching you work. But I'm not smoking. If I can lay it here for an hour, I can go wi'out there.'

She sat down with him in the kitchen, made no attempt to leave, and he found himself glad of the company.

'That reminds me,' she started. 'I seen that Joan Smith round here. Mrs. Oxford now. I meant to ask you.'

'She came about her son.'

'Hadn't seen her for years. Used to live near us. Too good to breathe. She lived with her mother when they were first married. Stuck-up lot.'

'Why's that?'

'Don't ask me. They was nobody to shout about. 'Er mother wa'nt. An' er young brother Walt used to play wi' me. 'Ad 'is trousers' arse 'anging out.'

'What was her husband like?'

'Smart young chap. I used to like him. They was a lot older than we was. Bit of a way with him. Natty dressed sort o' fellow. I was surprised to see 'er. Hair's gone grey, 'asn't it?'

'The son used to work with me.'

'You've changed jobs, 'aven't you?'

'How do you know that?'

'Can't keep much 'id.' Delighted. 'Our mester seen Eric Twine at "The Star". "Your neighbour's been made a manager." And d'you know what I said to our Arthur? I says, "I don't believe it. He's too good-natured." '

They drank tea together now while she reminisced.

'Do you know how old I am?' she asked.

'No idea.'

'I'm thirty-two today.'

'You don't look it.' She grimaced. 'Aren't you celebrating?'

'How can we? He's on overtime. An' I have to be about.'

He took from the cupboard a miniature bottle of brandy he'd been given for a Christmas present at work.

'We'll split this.'

They drank, and it seemed to sadden her. A waif, neglected, she drooped. She looked no more than fifteen with the short frock and the kid's bitten fingernails.

'I can understand it, how that poor woman went off her head. Gets on your bloody tits sometimes, don't it?'

'This street?'

'No, every bloody thing. Some days I could scream or take a chair-leg and split the kids' skulls in. But it in't their fault, poor little sods. It's me. An' it must ha' been the same with 'er. Maunging about the house all day. But if

I'd have gone in, I wouldn't have been welcome. Bringing me dirt in wi' me. And 'im. Looked at me as if I'd crawled out o' th' closet.'

'You frightened him.'

'Me? Him?'

'You didn't up with the skirts, did you?'

'I bleddy didn't. I've more about me than that.'

'Ah, ah,' he said, careful.

She looked at him, sharply, as if he'd cornered her intellectually, but then she scratched her belly. After a moment she tugged sideways at her dress, violently.

'I don't know why I did it wi' you, not to this day. I was that knocked about that your wife was dead. I liked her. She'd talk to me. And there she was, burnt to ashes. And I thought, "Look at that poor chap standing there, wi' note, not a bleddy thing. And I lay down on that settee and wriggled 'em off. You liked it; you can't say you didn't.'

'I didn't even know your Christian name.'

'Alma.'

'I know now.'

'I was in a daze, like. I knew what I was about, I don't deny. I'm not so soft as I don't know when I've dropped me knickers.'

He nodded. A solemn man.

'I'd hardly any idea what I was up to.'

'You say that,' she said, 'because you're ashamed of it, aren't you?'

'Why should I? You're a young, good-looking woman.'

'Well, then, you thought, "If I keep having it off with her, her husband'll divorce her and I s'll be saddled with her an' all them kids." You did, didn't you? I don't blame you.'

'I don't know what I thought.'

'Did you like it?'

'I was on you an' in before I had a chance to think. Wasn't till later that I told myself what a dirty hound I was. Man with his wife just dead.'

'An' what a dirty whore I was.'

'I expect so. But I was grateful. You did something for me.'

She examined her legs again, and stroked her tights straight, straight round her thighs.

'We s'll be in tears if we go on much longer,' she said, laughing.

'Have you told your husband?'

'What do'you think I am? He'd play bloody glory.' She stood. 'I've wasted enough of your time. I'll help you wash the cups.'

He put his arm round her belly.

'None o' that,' she said, pulled stiffly away. 'I'll tell you when I'm ready.' But she laughed again and patted his shoulder.

8

For the next fortnight Riley kept himself busy.

On Monday a phone call from Bowles informed him that he was to 'get clear' for the installation of a new machine. No amount of questions elicited the size of the fixture or what floor-space it needed, but when it arrived on Wednesday the engineers found no snags. Riley made objections, felt it his place to do so, and was surprised at the obsequious civility of the experts. But he refused to be awkward and when the operation was over, the new piece purring, he stood there satisfied enough, with Dyson, the maintenance man.

'Bit more responsibility,' he said.

'Nice little job, that. Neat. But it in't new, y'know.' Riley was taken aback at the enthusiasm. A girl was set on next day and she and Dyson soon had it in full spate. Every time the manager appeared the other remarked on the efficiency or the design, so that Riley grew suspicious.

'Does the job, and nicely.'

'Enid's got the hang, has she?' The operator.

'My grandchild, that. Smart, she is, and don't make no mistake.'

Towards the end of the next week, while Riley was making up the pay-sheet, he saw Addison, the chief cashier at the old office, swaggering along the factory floor.

'Hello, hello, my boy. Pretty set up.' He smiled at the secretary, pulled suggestive faces, left her smiling. 'Cosy. I'll say that. Kettle always on. Coffee for me. Black. Lot of sugar.'

Riley re-issued the order, resentfully.

'I just had to call in Haddon Street. Bit of hanky-pank going on there, but nothing to us back in the old bug-run.'

Addison fingernailed his moustache, shifted the wrinkles round his face and hummed, then sang, beating time, that his love dwelt in a northern land. Smirking, he pointed a finger at Riley and lowered his eyes to squint along it as if at a rifle.

'The latest,' he said. 'Bowles has got the sack.'

'Eh?'

'Thought that'd rattle you. Your friend Bowlesy's got the poke.'

'What's he been up to?'

'Ah, that's it. Nobody knows. Bit o' creature comfort with Pretty Polly. But he's done. Here today and gone tomorrow.'

'They've transferred him.'

'They have not. Erskine came down and he said personal to me, "We've had to replace Mr. Bowles." '

'And you didn't ask him why?'

'I said, "Yes, sir," and "Where's your backside, sir?" Replace. That's the word.'

'What's the secretary say?'

'She knows no more than the rest of us. There'll be a new man as soon as reasonable, Erskine reckoned.'

'Bowles's got another job?'

'Why didn't they say so, then? No, he's been up to some'at, somewhere, has our friend.' Addison, delighted, stood to receive his coffee, bowing to Miss Rogers, until she blushed. Riley thought he'd pinch her bottom.

'Can't be with the money, or you'd know, wouldn't you?'

Addison, sipping boiling coffee by noisy spoonfuls, explained why this was not necessarily so. Riley ribbed him good-humouredly. In the end, the visitor, draining his cup before the other had started his, said:

'He's been too clever, somewhere.'

'I thought he was efficient,' Riley said.

'Ah, but what at?'

Addison laughed, slapping his knee.

'The mighty are fallen,' he said, 'with a vengeance. I just came round to see whether they hadn't offered you the post. Or,' he gurned in delight, 'kicked you out. Bowles's appointment. In with him, out with him.'

For the next five minutes the parrot chattered, insinuated himself further into Miss Rogers' favour, clattered down the stairs, shouted to the workgirls as he would not have done back in Bowles's factories and drove off. The secretary made a special visit to find out about the visitor, praising him up to the skies. Riley laughed at her, flashed his scorn so that she backed out, rebuffed.

All afternoon he worried about impermanence, and later on whether to knock at Bowles's door. Slightly baffled as to his own motives, he looked the address up in the telephone directory before ravelling out what he'd want to say. If Bowles had got the sack, he'd resent or misread the visit, while Riley himself could get no advantage out of his thanks to a broken man. But Bowlesy was sly; he'd have a trick or two up his sleeve; he was boss-material; nobody would shove him around. Perhaps, Riley considered, his own motives were impure, and he'd like to see King Bowles up the creek, suffering.

At home he cleaned his shoes, laid out his best suit and white shirt, took a bath.

Bowles lived not twenty minutes' walk away, in a residential estate for the rich, a park with beech trees crowding the skies on the roads outside the mansions. Twenty-one Edgeworth Rise had an impressive wooden gate with a name, *Stannilands*, in gold letters. The drive wound between rhododendron bushes, a towering mountain ash with its cauliflower clumps of blossom, some bloom-thick laburnums to the house which consisted of two wings built at right angles, the main door at the intersection. White stuccoed walls, with picture windows, seemed impressively high.

A girl, eighteen, nineteen perhaps, with long fair hair

answered the door. She took his name, left him standing on the step.

Bowles stamped in, wearing a cardigan, shirt collar open, very untidy. As he looked Riley over he shifted his dentures noisily about his mouth.

'Hello, Riley.' Hands deep in pockets, Bowles waited. 'What can I do for you?'

'Mr. Addison told me you were leaving the firm, sir. And I thought that I'd like to come up to thank you for all you'd done for me.'

Bowles screwed his eyes, pouted his lips comically.

'That's not exactly what that sly bugger Addison said to you, if I know him.'

'Perhaps not in those words precisely.'

Now the other laughed out loud, savagely, took his hands from hiding and milled with them in the air. He gloomed at Riley, dark face dark, before poking a thumb into his cardigan breast, under one strand of his braces where he eased it up and down.

'Well, thank you. It's time I got out from Erskines.'

'You're leaving here.'

'I am. Glad to.' Again he rocked from foot to foot and waved his hands. 'I'll give you some advice, Riley. Don't underrate yourself.'

'Thank you, sir.'

For a brief moment, Bowles stared suspicion.

'You're worth a thousand sly sods like Addison. You're a worker, and civil. But don't be too polite, and once you've made your mind up, stick to it.'

'Thank you for all you've done for me.'

'That's all right.'

'I shan't forget it, sir.'

Riley shoved his hand out, and was touched with an unreasoning fear that Erskine's spies were recording this gesture towards a traitor. Bowles shook non-committally.

'Good night, then, sir.'

He let himself out into the evening freshness, closing the door timidly. Back in that hall with its oak and gold frames, behind that mock-Tudor door, Bowles did what?

As he legged it downhill home Riley knew exhilaration, in that he had done his duty, and with pleasure. But his former gaffer's puzzlement, uncertainty, touched him, confirming him in the belief that he'd done right. Not till he was past half-way home did he recall that Bowles had not worn his executive spectacles.

As he turned into Stoney Street, he whistled, nearly walked straight past Mrs. Oxford.

'Mr. Riley.'

'Didn't see you there.'

'Can I . . . ? Can I talk to you?' She was crying.

'Come on in.'

'I thought you'd gone out. I'd been waiting.'

Once they were inside the door she sobbed out loud.

'This won't do,' he said. 'Now, will it?'

As he spoke, he barely bothered with his words or with the woman, for his mind was back to the inconsequential brevity of conversation in that mansion. In a strange house, he'd gone up and said something that seemed both necessary but unimportant. He had needed, himself, to spit his thanks out. It would be memorable as if he'd stepped from the ranks and publicly thanked the C.O. This sobbing at his elbow seemed nothing.

He sat her down, proposed tea.

When he returned she had straightened her face, tidied her hair and could apologise. Rather brightly she claimed to like his cuckoo-clock. During the drinking of the first cup they sat in silence while he thought of Bowles's denuded face and flailing arms. She refused a second, and sitting straight-backed said:

'I've decided to leave my husband.'

Taken aback, he refilled, asked awkwardly:

'Have you told him so?'

'No.'

He coughed; this was devious.

'I owe him nothing,' she said. 'But it's no use walking out, unprepared.' She waited, pert smile held, continued, 'I thought perhaps you'd have rooms to let.'

'Here?'

'Or somewhere else.'

He hid behind his cup as she sat in command.

'I've had a part-time job at Stainforth's, the pastry cook's, for three years now. They've wanted me to go full-time for long enough. I can please myself.'

Riley said nothing as she laid down her law.

'I can support myself,' she said, 'especially if I get a comfortable place to live.' She stopped, fingers white on chair-arms. 'You don't understand me, Mr. Riley, do you? When he told our Frank to get out, I thought to myself, "Why should I stay here? What's to keep me? The boy's a grown man. Why should I put up with it when I don't need to?" That's sense, isn't it? He'd have to liven himself up if I went.'

'I see.'

'You don't.' Her voice crackled into laughter, as if he stood condemned with her husband for stupidity. 'I could please myself for once in my life instead of mothering those two great babies.'

'Well . . .'

'There's no affection, if that's what you mean. I don't love him. I don't see how anybody could.'

'What will happen, though, when you tell him?'

'He'll shout, and rave. He might try to hit me.'

'You don't feel any obligation, Mrs. Oxford?'

'Why should I? It's all give, on my part. Take, on his.'

He offered her more tea, and on her refusal packed the crockery on the tray which he carried to the scullery. On his return he said:

'Mrs. Oxford, when I met you tonight, you were in tears.'

'I know.' Shameless. 'I was that disappointed. I'd made my mind up to it, and then you were out.'

'It has to be me, does it?'

'No. Why should it? But I understood from Frank that you owned several houses, and it seemed sensible to try you. I was wrong. I thought you'd likely know somewhere even if you hadn't got anywhere yourself.' She used her priciest shop-voice.

'My other houses are let out to tenants.' He was boasting. 'I could put you up here, but I don't know if it would be wise.'

She laughed in his face.

'For you or me?' He scratched at his face, taken aback. She talked as if she'd been drinking.

'I understand your husband has it in for me already. Over the boy. And if you settled . . .'

'Does that frighten you?'

'I can look after myself, Mrs. Oxford. I was thinking about you. He might take it into his head to . . .' He allowed her a few seconds for imagination. 'Besides, you know what people are round here. There'd be talk. I'm a widower, an unattached man.'

'And you've got a bad character with women?'

He decided he'd had sufficient.

'If you hadn't been crying twenty minutes back, I should think you were pulling my leg.'

'I'm serious.'

'You don't talk like it.'

Now he looked her over again, this neat woman, as she adjusted her glasses, smiling prettily, with grey hair petalling either side of her parting, her feet together and hands finally replaced, re-clasped in her lap. He could not decide what was there. She'd married a loud mouth, had borne a nondescript son, had dodged round these two avoiding trouble and now, deciding on independence, favoured him with her counter manner.

'I see what you mean, Mr. Riley,' she began. She sat very still to talk so that he got the impression she wasn't the lightweight he'd imagined. She could be awkward, even

powerful, perhaps, obstructive. 'There are plenty of lodg-
ings all over the town. I could walk out now and fit myself
up half a dozen times in an hour in some streets. I know.
But I thought of you. Impulse.' The word stabbed him
with surprise. 'There's been a lot of talk about you in our
house since you've been made a manager. Ron was always
on about it. He was jealous. "Why don't you consult your
friend, the managing director?" That's what he'd say to
Frank when he was mad. And that's what he called you.'

She smiled again, a twist of the mouth, small, attractive.

'It's silly,' she said, 'to drag you into it. I don't know
why I thought of it. Bit of my own back.' She clasped her
knees while they sat in silence.

'You know one of my neighbours,' he said. 'Mrs. Scotten.
Alma Scotten.'

'Scotten? Oh, yes. Alma Humphreys, as was.' She made
a little dramatic performance of the act of remembering.
'They lived near us.'

'A rough diamond.'

'I haven't seen her for years. Alma was all right. She
was only a girl, then. The family weren't exactly my
favourites.'

'In what way?' Polite, polite.

'Didn't like work. One of the brothers got into trouble
with the police.' She relented, shifting her upright position.
'But Alma was a very attractive child; big eyes and she
used to sing a lot, pop songs, y'know, and stuff they'd learnt
at school. There was one we used to have. The headmaster,
old Boney Jonesey, always picked it. "Song of the Music
Makers." ' She hummed, ironically, beating time. 'I bet you
had it.'

He smiled back, not recognising the tune.

' "Come, music makers, rouse up a song
    To set the echoes ringing,
    A song of truth in the heart of youth,
    A song for the joy of singing." '

He still did not know it, but it brought back the smell of swabbed corridors and high glass partitions and the transposing piano being rattled into place by the two biggest boys. She had spoken, not sung, the verse with a diffidence that attracted him, made the situation unreal as though the break-up of a marriage had never been discussed, as if they were recalling minor pleasures for a radio audience.

She stood, pulled on ridiculously small gloves.

'I'm wasting your time,' she said.

Then he knew he'd offer to take her in.

9

There were no repercussions from Mrs. Oxford's move. She had her bits and pieces, mainly clothes, delivered in a van by a friend, a surly devil who kicked his way up both flights of stairs with her cases. Riley had exerted himself to persuade a plumber along the street to install a wash-basin in the third-floor bedroom, and he himself had bought an electric fire for the other which she'd use as a sitting room.

He finished both carefully, telling himself that he was doing himself good by preserving his property, drying it out. Mrs. Oxford herself arrived, inconspicuously, soon after six on the same evening, ate the food he'd prepared, and then rather chilly had said they must discuss meals. When she retired upstairs he had to force himself back into routine. His excitement still pushed; for the last two weeks he'd spent his leisure in her rooms, mounted Yale locks on her door, scrubbed the floorboards, washed the paint-work. The wallpapers were newish, only slightly stained, but he knew he wanted her to choose fresh designs so that he could serve her by redecorating.

It seemed foolish. He did not look forward to her love, did not want her thus; that was too dangerous. But up there, in those bright rooms under the roof, she'd settled cosily, and he below would listen to her moving about, and be ready with his lick of paint and screwdriver.

He'd expected the male Oxfords to poke their faces in.

For some reason he feared Frank, not the father, and prepared his mind for a cold managerial reception, when he'd explain that this was purely a business arrangement, invite the boy in, show him round, all. Why he bothered with this palaver to himself he couldn't determine. Frank was a nonentity, the father a braggart; he'd deal with both and sharp. Why the fuss then? He felt guilty. He robbed this poor pair of something he wanted.

Then for the next week he looked out in the street, watching for looming men, blocking his path, creating a scene. When nothing happened, he tended to forget, had to remind himself to hold all in readiness.

His contacts with Mrs. Oxford were, in fact, brief. She had her lunch cheaply in a restaurant not far from the shop she worked in; her tea upstairs. She had agreed that she would cook Sunday dinner for both on his stove. On Saturday, she worked in the morning, they pleased themselves, and though he hoped she would share his meal, she rarely did so, often going away to visit friends and not returning until midnight. However, she'd be up and dressed in time to see the joint, chosen by arrangement and fetched by him, in the oven so that it would be placed on the table with trimmings at five minutes to one. As the radio pips sounded, he had carved and both had begun. Together in silence, chewing, they listened to the news, and perhaps the commentary following, until they were ready for the fresh fruit pudding, both were slimming, and finally the cup of sugarless tea in the front room.

That Riley looked forward to, and was disappointed. They talked, but desultorily, and though Mrs. Oxford often took a second cup, to please him, he guessed, she did not stay there long. Sharp on to her feet, she'd put an apron across her Sunday dress, wash the dishes, and all would be cleared, over, by two. Now and then he plucked up courage to ask her back to the lounge, but she refused, smilingly, pleading letters to write. Then he'd sit to Gardeners' Question Time and drop asleep as if there were no woman in the house.

He'd thought it best to tell Alma Scotten what was happening, and she, as he expected, pulled his leg. That he did not mind and when she made out that she listened for orgies, and had not been disappointed, he joined her in bawdry. A sensible woman, under the muck, she was allowed her ribaldry about what went on or off in the attic, because it was a joke shared between them. Had he heard her making the same innuendoes to her husband that would have been different. He mentioned the new arrival to O'Brien once when he'd accompanied him to the hospital, but the man seemed utterly uninterested. His wife had received E.C.T. and improved; chatter about lodgers could wait.

Once when Mrs. Oxford was out Riley looked in her rooms. They were, as he anticipated, spotless but so tidy that all personality had been obliterated. No pictures; the calendar small, days unmarked. No clothes were to be seen or shoes. Her cosmetics had been hidden so that the dressing-table top was bare except for the runner and glass powder-bowls and ring-tree he had put there. Her wardrobe was not locked, but every dress hung spick and span. Tempted, he dared not rummage in the drawers among her underwear. A stickler himself for neatness, he wanted here some sign of flurry, a dropped hair-clip, a spill or scent of powder; instead this barrack-room perfection mocked him, as if she spent interminable hours slaving to erase all trace of herself. He needed a woman in the house.

On Saturday morning as she went out she put an envelope containing her rent on the thin shelf of the mirror hanging in the front passage. He kept a record in a ruled notebook headed 'Mrs. Joan M. Oxford', in which he wrote down the amounts paid and his signature, but did not show it to her. She might think he did not trust her. He modified his routine to allow her the run of the kitchen on Sunday morning, but had more leisure since the top floor needed no attention.

Occasionally he visited the local cinema, and once took Mrs. Scotten. She'd asked him where he was off to, said with her cheerful insouciance that she'd change her shoes and come with him. He replied that she must ask her husband. At this she looked abashed, the alteration in her appearance was startling, as if he'd made an obscene suggestion, but she called out to her husband who appeared shag-headed at the back door.

'Can I go to the pictures with Mr. Riley?' she asked.

'When?'

'Now, you daft bogger.'

'Well, I'll go t'our 'ouse.'

But he gave permission, and she was down, very clean, inside ten minutes.

'None o' that back-row stuff, yo' two,' Scotten called.

'You should know all about that,' she replied. 'You dirty ol' man.'

Riley insisted on paying for the seats, pressed on her a box of sugared fruits, but they said little, sitting stiffly side by side like a couple of old-age pensioners on an outing. It disappointed him, though he could not have said he wanted it different. Perhaps all his dealings with women were now to be cool like this, and he become the middle-aged man in the raincoat, satisfying himself with fondled enormous nipples of screen actresses. They called in 'The Wheatsheaf' for a half-pint, did not hang about. As she thanked him on parting she clutched the cloth of his coat, a desperate gesture, he hoped. Next evening, Scotten appeared himself to add his thanks. He was grateful because he didn't want to waste good working- or drinking-time at the pictures, while his wife didn't somehow fancy going off with a woman friend. 'She's tried it, mind. But it didn't suit.' The neighbour left, talking as expansively as he could, so that Riley grew suspicious that they were out to trap him into indiscretion, then mildly dejected at his new role of eunuch.

At the factory all was busy but not desperately so.

At meal-times the men and women discussed Bowles's successor, and once deputed Dyson, the maintenance man, to interview Riley about the matter. His blunt denial of knowledge was not taken altogether kindly, merely another indication of bosses' useless security. They talked of Bowles now with respect; he was a bastard whom you could trust. If he gave his word, he stuck by it. They remembered the time he sacked Ted Wilson, the union king, and got away with it, and locked the men out and had to crawl on his bended knees to entice them back. The women talked of his hands up skirts and the stories he told at the Christmas parties. Such reminiscence in this factory surprised Riley until he realised that a good number of his people had worked under Bowles's jurisdiction, or had husbands or relatives who did, so that when this place became part of a larger concern they already shared the broader mythology about the gaffer. Bowles was, had been, important in this town; not a smudgy photograph in the paper, like the Lord Mayor, but a somebody who'd actually spoken to you, more than once, on his rounds, remembered your name, and failing that said something so filthy or sensible to you, you hadn't forgotten it.

Riley would have liked to join these groups, to add his titbit about Bowles's house, but decided against it. The lance-jack holds himself aloof in his cubicle. He did speak to Miss Rogers, the secretary.

'They're all talking about Mr. Bowles,' she had said.

'Are they?' He relented. 'Did you know him, then?'

'I've seen him here a time or two since the amalgamation.'

'You didn't before?'

'Everybody has heard of him, I should think.'

He looked at her, wondered why she'd not married. She'd no parents to look after, had one brother who had been to Oxford and worked for Granada Television.

'Was he well liked, would you say?' he asked.

'In his way.' Riley laughed. 'He was a character.'

'I suppose so.'

'He was dreadful with women.'

'Isn't that just talk, Miss Rogers?'

'No, it is not.' Suddenly she blushed scarlet. 'I'm not

talking about myself.' She brazened it out. 'But some of the things some of the girls have told me . . .'

'Were they speaking the truth?'

'Nobody knows that. I just have to judge.'

'People like to boast of all kinds of odd matters, y'know.'

'You don't need to tell me, Mr. Riley.'

He invited her to sit, and they wasted five minutes in silence, while he allowed his head to buzz with a rigmarole of jagged ideas, muffled phrases, starts and foolishness. The rubbishy stream pelted on, regardless of him, as if controlled from outside, though connected vaguely with his past, but the triviality reminded him, if he caught himself out, of a cat on a keyboard, up, down, a deaf cat unperturbed by noise and only slightly put out by the uncertainty of footholds. He was a flitter-brain. On reflection, and he had to hold himself hard at it, he supposed everybody was similar. Once he stopped conscious thought, the idiocy of jumble tumbled back, like a badly focussed length of film. Underneath, he feared, some part of him encouraged this babel of poverty.

'I don't know, Miss Rogers.'

'What's that, then?'

'Human beings. I can't make 'em out. I can't make myself out, if it comes to that.'

Then she soothed, praised, buttered him up in her mildness. He didn't need her expertise any longer—he knew the factory as well as she did. But he enjoyed her company, this neat woman.

'You know, Miss Rogers, you do me good.'

'Now, Mr. Morley would never had said that.' She beamed.

'Would Bowles?'

'I never worked for him.' He'd spoilt it, again, but they smiled.

Major Erskine rang him.

'Riley? Bob Erskine here.' Christian name, diminutive,

to managers. 'How are things going down at Carnell & Bloom's, eh? Well? Yes. We're pleased. Bowles sent a very satisfactory report.

Riley outlined progress, mentioned the new machine about which Erskine professed ignorance. They made accustomed military noises at either end of the line.

'Bowles's gone. I expect you know.'

'Yes, sir.'

'I don't want to say too much. But he exceeded himself. It was no part of his business to instruct the directors.'

'No, sir.'

'He was admirable in many ways, Riley. Built the business up. Good relationships with the unions. Too good, for some of us. He wanted a free hand. Plenipotentiary, you know. Didn't do. I was sorry to see him leave, but it saved trouble.'

'I'd heard none of this, sir.'

'Oh, hadn't you, hadn't you, then? Say nothing. Trust you. Can take you into my confidence. Latest pay deal. That's what I wanted to speak to you about. But he wanted to settle the whole damn' tamasha himself, at a price we weren't prepared to pay.'

'He was very astute, sir.' Riley was not to be walked on.

'At one time. And locally. Not nationally. Things change. Saw himself as Santa Claus distributing largesse.'

'That's not the way the men regarded him, sir, I can tell you that.'

'I believe you, Riley, I believe you.' Erskine's dry cough sketched the ginger Hitler moustache, the polite ringed hand. 'We allowed him to resign when he'd fixed himself up elsewhere.'

'No word of this has got round, sir.'

'What's that mean, Riley?'

'In the factory it was given out he'd got the sack. They came round to tell me.' Mistake. 'But there wasn't any mention of trouble about pay, sir.'

'Matter hadn't come up,' Erskine said. 'Bowles was preparing his brief, he claimed.'

'I see, sir.'

'A good player on a bad wicket. But we employers are slightly better placed. Today. In a stronger position. We can fight, at least, with a modicum of hope.' Riley remembered Erskine's tactical talks; the boring voice and finger smartly indicating the obvious. 'Still we need help from time to time. Rang you about that, really. Want to know what your men and women are thinking. About pay. Conditions. Vital we know. But with tact, Riley. Bowles was good there, I'll give him that. Even so, there's no security of tenure in these managerial posts. You realise that. One error, you're out.'

Riley did not remember direct threats like that from Erskine in the army, but it was commonly rumoured in the sergeants' mess that a C.O. rollocked his company commander, his adjutant as he'd never chase his N.C.O.s.

'Still, we're pleased with you. But ask about. Your job is not to fulfil quotas, but to know where the men stand. The women, of course.' Erskine cackled. 'I'm coming round to see the place myself. Next week. Bring the new man. Bowles's successor.'

'He's appointed, is he, sir?'

'He is. Chap called Cooper. Young. Go-getter. Efficiency expert. He's on the make, on the way up, but he'll do, he'll do for the time being. We all need shaking up.'

'In what way, sir?'

'Way? That's for him to decide, isn't it?' Menace, a second time. 'And he will.'

Between them they fixed the day of the visit. Immediately Riley sent for Dyson and for Miss Rogers. He invited both to sit down, described the phone call. The secretary smiled, gushed that Major Robert had not been here before, and cooed inanities about his taking a more active part in running the business. Then she wondered aloud about the acute Mr. Cooper.

Dyson glowered, humped himself from ham to ham like a sulky child, then pushing out wet, red lips.

'Don't know their arse from their elbow,' he said.

Riley waited for him, face pleasant, to continue.

'These fellows coming round. Deal with bits of paper in an office. All they know's a ten-quid note when they see it.'

Riley inquired politely whether he should inform the work-people, but Dyson, acting indifference, said he'd pass the word.

'We shall have to have the place spruced up on that day,' Riley said.

'Waste a week, bulling, for half an hour.'

'That's not what I said. Arrange for the clean overalls to be issued that morning.'

'Ay, bull.'

'Yes, bull. The floors clean. No waste lying about for days. I don't mind slovenly habits as long as they don't get in my way. On this day they will. Are you going to tell 'em, or am I?'

'Please yourself.'

'I'll tell them, then, but you can give 'em a preview. With comments. Bolshy as you want, as long as they know what's what. I'll issue the official order.'

'They won't like it.'

'Hasn't the union got a pay-claim in?'

'Well, if they have.'

'Cooper'll be the man who argues it out for the directors.'

'I don't see as that's got much t'do wi' it.'

'If you don't, you don't.' Dyson affronted rolled his head. 'Tell 'em old Bundook said so.'

'What?'

'You heard. I'll issue official orders later. But I want 'em acted on.'

Dyson shambled off, lugubrious, but delighted to act as messenger.

'I don't like him.' Miss Rogers. 'He's rude.'

'Not half as rude as I shall be if they don't jump to it.' They nodded agreement. 'The tea-break's about due. Gives him chance to say his piece.'

'I wouldn't trust him.'

'I don't. But he'll get the idea across. And attract some of the blame. Then I tell them exactly what's what.' He moved smoothly to her, took her by the warm crook of her arm. 'I think two sweet coffees here will be in order while they learn the worst downstairs.'

She leaned on him slightly; he felt her left breast on his jacket, but though she seemed friendly, there was a poise about her, a smartness of dress and stance that showed she need stand no nonsense from him. Her hair brushed his face as she moved away. Sweetly.

The work-people were all compliance, and made a point of asking next day about Cooper; Riley answered, politely cheerful.

'We don't know till we've seen him, do we? Said to be quick. Efficiency king. We know what efficiency means to that sort. I don't need to tell you. Redundancy.' He'd acquired managerial threats easily. 'But we don't know. Young chap, on the road up. And if you and I stand in his way to the board, we know who'll get trampled on.' Pause. 'Me.' And the one or two listening bystanders joined the uneasy laughter.

The visitation passed without incident.

Girls stood, cleanly, in Sunday make-up at their machines while the men in the storeroom managed a heavy day's work without mess. Riley and Miss Rogers had straightened their rooms, and Dyson had even cleaned the highest barlights. All the loudspeakers functioned, and heavy rain outside gave the factory a comfortable air.

Cooper was a round-faced man, who slapped his kid gloves against his white military raincoat while he stared up and down. Neither he nor Erskine knew what to look for, but while the major scraped his mind for a few relevant questions about paint-work or maximum and minimum

85

temperatures and asked one or two of the staider women how they liked the work, the younger man could barely sling a word at Riley. Exactly as in the army, a man polished his leisure time away for a general and his entourage to walk past unnoticing. The lack of notice was the hallmark; too smart to be seen. An unshined toecap or cloudy button would have brought hell down.

They tramped upstairs to the office where Miss Rogers issued coffee and biscuits and Cooper tested Riley for five minutes. After initial hesitations, Riley enjoyed the quiz as soon as he realised he'd not met his match, that he could point out flaws in the other's reasoning, present snags or qualifications the other hadn't thought of. In the end he summed up adequately, thought Erskine watched him with new respect, but found Cooper faceless.

'Good,' Erskine said to Riley. 'Good. What d'you think then, Geoffrey?'

'All small concerns are uneconomic. Must be.'

'But this does what's necessary at present.'

'In view of the price, yes. I don't deny it.'

They looked at Riley, guilty, nabbed thieves.

'You'd close the place down, then?' Riley said to Cooper, aggressively, speaking for his men.

'He didn't say that.' Erskine's voice twanged far back, aristocratic.

'We think, we must think in terms of expansion. Suppose we did, you couldn't meet demands, either in quantity or sizes.'

'I could step my output up.' Riley had prepared a short typed statement; he passed copies. Both read.

'Good,' Erskine said. 'Very interesting, Riley, this. Think so, Geoffrey?'

'Neat,' Cooper answered. He shrugged. 'If we move big, well.'

'Drop in the ocean.'

Riley sat deflated, neglected. This young jockey, with his schoolboy's moustache, his scowl and Old Etonian voice, sniffing his coffee-cup as if it were hemlock, wouldn't bat an eyelid if he had to blow the whole place to smithereens, employees and all.

'Keep this up,' Erskine said, tapping the plan with his fingernails. He shook hands, and made for the outer office and stairs. Cooper nodded, locked his fingers behind his back and followed. The major paused to thank Miss Rogers for coffee; Cooper nodded graciously. In the outside porch, Erskine wrinkled his eyes, touched his moustache and said, 'You've not got me a note on pay-claims?'

Riley took out his wallet, passed another memorandum, this time handwritten.

'First inquiries,' he said.

'Splendid.'

'I'll have more information.'

'I'm sure you will. You've taken to this like a duck to water, Riley. Good.'

Cooper, eyeing a spouting drainpipe, did not speak as he stepped out, avoided puddles, reached the back seat of the Bentley.

10

Riley discussed the visit with his people.

Dyson led an official delegation to him on the shop-floor at lunch-time. They wanted to know what Cooper thought of the place.

'Hard to say.' Riley sat easily on the edge of the table. 'He's a whizz-kid, and thinks all this is out-of-date.' Dyson began to demur, truculently, but stopped as the manager held up a hand. 'You say some of these machines are new. So they are. But this chap's all for very fast expansion. He wants a dozen factories, or their equivalent, for every one or two we've got. Talks big. And if he manages this, then he thinks our sort of place'll be of no use.'

'We'll be out.'

'Not of necessity. If they take over, they'll need men they know. We're getting so big, even now, that the high-ups don't know you and me by name. But they'll use anybody useful. A good workman's worth money.'

'When will all this happen?'

'Never, I hope,' Riley said, saw them smile with him. 'If it does it'll take time. I don't know. Cooper might blow bubbles for a bit, then flit elsewhere.'

'Did he seem a fair man?'

'I've no idea. He was astute once he was up in the office. Whether he'll play fair, I can't say. He would if it suited his book. Don't see why not.'

Riley enjoyed the exchange of ideas, and noticed, with surprise, that the men and women listened with great seriousness to what he said. They watched, and nodded, expressed approval or disagreement in a subdued way, politely, without temper; they talked to a boss.

Soon they touched on the topic of pay. Again Riley raised his hand, and again commanded silence.

'Before you say anything more. You've got a claim in. Or at least negotiation's started. Now, I'm the enemy.' Some laughed, but one grave woman nodded. 'My job is to keep you working and happy. They're not incompatible.' He coughed. 'I hope.' Sergeant's clumsy pep-talk. 'I'm pleased to chat to you. To listen to what you've got to say. But you must remember the directors, or one of their underlings, will quiz me. I'll be glad to hear you. But wouldn't it be better to see your union man first? He mightn't think it wise.'

'Bogger 'im,' said the woman.

'Not today, baker,' Riley answered, and they laughed. 'I want to be fair. You've done me well. I'd help you out if I could. But you might give something away, in an informal talk like this, that your union thinks better kept back until the pay-talks proper begin.'

As he expected, this opened their mouths wider than ever. They chuntered about the union, closed shop, cost of living, as if amongst themselves. He was pleased with their moderation; they seemed unmilitant, old-fashioned, even the youngsters. Riley allowed them to say their piece, did not interrupt and left casually ten minutes before the starting-bell rang, while they continued argument.

However, he was surprised when Dyson presented himself to suggest that the union representative would like an interview, at four o'clock.

Riley refused, saying that as this was obviously unofficial it had better be done in private time. Dyson, slightly unprepared after yesterday's bonhomie, agreed, borrowed the phone while Riley diplomatically waited outside, though he heard every word, and then decided the lunch hour of the following Friday would suit everybody.

Now, Riley was nervous.

He gobbled his sandwiches, fiddled at the mirror, went

three times to the urinal; at twelve-forty-five he bit his lips, followed the arrival, the jovial, coarse exchanges with the work-people who paraded in expectation, listened to the confident quick clatter of shoes on the staircase. Miss Rogers held progress up for a moment, asked the two to wait, came in to announce their arrival. Riley read a type-written sheet, found he'd understood nothing.

Dyson ushered his companion into the room, closed the door. Riley stood, progressed round his desk, shook hands with the union man, a cold hand, limp-damp, showed the visitors to chairs already placed. Without hurry, once they were settled, he returned to his chair, unhurrying.

'Now, Mr. Riley . . .'

Riley held his hand deferentially up.

'You gentlemen will join me in a cup of coffee.' He rang the bell, waited for the secretary, made his demand in leisurely politeness. He waved his antagonist on.

'Mr. Riley. I'll make myself plain. My name's Maddison, and I'm branch secretary. My members have asked me to call on you.' He waited, but Riley merely stared. 'You've no objection.'

'None.' He was made to wait for the word.

'I understand there was some discussion between you and my members about pay. And in the course of this you drew attention to my union and its negotiations. I don't want to be misunderstood, but I believe you made it clear that your opinion would be canvassed by the directors. I do not want to step out of place. Nor make wild accusa-tions. But isn't that, Mr. Riley, provocative? Or, to use a less loaded word, dangerous talking? At this early and deli-cate stage, when both sides are preparing their case . . .'

Riley allowed him to run on, stared down at his desk, or now and again straight back at his opponent's eyes. He could have laughed out loud. This Maddison, a bald lined man, had nothing to say in thousands of words; perhaps he needed to hold his place, assert himself by bellicosity and had therefore slapped himself down in a manager's office to make threatening faces and string out menacing feeble sentences. Miss Rogers interrupted the flow with a tray. Now Maddison and his companion were snaffled, needing both hands to manage coffee and biscuits, while Riley stirred his cup comfortably on the desk.

'Please go on, Mr. Maddison.'

He obliged. Sentences circled; questions were hurled; the tone hardened, quieted itself, exploded, snarled. Riley waited. In the end Maddison stopped, a frown, a thrust-out chin indicating aggressive intent.

'Mr. Dyson?' Riley almost theatrically gestured that the floor was his, but Dyson, unprepared, wriggled, sucked his coffee, claimed Maddison had said it all.

'Thank you.' Now for the other. 'I don't quite follow you, Mr. Maddison.'

'In what way?' Snapped.

'As I understand you, you are prepared to fight me, or my employers, or anybody else for the rights of your members.' Maddison growled assent, assumed a fighting face. 'I knew that already.'

'What you said the other day constituted, in my humble opinion, provocation.'

Riley nodded; when there was nothing to argue he'd be silent.

'I don't want to overstate the case, as you understand. Good relationships between union and management are a prerequisite of modern industrial . . .' He was away in strongly delivered phrases, so that for the moment Riley believed in his belief, his sour sincerity, until he considered what was said. As he received no answer, Maddison talked louder, rattled cup, spoon and saucer, leaned forward, red of face. At the end of a raucous paragraph he dropped his voice, hissed, 'It's my duty, Mr. Riley, to make you understand this or to warn you that otherwise you may well put yourself at peril.'

Again he halted; Riley put his hands in ironical prayer before his face.

'Is that all, Mr. Maddison?'

The other glared, but added nothing.

Riley now looked hard at him, then, modestly sighing, dropped his eyes.

'Thank you very much,' he began. 'I appreciate your frankness. And I'll tell you, before Mr. Dyson here, that any time you wish to put your case to me, you are welcome. All you have to do is ring my secretary, and she'll arrange a time convenient for us both.' He paused, but not for long. 'As for today's business. The discussion which took place did so, as Mr. Dyson will tell you, at the invitation of my work-people. And I'll tell you, if they invite me again, I shall stop again and talk to them.' He checked Maddison with a raised finger. 'If you advise them against such discussions, that is, of course, your business. But I think, and Mr. Dyson will confirm this, I specifically warned them, and asked them to . . .'

'I've no objection to that, as well you know. I'm not threatening anything or warning anybody or chucking my weight about unnecessary. I'm just reminding you there's a union, that it's prepared to take action if necessary and if driven to it.' He talked on, but the apology stood, rock in a torrent.

'And,' Riley said, 'you wanted to have a look for yourself who's in charge here, eh?'

'Ay.'

'Don't blame you. Very sensible. You won't find me unreasonable. My job's to keep this factory running efficiently, and that means seeing your members are contented. I shan't forget.' Apology in return. He stood.

Maddison, with nothing to say, added a couple of paragraphs and the three moved together, the secretary still in verbal spate, to the door. A hand-shaking ceremony and they were gone. Three minutes later Dyson returned cheerfully by the same entrance.

Upstairs Riley, trembling at his desk, was elated. He'd shown them his mettle, peaceably. It did not do to scold, or squabble for a start, but merely to exchange courtesies of awkwardness.

'He tried to frighten me,' he told Miss Rogers.

'And did he?'

She handled his sleeve; she often touched him now, could barely enter the room without encroaching on his side of the desk to sidle up to him, brush past him, finger his suit. He did not object, pleased to give pleasure.

He saw Vaughan, the union organiser, in the street a day or so later.

'Had a visit from one of your underlings,' he said.

'Who's that now?' Fruity South Wales.

'Maddison.'

'Oh. Bullshit Bill. What did he want, as if I didn't know? Let me tell you. The union looked after its members, so watch your step. He didn't want trouble, but he could hand it out. Mind your lip with the men; they might be simple, but he wasn't.'

Both laughed, marched into a pub for halves of bitter.

Vaughan, chuckled still, but tapped Riley's arm.

'Maddison's all right. Keen. Keeps the men up to scratch. Does the chores willingly and makes faces at minor management like yourself.'

'Is that good?'

Riley was unused to the chatter of the lunch-time bar, the black girl in hot pants and hexagonal dark glasses serving, but enjoyed the exchange. He held his shoulders back, appeared proud.

'Yes. I've no time to do it. What with the day-to-day administration and the real fights we have got on, I'm hardly in my own office, never mind yours. So we have Billy stirring it up.'

Riley outlined the pretext for Maddison's visit.

Immediately Vaughan's face became wary, coldish, but then he drank and smiled again.

'It doesn't do, my friend,' with pulpit unction, 'to be too scrupulous.' South Welsh pronunciation. 'When the manager tells 'em to send for their union representative before they talk to him, they suspect he's up to some monkey business. And so would I, fellow, so would I. Trouble is there aren't many honest men in your walk of life.'

'Now, then. You're in management yourself.'

'Too bloody true, boy.'

'Did you never think of . . . ?'

'Working for the other side? Chance'd be a fine thing. And by the time I'd got a few paper qualifications and some experience I was too deeply committed. I'm in for another promotion tomorrow. I shall get it, too. And we pack our traps and sell the house and set off like scalded cats for Manchester, uprooting the kids from their schools and my missus from her job and all for another two bloody hundred a year and a shuffle up the stair.'

'How far will you . . . ?'

'That's easy. I'm about there. A lucky run or two and I might do a touch better. But I'm in my forties, like you, and they've got me written off as a good middle-range man. It would be a miracle if I managed anything more, now. But I tell you this. I don't mind.' Forefinger tapped Riley's lapel. Everybody touched him. 'I'm busy. I like the work. I haven't stopped yet.'

'And you hope for something . . . ?'

'Of course I bloody do. I'm human.'

'They made me a manager,' Riley said, humbly. 'I think they wanted somebody on the cheap.'

'I know what you get. It's not too bad, as things are. And if you want my opinion, you're the ideal man for that place.'

'From your point of view?'

'And theirs. But my people like you. "Bundook's straight." That's what they say. "Struts a bit. An' slippin' the secretary a crippler." ' He laughed, punched Riley's upper arm, and they drank another half. 'They like that, you know. Dirty sods.'

Riley felt above himself as he walked for ten minutes among car-din to his factory. He wasn't badly paid. They liked him. Straight. A man. He inspected lilac leaves behind a brick wall adjacent to acres of concrete, skyscraping offices. A bulldozer would soon uproot the shrubs and the line of privet and the flagstones of the garden path and who could complain? But seventy, eighty, a hundred years ago a decent bricklayer had completed that wall, and what? Gone home to beat his wife, booze himself, shout in a prayer-meeting? He was dead now.

His mood changed.

Vaughan patronised him because he was a nonentity, not worth fighting. Buying half-pints from pretty black ladies, in a cacophony of men with stuffed wallets and shouting laughter, was a fool's game. The beer turned sourly in his stomach all afternoon. He cleaned his teeth twice, kept well away from Miss Rogers, feeling that he'd smirched himself.

At home he had already begun his cleaning when he heard Mrs. Oxford come in. She went straight upstairs.

By eight he'd finished, was satisfied and sat in front of the television. A noisy quiz-show dispersed his interest, and he was considering going next door to inquire after Mrs. O'Brien when he heard a knock at the back.

'Mr. Riley?' Smart voice under jaunty trilby. Nodding. 'My wife lives here.'

It took some seconds to connect, to concentrate on those last four words, revise the stereotype and decide that this was brutal, swilling Oxford.

'Come in.'

They went sedately into the lounge where Oxford perched with his Alpine hat on one knee. In his youth he'd have been handsome, Riley decided, for even now he kept an aquiline straightness, a pride of posture, that the watery eye, broken veins on his cheeks, could not dull. His hands were misshapen, cracked with work, but he'd shaved, put on a clean shirt, a fancy tie, his best suit, shoes smooth as galoshes. It seemed pathetic.

'Did you want to see your wife?'

'To see about her.'

'She's upstairs in her rooms.'

'Rooms?' The word echoed, softly. 'She don't live with you, then?'

'She lives in her own place on the top floor.'

'She lives with you, Mr. Riley.' The sentence was urged strongly, but tailed into the weakness of the name.

'In this house, yes.' The conversation took the exactly expected line, but Riley trembled. When he glanced at the visitor again the man seemed uncomfortable, uncertain, shifty.

'You mean to say . . . ?' Oxford.

'Yes.'

'She's not living with you.'

'No. Not as you mean. She's a lodger.'

Oxford scratched his poll, but not inelegantly, and moved his hat from one spot to another six inches off. It seemed to mean something. After a pause he said:

'You're not having her?'

'No.' The word thumped.

'You've had her, though.'

'You mean sexual congress with your wife?' He slapped that pompous phrase down. 'Her stay here is a business transaction.'

'How can you prove that?'

'I can't. I'm telling you.'

Oxford seemed momentarily convinced, or diverted, as if he'd thought suddenly of some vast, important truth.

'Can I see her, then?'

'I'll need to go and ask her.'

'I'll do that.'

'I don't know,' said Riley, 'that I can allow . . .'

'It's my wife. I shall do as I bloody well like.'

'Not in my house, you won't.'

Two schoolboys boasting, spitting, peeing up the lavatory wall. Absurd. Not at all. In its infantile fashion, serious. They sat, looking for surrender. Together both rose to their feet.

'I want to see her,' Oxford began.

'That's up to her.'

'If you're going to act awkward . . .'

'Yes?'

'She's my wife, when all's said and done.'

'She's entitled, Mr. Oxford,' Riley said, 'to privacy if she wants it.'

'Ne'er mind what she's entitled to. Just because you've got a bit of a boss's job, now, you're not laying the law down to me, I'll tell you that.'

Riley did not answer, felt excitement, watched the other's eyes.

'Now, gerr out o' my way before I shift yer.'

No answer except for Riley's bleak stare.

'Bleddy well move when I tell you.' Oxford's face swelled red, blubbery. Suddenly he lurched a step towards his opponent, aimed a blow, a swinging smack with the first lightly clenched. Riley shoved a protective arm up, ducked, but felt the lash of pain on his hand's back, on the top of his head.

Without thinking he jabbed his left hand into Oxford's face, and then swung a right, a quick punch which stung his knuckles. Oxford's mouth gaped; his expression sagged to glazed surprise, a frightened gasp. Riley kept his hands up, but the other touched a cheek, fingering his wounds.

'I've been taught to look after myself,' Riley said, in quiet.

His voice, very low, shocked him by its hoarseness. His vocal cords were coated with aggression.

Oxford stood still, helplessly, a palm half covering his face. His eyes stretched wide, and wet.

'Sit down,' Riley said. 'Let's have a look.'

He was allowed to take the other's hand away so that he could see the reddened flesh.

'Don't think it'll be much,' he said. 'Does it hurt when I touch it?' Oxford's exploring hand joined his.

'A bit.'

97

'Sit down, will you?' Oxford obeyed. Now Riley felt generous, as if the two blows had settled his superior status. 'Would you like a cup of tea?'

'I want to see Joan.' Mulishly defeated.

'I'll go upstairs, then.'

Oxford's hat lay crown downwards at his feet. Riley picked it up and dropped it on its owner's lap. Insultingly. He looked down again at this man who stared at the wall, whose shoulders were held square inside a newish suit. Ordinary. His face stood in shadow from the light behind so that no mark of fighting showed. The right hand had picked the hat by its crown and was moving it, thumb and two fingers, like a huge draught or pawn.

As he mounted the stairs, Riley paused, breathless, leaning on the wall.

Mrs. Oxford appeared at once. He spat his message out. Without surprise, but flouncing a little, like a rebellious child, she said:

'I'd better come down and see him, then.'

Riley returned to find Oxford as before, stiffish, cutting a figure, man at barber's, in dentist's chair.

'She'll only be a minute.'

'Thank you.'

'Face all right?'

That did not get answered, and they remained, one up, one down, until they heard the descending footsteps, the decisive knock. Riley opened the door, waved her to her seat.

'Would you like a cup of tea?'

'Not for me, thank you.' She wanted no social fripperies.

Back in his kitchen, Riley, cut off from television, cleaned his tankards, the fish knives he never used, then decided to scour his stove. He had just sprayed his oven, was opening the back door, when he heard the Oxfords at the front. He moved into the passage.

'Everything . . . ?' he began.

Mrs. Oxford patted her hair, which fluffed less neat than

usual. In the corridor's half-light she seemed fatter, more frumpish.

'He just wanted to know if we could talk about things,' she said, each word dull and separate.

'And what did you say?'

'I told him that things were better as they are.'

She finished the poking at her hair, faced him.

'He wanted you to go back, then?'

'Not in so many words. He's worried about Frank. He'll get himself into trouble, he said.'

'In what way?'

'Don't know.' Voice brightly metallic, then back to greyness. 'It might be just a cock-and-bull story he'd made up. To get me back.'

'You're not going?'

'Not as I feel now,' she said.

He took a couple of steps towards her, circled her with his arm so that her face rested, down, on his shoulder. She did not speak, nor struggle; man's body stood against woman's. He touched her hair, her neck. Her right hand groped his sleeve. In the silence of the narrow place he could hear both breathing, noisily. Though her fingers massaged his arm, she seemed wary; he did not know why he thought this, except that he perhaps expected it. He kissed the top of her head, smelt the lacquer, felt its hard crust. With a hand on her buttocks, he pushed her in close, but she made no resistance.

In the end, she looked up, spoke brightly.

'You're hurting me. Crushing my glasses into my face.'

He allowed her breathing room, but did not shift his arms.

'This is silly,' she said, without enthusiasm.

'What is?' into her hair.

'To walk out on one man into the arms of another.' She leaned away from him. 'We're not going to be lovers.'

'How do you know?' He laughed. He was somebody.

'Let me go,' she answered.

He patted her on both cheeks of her buttocks, and stepped back. He expected her to run upstairs, but again she moved to the mirror where she inspected her eyes, touching the corners, tautening the skin.

'I don't know why he came,' she said.

'He wanted you back. And he's curious. He thought you were sleeping with me.'

'Is that what he said? If I'd have known that, I'd have given him the length of my tongue.'

She resumed her inspection, reminding him of a teen-ager with blackheads. He smiled.

'What sort of man is he?' he asked.

'Ignorant.' Contempt slapped the word into his teeth.

'He didn't seem bad. Not to me.'

Now she swivelled into the middle of the passage where she struck a pose, one hand on hip.

'Did you hit him?' she said. Teeth showed white. 'His face was marked, and his eye all watery.'

'He slung one at me first.'

'And you?'

'Returned. With interest. That's all there is to it.'

She smiled, rapt, engrossed in her thoughts before she took his lapel between finger and thumb to massage it.

'You struck my husband.'

He kissed her inimpeded, alive to her cynicism, his own lust. Not until he'd possessed her did he remember the grease dissolving from his cooking-stove door.

I I

Cooper, the new man, ordered Riley up to see him.

In Sunday suit the subordinate returned to the old factory, looked into his former work-place where he spotted, already, one or two unfamiliar faces. Addison charged on him, breezy, with the big hello, hand-shakings, pawings, arm-in-arm conducted tour. Furniture had been shifted round. Solemnly he shook hands with Frank Oxford, but they exchanged barely a dozen words, though they perched opposite one another for some minutes. Riley thought there ought to be some saw, some adage, to sum or right the situation between them. The boy looked vividly alive with his long hair and his pale, aristocrat's features, like a Lord Byron, bearing the world's sorrow or knowledge behind the dark, handsome eyes, the lips. While he did not speak, the image was maintained; as soon as he opened his mouth, the accent, the clichés dispelled it. He was his mother's boy, and he and her lover should have had words for each other. They had nothing, except when the young man called the older, 'Jack.' Addison was loudly formal with his 'Show Mr. Riley . . .' or 'Let Mr. Riley try this little gadget.' It seemed a sad place, busy, soulless, forgetful.

Upstairs, Pretty Polly, Bowles's secretary, had gone. The new girl was more interested in her nails than her visitor. This shocked Riley. Bowlesy's woman kept you there on tenterhooks while she worked, explaining the delay. Then you felt matters of importance were being decided while you polished your seat. Now this new kid with her manicure set and her chattering, demotic conversation with some other typist over the phone showed she was waiting at ten in the morning for five in the afternoon. So much for the super-efficient Mr. Cooper.

'He'll see you now,' she said, and surprisingly stood to open the door.

'Sit down, Riley.' Cooper signed two documents, and put his expensive pen into an inside pocket. He puffed, an odd sound for a young man. 'All well, up the road?'

He allowed Riley a few sentences, while he blew frog-ugly faces, then stood, walked to the window, back to the visitor. Suddenly he turned, said softly.

'Place looks like a shit-house, if you want my opinion.'

'In what way, sir?'

It was exactly like the army, where superior rank gave one the right to blast underlings as rudely, as obscenely, as could be. They, in their turn, kept straight faces, because one never knew what idiotic behaviour would reap commendation or what brain-work bring down calumny. As one took the violence of the rocket, thumbs along seams, one attributed it not to one's shortcomings but to the quantity of whisky swallowed or bridge hundreds forked out for in the officers' mess the night before. Impassivity paid.

'Filthy-dirty, like some dunghill.'

Cooper wasn't fluent. Riley could have handed him a few epithets or tips. Perhaps he meant what he said. Riley didn't speak.

'This holiday we're having it painted.'

'Very good, sir.'

'I shall expect you there. Had you arranged to go away?'

'No, sir.'

'That's it, then. It's a good time with the people out. Any query?'

'How long will it take?'

'How in hell should I know? They should have it done inside the fortnight. That's up to you. That's why I want you there.'

'At that time, sir,' Riley said, 'there's normally the annual overhaul of the machines.'

'Is that a long job?'

'This is my first year, sir. But I imagine it took a week. The first. In case there were big repairs.'

'Big repairs. How likely's that?'

'Not very, I should think. I'd need to consult the maintenance man.'

'What do you suggest, then?'

Cooper stepped over to his desk, and, podgily erect behind his swivel-chair, slapped his clenched right fist into the palm of his left hand in front of him, then behind his back, and once again to the front. After this athleticism he sat down.

'Do the machines first week. Then you can put the painters off if necessary.' Riley spoke slowly.

'Off? I'm having that place smartened up, Riley, if it kills you in the process.' He laughed, wheezily, at his own wit, and flicked a table-lighter under his cigarette.

'If it's a case of paint or machines turning when the men and women come back, I know what I'd choose.'

'I've chosen. Both. Up to you. You're the manager, aren't you? That's what you're paid for.'

Riley knew he should keep his mouth shut.

'I'm not the manager of the painting contractors.'

'Never thought so. This is just a shade tricky, Riley. Needs a bit of brain-power. Up to you.'

'Right.'

'Good.' What those two words conveyed, neither knew; neither cared overmuch.

'I'll talk to the men about getting the overhaul done first week. What they'll say God knows. I shall have the unions round my neck, but I'll risk it. And if you can, get the painters pared down to a week.'

'Should be on.'

'You can apply legal sanctions, can't you?' Riley asked, bolder now. 'Have a strictly enforcible date of completion.'

103

'What, on a little job like this?' Cooper laughed, patting his fingers stubbily on the desk. 'I don't use steam hammers to crack monkey-nuts.'

'Get them to do the outside last, then. They can finish that at their leisure.'

'More like it.'

'I'll see Dyson straight away. And ring you.'

'Don't bother.'

'You've got to give the paint contractor a starting date?'

'I'll let you have his number.'

Exasperation dried Riley's mouth. He wished he were standing so that he could lean, tower, over this podge-jowl twiddling his fat fingers.

'I'm not being awkward for the sake of it,' he said.

'Never thought you were.' Cooper flicked ash largely.

'I set the snags out because your pay and mine, as well as profits, depend on getting this right. I'll do my best.'

'I'm sure you will. And we'll see how good it is.' Condescending bastard. 'You were in the army, Riley, and you know when the C.O. issues an order he doesn't expect to supervise the carrying out, does he, now?'

'No, sir.'

'And what's that tone mean?'

'Nothing. If the C.O. orders a barrack inspection he'll get it. If he wanted a mass-suicide, he wouldn't.

'Now you are talking like a bloody fool, Riley. I want your place scrubbed up in a fortnight, no more, no less.'

'And if the men and girls come back on the Monday, and their machines are still in bits.'

'Some sod'll jump, Riley.'

'Me?'

'Amongst others.'

Cooper's eyes protruded, his cheeks burst, flush-mottled. But the posh voice dropped quiet and the fingers rested chubby and dead now on his desk. Riley imagined the shining brown boots together out of sight. Well lined. Thirty-odd-thousand farm-house out in the villages. But his name was plebeian; some black-handed ancestor ringed beer-barrels years back. And now here sat milord god. By kind permission of the commanding officer, Lt.-Col. K. R. F. Cooper.

'I know what the labour force is like, Riley. And if after they've been on beer and bollocks for a fortnight, in Blackpool, they come streaming out on strike because they can't stand the stink of your paint, you'll catch the blame. Your head will fall. Give them management, and that doesn't mean bowing to every whim that blows their empty heads up; it means coming down on 'em, letting 'em learn that when you say, "Thus far and no further", you mean it. Paternalism, if you know the word, Riley. Father knows best. How old am I?'

'I beg your pardon.'

'How old d'you think I am?'

'Thirty-five, forty.'

'I'm thirty-three, Riley,' Cooper said. 'I've been in management proper since I was twenty-five. You think this job's top of the tree, don't you, that my predecessor Bowles was pretty near king of the city? I don't. I was in for two positions at the same time, one I wanted, and this. The other was a management consultant affair, and they decided in the end I hadn't a wide enough experience. Surprises you, doesn't it? These fellows can be as old-fashioned as blue buggery, I can tell you. So I take this. Biggish concern? Needs expanding. Started already. But I want to finish on fifty thousand a year, and I don't think that's on in this seat. See?'

Riley inclined his head. He blamed his face, as usual, for the confidence, but in the forces ambitious young officers used to unburden themselves on him exactly like this.

'Yes, sir,' he said, as if it were important.

'And now you're wondering why I spill all this to a trumped-up army sergeant they've made a manager, eh?'

Angry, Riley said nothing, pulling his lips in, disguising nothing.

'One,' Cooper said, bending the index finger of his left

hand back with that of his right, 'I don't have many people to talk to. Two, you're a decent man. Give us a day's work for a day's pay. You're frightened of your own shadow, but you've come into this sort of responsibility late in life. Third, I like people to know who I am and where I stand. "Cooper's a bastard." Fair enough. As long as they know what sort of bastard. Your friend Bowles, of pious memory, was efficient. He knew all about these factories and their equivalents. He'd found out where and how the men lived and what they wanted. He knew the unions, and the representatives and the trades councils and the exporters and the men from the ministry. He knew the women and their dislikes and their fancies and the colour of their knickers from all I hear. But the difference between me and King Bowles is that I think this concern's chicken-feed. Understand?'

'Yes, sir.'

'And I know just that you're thinking. That I'm riding for a fall that'll squash my big head into lemon-juice, and serve me bloody well right. That's not far out. This firm's no family sentiment for me. Make or bloody break, boy. This concern'll go or the shareholders vote me out. And that's just how I like it. So when I say, "Riley, get that piss-corner of yours cleaned up in two weeks", I want to hear no more of it until there it is shining next time I happen to look that way.'

When Riley left, Addison was waiting for him with a cup of coffee. 'Well, what had King Dick to say for himself?'

'Bumming his chat.'

'Eh?'

'Boasting.'

'Ay.' Addison rolled his eyes, appearing to swoon. 'About how much money he'll make and what he'll do to you if you're not up to the mark. I've had some.' He sucked boiling coffee from his spoon. 'Can't understand it. If I asked him to tot the books up, or get a wage-sheet out, he couldn't do it. Now what is it he can do?'

'He makes soft herberts like you and me jump.'

They laughed. Nobody liked Cooper. He talked big to selected individuals, but he could be cheated. Addison ran fire with anecdotes, but Riley sipping his coffee, noticed that he himself wanted to be back, to sort out the annual holiday, and that was sign enough that Cooper knew what he was about.

In fact, he found no trouble at all. Dyson and his colleagues from Humphreys, Day Street, agreed to manage the overhaul provided overtime was granted. They'd be in the second week at the heating system and lights as well as tinkering with the brickwork in the cellars and no amount of painting would interfere with that. When Riley rang Cooper's officer for the phone number of the painting contractor, to make sure their work would be over inside the second week, he found it had already been arranged. Efficient Cooper.

As he walked from the bus in hot sunshine the lime-flowers were out and he smelt their sweetness as a kind of reward. He'd shown his mettle again. In his way he was grateful to Cooper for the opportunity; Bowles would have organised the lot. Under the ash tree in his front garden Riley leant on the wall in the warmth of the paving-stones and his self-satisfaction. A black Rover saloon drew up. An imperious finger.

'Thought it was you.' Cooper. 'Am I right for Tattershall Drive?'

Riley briefly reassured him with precise instructions.

'This where you live?'

'Yes, sir.'

Cooper glanced it over, vulgarly poking his ear.

'Damn' hot, isn't it? I'm just calling in on Sir Louis Baird.' A property magnate who still lived in his father's mansion, white Georgian, half-way up the hill on Tattershall, with acres of sloping treed garden behind wrought-iron gates.

Mrs. Oxford came down the street, saw both men, bowed

her head like an old-fashioned retainer and scuttled down the entry.

'Your wife?' Cooper, rudely.

'I'm a widower.' Bowles would have known.

Cooper looked affronted, covered the expression, and laughed loudly as, waving, he drove powerfully away, leaving Riley exhilarated.

There was no sign or sound of Mrs. Oxford in the house, though she was back unusually early. He went upstairs, found her lying shoeless on her bed.

'Oh, it's nothing, nothing,' she snapped. 'We weren't busy so I came out half an hour early. That's all.'

He did not like it.

'What's wrong?'

'Oh, I don't know. Everything. Everybody. I'm depressed. That's all. I shall have got over it by tomorrow.'

He made a pot of tea, cut sandwiches and wisely left her. She barely spoke to him while he was there, but moved restlessly on the bed, the legs of her tights rasping. As he closed the door she thanked him grudgingly. He did not reply.

12

Riley learnt next day, by letter, that his neighbours, the O'Briens, were away.

He received a note and a postal order for a fortnight's rent from the husband. With a gush of crude affection he read the few lines, informing him they had gone to the 'wife's brother in Northampton for the change'. Why had the man bothered with the money? And all this had happened next door, in silence, while he sparred and kowtowed to Cooper and coupled with Joan Oxford.

O'Brien had fetched his wife from hospital, with the fuss and expense of taxis, had carted her, dressed to the nines, with her luggage, down to the bus station and on and off long-distance coaches. And she? Stared round at the rush and hullabaloo of the world, memory pecked hollow by E.C.T., until her relatives appeared like grotesque characters round the edge of an X-film ritual burning. But O'Brien had coped, for and with this raddled parcel whom he'd once stripped and snapped. Greater love hath.

He knew he was indulging himself to wallow like this. Probably Mrs. O'Brien had nagged her husband into buying the postal order, and thus honesty sprang from inadequacy. He knocked on the Scottens' door.

When the kids had been cleared, Alma detained him in the kitchen. She rinsed her hands under the cold tap, saying:

'I s'll be glad when this bleddy lot's all in bed. If they ever get there.'

She catalogued the O'Briens' affairs, and enlightened him with a malicious account of a panic-stricken husband clucking up and downstairs round a wife who merely subjugated her old man because that was all she knew how. In Mrs. Scotten's sharp view, O'Brien should have been locked in the 'sylum, not his wife.

'What she wants is a bleddy good boot up her bum. That'd settle her nerves, the silly cow.'

Riley laughed, because her indignation burst so furious. A child sidled in at the cackle, eyes wide, picking his nose.

'You women should stick together,' Riley said.

'Woman? She's an 'ag. A stringy 'ag.'

'But she's been very ill.'

'You can call that ill,' she scoffed. 'All she's doing's forcin' that slave of 'ers, that skivvy, to do as 'e's bid. That's all her badly is.'

'You fancy him, then?' he asked, catching her mood.

'Him? I'd sooner 'ev it with a pea-stick. Eh, and that reminds me. What are you doing with Joan Smith, as was, up your stairs?'

'Lodger.' They'd discussed it before.

'How-de-do, howdedo.' Mrs. Scotten rolled her eyes. 'I hear her clipping up the entry on high heels. You'd think she were about twenty-one, flouncing about. You watch her, Mester Riley, or she'll have you.'

'In what way?'

'What way? You ask me. Don't give me that. Trapped. She'd like to be rid of her husband. Not genteel enough for 'er. Wants too much knob. So gets round you.'

'She doesn't live with me.'

'And you've never had it with her?'

He blushed like a youth, with a heat of embarrassment, so that even she turned her face away, clipped her child out of the kitchen, muttered, 'Don't take any notice o' me. I'm only pullin' your leg.' After the brief period of remorse, nature reasserted itself so that she said, 'Them Smiths was nobody. They thought they was, but they wasn't.' Then she came across to him and gripped his arm by the bicep. There was nothing of Miss Rogers' tentative touch there;

it seemed she warned him to get hold of himself, face reality. 'Funny,' she said, 'who you fall in love with.' She launched into a recital of the life of the middle-aged Grocer— R. Brown—Confectioner at the corner shop who'd fallen for a girl, young enough to be his daughter, who sometimes helped out in the evenings. 'There they'd stand cuddling and kissing behind the counter wi' half the street looking on. She were engaged to somebody else but she chucked him up. That didn't matter. Now they're married. Happy as kings. Haven't have no family up to pres, but I suppose o'd Arthur's not got round to it yet.' She laughed coarsely. 'What d'you think she could see in him? Fifty-odd? Ugly as an empty coal-cellar?'

'His bank-book.'

'Could be. Could be. I wouldn't marry him, not if he was Getty. She don't mind. All smiles. Plump as a puddin'. Good job we're not all alike.'

She slapped his rump, then heaved on his pullover, dragging it awry.

'Don't do anything as I wouldn't,' she said. About her vulgarity there seemed a common sense, almost a righteousness, which left him both vulnerable and aware of his need.

'Come in and see me,' he pleaded.

'You want a harem,' she said.

'I don't know.' He scrubbed his face helplessly, unable to respond to her joviality. For the minute he knew himself incapable of decision, of straight thought, and yet suffused with a violence of emotion, a welter of sorrow. Tears welled from his eyes in spite of an effort of will. He was a wraith, able to observe, but not to intervene; a victim, worked over, killed all the day long, by a world knowing neither pity nor sense. This woman, Alma Scotten, could save him, with the tide-mark round her neck and her grubby fingers, chewed nails, slatternly short skirt. She represented reason, spicy picture-postcard variety, but the only thing of value amongst the whirl and worry of his factory and his mistress. She demanded nothing except that he should stand and listen to her smutty badinage. When she'd seduced him she'd made no counter-proposals, no demands. An act of sex was itself, offered out of generosity or curiosity, but the beginnings of no blackmail. His body hung in chains of sorrowful violence. A child again, dominated by the unfairness, the inequity of his tormenting world.

'Come in and see me,' he begged.

'I'll see.' She laughed.

He stumbled from her back door, knees knocking, in weakness that ripped the bones from his body. When he'd walked next door twenty minutes ago for a gossip he'd been perfectly well; now he staggered, clawing for support, from gate to wall to drainpipe to door to washing-machine. This killed him like cancer or thrombosis, but no pain sharpened in him, only lassitude and multiplying sense of unease. It ruined him like an earthquake shifting foundations; he'd found in seconds that the fabric of his living was undermined. That childish explosion of tears, though that was understandable, had acted harbinger to his witless, godless draining of strength, of motive, of care, until he flopped now across a chair like a colourless jelly, a sodden heap of rags in a wet hedge-bottom. Even as he recognised his inability to struggle, he hardly believed the messages of surrender signalled in from every nerve-end. He'd see the doctor. A tiny live cell in his brain cynically demanded what he'd get there. If it was the old man, a pep-talk; if the young quack, a prescription for pills. The thought, it seemed not to come from himself, but to squeak from the devastation round it, pleased him so that he repeated the words 'pep-talk, pep-pill', under his breath, like a crone, a drunk, a tramp. That repetition made him, saved him. Pep. Pep. Pepper. Peppermint. He sensed himself talking, pulled himself up to listen, recognised the words and their origin and without any sense of diminution of either misery or weakness realised he could move, would do so, towards the wall-cabinet and the miniature bottle of brandy.

He gulped, minutely; choked.

Coughing, he waited, and waiting knew his strength. This spasm, this earth tremor, of irresolution, of feebleness, had not finished him. Moistening his mouth again at the dwarf neck of the bottle, he noted, forced himself to see the room, to name the contents of this drawer, that cupboard. He could do it. He was not sure whether he could walk across to it, but he knew exactly where the pickled-onion jar was.

Being so, he would approach, touch it.

He stood. Yes. Walked. Done, legs flabby, but walking. His arm opened the sliding-door with normality. Jar? Where? He had come; it had gone. His whole understanding lurched, ducked, as it were, into uncertainty; no orders were issued to the searching eyes. Pulling himself upright, he looked again, failed, began to move tins, bottles, packets. There. He must have passed it over three or four times with his eye before he registered it, but now it revealed itself, red top, gay label, shapely onions. He lifted it, in triumph, felt its round smoothness, replaced it, recognising his foolishness, then, groggy, smiled at the recognition, before he made instant coffee, and sat.

Half an hour later, when Frank Oxford and his father knocked, Riley still stared at the wall.

'Do you want to see your mother?' he asked.

'No. You.'

Father and son came in, sat in the kitchen where Frank praised the size, the neatness of the place almost proprietorially.

'My dad said we ought to go an' see somebody,' he began, preliminaries over. 'Solicitor or something. But I said, "Jack Riley. He's our one." '

Riley watched suspiciously.

'It's making my dad bad,' Frank said, handsome in the clean summer light from the window. 'She'll neither write nor answer.'

'Your mother?'

'Yes. We've written letters. I have. And me dad. Nothing happens.'

'You know where she works,' Riley said.

'No.' The boy shook his head, with a heavy flash and swirl of hair. 'We can't go creating in the shop. Make her worse. Me dad's in a poor way. It's shook him.' The defective grammar added power. 'Just clearing out like that. It's not as if she's a young bird. She's a married woman with responsibilities. She can't just pack her traps. I mean, it's not too bad for me, but me dad. He's used to havin' her there. And all the talk. Poking noses in; you should hear some of 'em.'

'Haven't you spoken to her? Since she left?'

'I've seen her a time or two in the street. She might be a stranger. All right, y'know. Pleasant. But she doesn't care. Never asked about me dad. Just a few words and then, "Well, I'll have to be off now," and she's gone. That's no way, I'll tell you.'

'Did you never ask her?'

'What do you think? "Look, Mam," I said, "what did you go off like that for?" And do you know what she said? "I'd had as much as I could stand, Frank." "As much o' what?" I said. "If you don't know, it's no use telling you," she said. That's all the sense you get out of her.'

The youth spoke with an air of grievance, as if he ought not to have been called on, and yet fluently. While his father sat, glum, red-faced, different jaunty-feathered hat on one knee, dumb as dog-muck, the boy sulkily put his case, with undetailed emphasis that made its effect. He'd something about him. It wasn't everybody who'd expose his mother's unreason and his father's incapacity so explicitly, and without any exhibitionism. He spoke what he'd thought, what he'd seen, what he'd talked about, but sensibly, like a grown man. Riley was impressed, looked twice at the well-wrought features, wondered.

'Can I ask you something?'

'Yes.' The boy replied, but looked at his father.

'Why did she go in the first place?'

'I don't know.' Frank scratched his head. 'Everybody gets fed up some time or another. I know I do. But it won't be long before I leave home any road. She thought she'd somewhere else to go. But she's married to me dad. All that time. Twenty-one years, is it?' He looked up, eyes grave, almost dark, blue, beautiful, and said, 'Everybody'd go off given the chance. Old people have to restrain themselves. She should have thought of her husband, in her place.'

'Did her husband think of her?' Riley asked the question without compunction over Oxford's head.

'Yes, he did. I'm not saying he was perfect, but when I was a boy she was ill for a long time and he came home every dinner-time and fed her, and did the shopping and housework. Yes. And look at him now. He's done.'

Riley, touched, faced the father.

'What did she say, Mr. Oxford, the other night?'

'Nothing. Nothing.' The voice clogged rough in his throat. 'She was better off. That's all. She wasn't coming back.'

'She gave no reason?'

'No. Except she was better off.'

'You asked her to come back?'

'I begged of her.'

Riley nodded. He could not be sorry for that hoarse, unpalatable voice.

'We thought,' Frank said, 'you could have a word with her. Or else suggest . . .'

'I don't . . .'

'You'll know her a bit now. We don't think no wrong of you taking her in. You'd do it out of kindness. Like you did wi' me.' He floundered. His hands searched the air for vocabulary. 'But you've got a position. I mean, you're a manager. You have to talk to people, to see what they want.'

A tremor of former weakness touched Riley's limbs.

'You both want her back?'

'Yes.'

'Mr. Oxford?'

A miserable, red-faced nod. The man had all the signs of smartness, but was limp, ugly, half-formed. No wonder she'd walked out.

'Thank you, Mester Riley.'

Oxford spoke, in a voice like a cough, forced up. But he'd thanked the adulterer. Riley felt no shame, merely a sense of mild amazement at the ironies of the world. Frank, smiling now, fingering his long hair back from his high brow, became voluble in thanks, until he clapped his father on the back, said they'd take up no more of Mr. Riley's time.

'One minute,' Riley said. 'I'll speak to her. But beyond that I can't promise anything. A few words here and there don't cure matters that have been festering for months, y'know. I'll speak. I'll tell her you've been.'

'Tonight?' Frank.

'If she'll see me. That's up to her.'

'How will you let us know?'

'I'll call. Or you can drop in here. I'll ring your office.'

The two left, and Riley sat. Why, when he could so easily have turned them down, had he promised with such readiness? He was sorry. As he'd no intention of breaking off his liaison with Joan Oxford, his sorrow wasn't worth much. He wanted to stir it up, to set them all kicking and leaping on his say-so. Despicable. A hypocrite. Trouble-maker. And this after the evening's warning. God is not mocked. No, he denigrated himself. He'd agreed because that was easier than refusing. Yes, sir, no, sir. He'd saluted and agreed until he could do no other. A no-man. Mr. No-one. Like a man made of smoke.

He forced himself upstairs.

Joan Oxford, bright in a multi-flowered dress of orange, yellow and black, with a plain unmatching cardigan above, seemed to be waiting. Her hair, touched now barely with grey, curled prettily, but her face pinched sour.

'I saw them go,' she said. 'What did they want?'

He thought of her, sitting at the window, squinting into the street for something to happen. He'd always imagined her fully occupied up there, making, mending, planning.

Briefly, drily, he told her. She said, 'Uh,' sat heavily down by the chair still by the window. Uncomfortably he waited, but she seemed in no haste to speak.

'I told them I'd see you, speak to you,' he said, in the end.

'Did you?' No looking up. 'What good will that do?'

'I didn't say it would do anything. I just said I'd tell you they'd been.'

'I know that.'

'Frank says his father's very upset.'

'That'll do him no harm.' Vindictive. 'He misses his comfort. What did he say for himself?'

'Hardly spoke.'

'Left it to Frank? That's typical. If he could shrug it off on to somebody else, he would.'

She dusted the sill with the flat of her hand. 'He didn't say anything about Frank, did he? About him going wrong?'

'No.'

'What else, then?' She snapped; he saw he could give no right answers.

'They want you to go back to them.'

'And what do you think?'

'That's not for me to say.'

She whirled up from the chair, in a flurry of anger that stabbed with surprise. As she stood the wildness disappeared, the violence solidified into sulkiness.

'After what you've done to me, you say that?' Each word was clear as from a glass harmonica. For a moment he thought the words, small ringing, chimed in his own mind. Shocked, he stepped across, took her in his arms. Awkwardly she struggled; he held on. Viciously she kicked his shin. He hurled her off so that she hit the dressing table, tilting the mirror with a flash of sudden light, spilling the contents of the runner and its tray. She dropped slowly to one knee, then both, her right arm across the now bared, polished surface. Fury roistered in him. He could not see, would not, this woman on her knees like the cover pictures of some back-street newsagent's novelettes.

She got up without a sound, ignoring the brush, comb, broken glass on the carpet. A hand smoothed her dress, adjusted her glasses before she looked at him, almost primly. This done, she went to the connecting door, opened it, walked through, then smashed it back so that the floor-boards shook, the window rattled and a postcard pinned to the chimney-breast fluttered down. He did not hear her on the stairs; she'd be in her bedroom.

Sighing loudly, he knelt and picked up the glass, swear-ing, sucking, when he cut a finger. He snatched the even-ing paper and parcelled the fragments. Perhaps it was possible to mend them. Still down, finger in mouth, he rested his forehead against the embossed handle of a drawer, before he replaced and smoothed the linen runner, bloodying it on its dragon design.

When he had satisfied himself he laid the newspaper bundle by her wastepaper basket and let himself out. On the corridor he waited but could hear no sound from the bedroom. He knocked politely. No. Again. Nothing. He did not swear out loud, walked away.

He was surprised to find, in his armchair with biscuits and tea, that this encounter had stimulated him. Without trace of weakness or pain in the limbs, he recalled the quarrel but found not only that his mind dismissed it as trivial but also that his nerves, his body, did likewise. Diminishing returns. He completed his evening's chores.

13

Though he could easily have confronted her, Riley did not face Mrs. Oxford until the week-end. If he heard her about, he kept out of her light, and on Friday evening failed to make his now usual call for the rent.

That had been recently the subject of a small altercation. He'd suggested, hesitating, that he didn't think he should collect. She stopped him.

'No. Don't say that.'

'But, Joan . . .'

'I know what you're going to say, but I don't want to hear it.'

'That's silly. It just . . .'

'I'm going to pay my way, be independent. That's what I came here for.'

'Well, it's, I, you . . .'

'No, Jack. That's enough. I want you up here on Fridays collecting.'

He'd felt put into his place, then, morally smeared, condemned. Money was money. She'd no idea, clearly, that his offer had cost something. He'd never had a surplus to chuck about.

After a day's thought he'd written a note to Frank Oxford claiming shortly that he'd broached the matter and watched her blow her top as result. He put it in slang, jauntily, as if to trivialise or suggest that the matter rested incomplete and he'd try again.

On Saturday he heard her trot in from work, and waited. At the end of half an hour she came down, presumably for the laundry parcel which was placed on top of the meter cupboard in the dining room. When she emerged, he stood ready in the corridor, but she walked straight past him and upstairs without a word. She'd looked in front, with that awkward bundle balanced before her; her effrontery took him aback. Puzzled, he sat down to think it out, decided after twenty minutes that he'd decided nothing, and stood, determined to knock on her door. It was as if his body had taken the decision in spite of his head.

Knock politely.

She opened. 'Yes?'

'I've come to say I'm sorry.' He'd not quite prepared himself, but she nodded and dropped her eyes. For a moment he thought she might close the door in his face with a saintly, reproachful speed of forgiveness, but, no, they remained. 'I said, I did things I'm sorry for, as I shouldn't have done.'

Did he mumble, did he, in fact, speak at all?

She nodded again.

'Come in.' Wearily, as if this were a duty to be trudged through. 'Sit down.' As if in the dentist's waiting room.

'I was upset,' he said, at last. Clearly she'd no intention of speaking. 'Seeing those two sitting there, it upset me.' She made no comment, still stood. 'I don't know why. I thought I'd like to do something. For them. If I could.' She did not help him. 'I don't know. I'm all muddled up.' Now she fiddled with a chair-back. 'I felt rotten then, and I've felt worse ever since. I took you away, like. Your husband sat there so thick and pudding-faced and Frank was lively and young. And he was talking, well, if you know what I mean. And I thought, "It's his mother and his wife." I don't know.'

He did not; that was correct.

She moved over to her dressing table, bedroom furniture in her sitting room, now restored straight, and picked up a brush and set about her hair. It was a strong performance, the hand flying through firm strokes, the sharp swish of the bristles dry and masculine. Abashed, he watched, uncertain why she acted as she did. Was she making time, or deliberately neglecting him, expressing scorn? Or was it involuntary, the rush of a distraught woman to do what she knew she could? In the end, she laid her brush down, straightened her skirt.

'I think I shall go back, then,' she said.

'Will you?'

He'd answered gruffly. He felt relief. She'd go. His mistress, back to her man. Why did he not know what to feel? Did he want her? Would he fight for her? Apparently not.

Very slowly, he pulled himself nearer the upright.

'When will you go?' he asked.

'There's no hurry.'

'I don't suppose there is.' He coughed, a nervous spasm. 'I shouldn't have shoved you over,' he said. 'I didn't know what I was doing. It was wrong. That isn't why you're going, is it?'

She shook her head. All's uncertainty.

'You're not going back because of what I did?' he asked. He seemed to be pleading against his own will, as though some part of him had taken over. And yet it was spurious. There was no furore in the genitals, or suicidal self-pity, or husbandly desire or brotherly love. He supplicated like an actor; this was the role.

'No, Jack.'

He put his hands out to her, half-shocked by his hypocrisy, and she took them, stepped closer, loosing them to clasp his head softly into her belly. He smelt the dress, closed his eyes into a quiet orange darkness and was still, back to childhood, to his mother's breast with her apron lifted to symbolise protection. Now sex stirred, but she would not let him move. He groaned. That spoke sufficiency.

'I didn't get tomorrow's meat,' she said, breaking away.

'Never mind.'

'I was that mad with you.' Her voice schoolgirlish, she'd picked up the hairbrush, begun work again.

'I got a joint in,' he said.

'If I had,' she answered, 'that would have been a waste.'

They began to laugh, the pair of them. Warmth gushed in the room, pleasure.

'You go down now,' she said, 'and I'll see you later.'

'You were mad with me, then?'

'I could have killed you.'

'That's not why you're going, though, is it?'

'No, Jack. I've told you. It isn't.'

She ushered him out, both gloomy, now, middle-aged, awkward. He walked downstairs, under narcosis, in a poisonous, comfortable apathy. Ten minutes later she came down, kissed him, and asked when she should leave. They made friendly love.

Next morning Riley woke to deep desolation, just recalling his nightmare, his incarceration in the cellar, with the Macmillan figure. No help appeared there; his despair degraded and yet once he began to attach words to it, to describe it, lost something of its terror. He imagined that he must equal Mrs. O'Brien in this worldless hopelessness, this inhumanity, this dredge of death which left him appalled. His breakdown, his weakness after the interview with Alma Scotten, was nothing, an aberration, a failure in the machine, to be feared but understandable, with a cause. The other was hellish, the application of a restricted intelligence to a limitless despair.

He sat on the side of the bed. Morning shone outside; a blackbird shouted in the ash tree, but, grey-faced, he was afraid to listen.

14

The clean-up of the factory during the annual holiday went without hitch.

Maintenance men were efficient; far from ganging up with Dyson, they chased him into surly speed. The painters whistled and howled with their transistors, swung like monkeys on and in the roof, were never wonderfully careful, but made a satisfactory job. Their foreman, a youngish cynic, with a Pancho moustache, ridiculed the project but kept his lads, long-haired yobbos, noisily busy.

'Whole bloody lot'll be shabby in three months,' he said to Riley.

'Nothing's perfect.'

'They should make factories look like factories, not bloody drapery stores. Nob'dy likes working here; they should admit it and gi' ovver the bull.'

'You'd have the place thick with dirt, would you? No radios?'

'I never said any such thing. Clean, yes. Bit of music, fair enough. But when you've got your eye down to a machine that don't alter its product from the first to the thi'ty thousand and first, you don't give a monkey's whether there's a purple stripe round the walls or the ceiling blends with the supervisor's arsehole.'

'What the answer?'

'Shorter hours. Plenty of breaks.'

'Nobody'd do any work at all, if that were the case.'

The man dug his hands into the front pockets of his paint-bedraggled overalls. His moustache added lugubrious calm to lively, bloodshot eyes.

'So they all say. But there's plenty of labour to hand, as I see it. It's the work to supply 'em wi'.'

Riley enjoyed his supervision, at first.

There was little to do, and during the painting he was cleared from the office. He'd begun during the maintenance week to reorganise the files, but lost heart after two days, and, half-scared Miss Rogers would not approve, had returned all to its place. Thereafter, he read, a book on Devon, a cowboy romance, a life of Lord Nelson, listened to the women's programmes on the radio or once or twice vainly skimmed the pages of the technical manuals which had been turned out for the annual inspection. Once or twice, when nobody observed him, he'd done a little cleaning up on his own account, but by the second week, with a full day's metallic whine of Radio One, the stink of paint and his sense of unemployment he became edgy.

Joan Oxford hadn't returned home.

Clearly she wanted a performance, conferences, protocol, agreements, worship.

Once he'd decided to spend a day at the seaside, he invited her to join him. She refused, smilingly. He knew.

'Not now I've decided to go back, John.' She began to use his proper name. 'People would talk, and it would complicate matters.' She was loving so that the two embraced about the house stroking each other, like kids. He did not remember such tenderness for his wife, nor such manifestations of it. Certainly he could not understand why a woman who'd made up her mind to return to her husband should show such avidity, however gentle, for another man's caresses.

He set off early for the coast, and relished the coach journey with smart middle-aged companions or pensioners, cloth caps and raincoats, toddling aboard, disposing of their lunch bags. The jokers, the stupid, the incontinent, all, as expected, appeared and acted to type through the flat Lincolnshire countryside.

'Should 'a gone the other way,' the know-all said.

'Through 'Orncastle. More interesting like. Bit of up and down. 'S called Wolds.'

'Want to get there before the pubs close, y'know,' the wag shouted.

'Is he thirsty, then?' they asked his wife.

'Ah. He'd drink the sea dry, he would.'

Though the day sparkled with sunshine, breezes whipped briskly in from the water. Beaches were crowded and bright with bikinis and windshields. Riley had never seen people so busy doing nothing; all appeared to work hard even when they were loafing, acquiring a tan, for they'd leap up, change position, oil this arm or that shoulder, turn again, alter angle, miss no ray, no puff of ozone. Children pestered and struggled, parents revealed themselves patiently childish, petulantly loving. On the wide, flat, paper-littered silver sands human insects wriggled and exploded and stuffed and yawned and goggled and God's will was done. Be ye, therefore, perfect.

As he stood on the promenade, by a freshly painted shelter, preoccupied and observant, he remembered that he had not been to this place for over thirty years. And yet there seemed little difference: the villas, the arcades, the clock tower. Surely fashion must have changed; then they wore legged cotton bathing suits, panama hats, cadies, directoire silk knickers. Thirty, thirty-two, as a boy. If he waited as long again he'd be well up in the seventies, too old for the concrete steps and the dodge between traffic. Perhaps he'd never reappear; perhaps this was his last time. He stroked an iron post. His own father hadn't managed sixty. Make the most of it, Riley. A shouting urchin whirled by tugging at his kite; a lobster-red man drew his shirt on. Human behaviour, infinite variety. A young wife's belly sloppy with recent childbirth. Hopeless castles in the softness of the sand. A newspaper over a sleeping face. And the voices, strident, competitive yells and shrieks, and away, level in the distance, like steel, the polished sea. Last time, Riley. He grinned, poking his nail into the paint of the post.

He could come again on Sunday next if he wished. But he would not. And next Tuesday, weather permitting, there'd be a new cast for the same play. He whistled, turned away, was greeted by one of the hands from the old factory who introduced his wife. Both treated him with respect, mistering him, shaking hands in the end. Well, it boosted his ego.

But he was glad to get home, face burning, relieved that Mrs. Oxford did not come down.

The painters finished on time, and Riley, daring, rang to ask Cooper if he'd come to inspect. A secretary was found after a search; Mr. Cooper was in Ibiza; it would be the end of next week before he returned. Riley swore, but without venom, going through the motions. Cooper acted managerially, and quite right, sod him.

On Monday when the workers came in there was noise and talk, but they had their machines flying, even though they seemed to stare, as at dangerous animals. Lying baking on a sandy towel and three days later watching cardboard folded and stapled and packed at the touch of a lever.

By Wednesday, Dyson had come up with a complaint.

'That little bogger Sampson's nicked some'at out of my locker.'

'What?'

'Half a bottle of whisky.'

That was the cause of his hesitation. Alcohol must not be brought on to the premises, according to the printed rules of conduct.

'What would he want with that?' The lad was an undersized fifteen, had started at Easter.

'How the bloody hell do I know?'

'Look,' Riley said. 'Simmer down. If you can't state your case without all the bawling and swearing, go elsewhere.'

'Well, he . . .'

'Is that clear?'

Dyson glowered, but nodded, shrank a little into his overalls. Riley invited him then to pull a chair up and heard the grumbling farrago.

'Ask him to come up at dinner-time. Ask, mind you, not tell. And you come up with him.'

Riley waited for them at the beginning of the break, but they did not appear. No sooner had he unpacked his own sandwiches then he heard the pair clattering up the stairs to Miss Rogers' office. He replaced the top of his coffee flask, and hid his lunch in the cupboard. This time he did not invite the two to sit.

'Do you know why I asked you here?' Riley said to the boy.

'No.' Merry about it.

'Mr. Dyson didn't tell you?'

'No, he didn't.

'And you can't guess?'

This time young Sampson hesitated.

'I see you have got some idea, then. Mr. Dyson thinks you've taken something from his locker; have you?

'No. I have not.'

'Not a bottle of whisky?'

Again the boy stopped as he was about to speak, scratched his head, bit his lip.

'Oh, that,' he said.

'What about it?'

'Well, for one thing it wasn't in his locker.'

'But you took it?'

'Only for a joke.'

'Where is it now?'

'Down the loading bay.'

Patiently Riley listened, twice stopped Dyson from intervening. The cross-examination rambled among trivial rancours. Dyson, having a quick sup, had left the bottle on top of the lockers. He'd been teasing the boy on account of his size, asking him when he was going to get married, telling him that Fat Mary, one of the machinists, fancied him. Sampson took the bottle to get his own back. No, he oughtn't to have done it. Worse, he'd had a taste of it himself, but out of curiosity. Yes, he'd let another youth have a drop. He'd then split to Dyson. Anyroad, Dyson pinched things . . . Before they'd finished the lad was in angry tears, and Riley furious.

'Now,' Riley said, solemn. 'You give it back to Mr. Dyson. We'll judge then how much of it's gone. And don't do anything so daft again or there'll be trouble, serious trouble for you, young man. If anybody makes game of you so much you can't stand it, come up here and see me. Do you understand that? I don't want you traipsing in here every time anybody calls you or bawls you out, but if anything's wrong that you can't set right, come and see me. Clear?' The lad gulped, head down, fingers groping at his tears. 'Right, now, just go next door there to the lavatory and give your face a good wash. Here's the key. Leave it in there.'

Sampson lifted his eyes in a quickness of panic towards both, grabbed the key and shuffled out, leaving the door ajar.

'Shut that,' Riley snapped at Dyson. Anger rucked still, and when the subordinate returned, in obedience, neither spoke for the minute. Riley sighed, lifted his head, put his hands flat down on his desk. 'You should be bloody well ashamed of yourself.'

Dyson's lip dropped.

'You're not going to talk like that to me,' he said. 'Cussing and swearing.'

Riley rose, walked round the desk.

'I shall talk to you as I bloody well like,' he said. His anger died because he faced a frightened, crouching, grey-faced sixty-year-old. The man looked pinched, ill, with a tuft of unshaven white whisker on his lower lip. 'Leave him alone in future.'

'I never said much.'

'Enough to torment him into getting his own back.'

'He's mardy.'

'The more reason to leave him alone.'

'You can't tell me 'ow to talk to folks.'

'I can. I shall.' The anger which burnt at the sight of the shamed lad was out. Here stood a silly man who should have known, who did know, better. 'Draw that chair up, Mr. Dyson.'

Riley considered. He should leave the man there, having made no threats, exposed no weaknesses of his own. But he could not. He was father to these men and women; a wry smile twisted his face at the thought of their comments on that notion put bluntly to them. He fiddled with his pencils, a managerial ploy, though his stomach strained, bubbled with hunger.

'To a large extent, Mr. Dyson, I depend on you for the welfare of this place.' Now he'd begun the pack of lies, he'd continue with this child's game. 'It's a live-and-let-live affair. But the older people, the more responsible, have to give more than they take. It's not the nature of things; it used to be different when you and I started. But it's the way the world's organised. It's a young man's paradise these days. A kid's playground. We don't like it, but I'm afraid we've got to put up with it because we can't change it.'

He yapped on, barely heeding what he said, or minding the logic of his position. He cleared his grouses as a bronchitic shifts phlegm. Dyson did not even bother to feign interest, but in a pause grumbled churlishly about young Sampson and another such yobbo who egged him on. Neither man listened; both mentally elaborated their own ideas like dismal church organists improvising on and trivialising some well-known tune.

Twenty minutes later Riley stood, interrupting Dyson.

'I shall have to shove you out, now, Mr. Dyson. But there are two things. One: don't bring booze here.' That word softened the rebuke. 'And I don't know what the truth is about taking things. Waste is one matter. Winning something of the firm's is different altogether. But we'll leave it at that, shall we? And don't forget, Mr. Dyson, that I depend on you.'

Dyson shrugged surly; he'd listen to soft-soap.

'Is that an accusation?'

'No.'

'Then you've no right to say it.' Off we go.

'Go on, then,' Riley said. 'Let's hear your piece.' Open war.

'You've no call to accuse me of stealing. You've no evidence because I've taken no'te.' Dyson rang the changes on these three statements, and as he continued, his face reddened, he spat his words louder, nostrils stretched whitely and wild. Riley watched him, not listening; he knew the value of bluster; he'd not served in the army for nothing. He eyed the storm from shelter, did not get wet. The accusing voice squeaked higher; eyes blurred, tearful. Here was a scruffy sixty-odd-year-old, probably guilty as hell, in a lather, a gruesome tizzy without need, shaking his heart, his blood, getting nowhere.

'Ummm.' Riley made the deep sound, humming, in question. The other stopped. 'I made an inventory of the tools here while you were away and compared it with the official list. It was very short.'

'Yo' don't know where all the things's kept.'

'Perhaps not. But I know the difference between borrowing and keeping.'

'You can check any time yo' like.'

'Name a day,' Riley said, grim. 'Next week, after Monday.'

'All right, then.'

'If you're awkward, so am I.' Boast; leave it. That was best.

'I 'aven't took nothing.'

The man cringed; his outburst had dried the blood from his veins. Riley waited, steadily clicking upper tooth on his lower set, rhythmically, audible. Then he nodded.

'I believe you.' He did not smile or relax. 'What day?'

Dyson wetted his lips.

'About Tuesday.' That first word, that modifier, saved him from abject surrender.

'Tuesday, then.' Riley went to the cupboard, fetched out his sandwiches and vacuum-flask. 'Tuesday.' Dyson made for the door.

That night as Riley left the factory he wished Dyson, who went through the motions of work, a pleasant good evening. He received no reply, and concluded he'd made an enemy, that he should expect this, that his position entailed such. None the less, he was glad to find O'Brien shouting to him from the back door when he arrived home, inviting him in.

When he entered he found his neighbour sitting by the table and in front of the fire, handling a tray on which stood two glasses and an unopened quart of beer.

'Business first,' O'Brien said, shoving across his rent book and arrears. Riley counted, signed, thanked, and the book was put away. 'I hope you'll join me in a glass of ale, Mr. Riley, because I want your advice.

'You don't need to pay for that with beer.' Jovially.

With clumsy ceremony the glasses were filled. There seemed something sad about the man, as if his elbow-weavings, his hand movements exorcised, or failed to, tragedy about to be announced.

'My wife's very ill,' he said, after the first mouthful. Riley was not surprised.

'Is she in hospital?'

'Yes. We come back yesterday, by amb'lance. They took her in straight away.'

'Mental?'

'In a way. And yet in a way, not. Her whole body's broke down. The system don't function.'

'What the cause?'

'They don't know. At least not yet. This consultant's got her in for observation.'

'Is it caused by the mental trouble? Or was that a first sign?'

'I don't know that.' O'Brien took three inches of ale from his large glass. 'This doctor as she seen said it was as if the whole system of signalling had broke down. I didn't exactly get it; he wasn't much good at explaining, not for his position, and kept using words I didn't catch. But I got the drift, like. Her body isn't living properly. One thing he said was, "Interdependence has gone." '

'And what do they hope to do for her?'

'Observation. I mean she's not too old. That's what they said, themselves. She in't senile, is she? And they'll decide.'

'Did she know? I mean, could she . . .?'

'How can you tell? She just, well, she was like a house with the lights being switched off.'

'On your holiday?' Riley asked, to air his voice.

'No, before. Before. In the 'ospital—when she got depressed. I thought when we went away she was a bit better. Ate a bit. Said a few things. Laughed. Looked at the telly with us, took a bit of interest. She keeled over one morning, and it was bed after that. I thought it was a stroke, but they said not.'

'Is she in much pain?'

'They don't think so. And she don't rouse herself enough to tell 'em. She'd shout soon enough, wouldn't she? You never know with women.'

'I'm sorry.' Sipping. 'You said you wanted to ask me about something.'

O'Brien began a curious movement of his hands, plucking at his pullover and his trousers. It would exaggerate to say he wanted to strip himself, but a violence hovered, a ferocity about the fingers. Perhaps this seemed like a limbering up. At last he finished, humped his small paunch round, played a tattoo with his lower lip.

'I was deceiving her.' The words plummeted.

'In what way?' Riley knew he must speak.

'With a woman, another woman.'

'Before this happened?'

'Oh, ah.'

'Did she know?'

Now O'Brien considered again.

'I can't answer that. She was the suspicious sort, but I don't know how she could. She never said o't, any road.'

Two middle-aged men and a beer bottle. Enough to make the cat laugh.

'And nah,' O'Brien said, 'it's come to this.'

'It . . . ?'

'It's a judgement, in't it? On me?'

Riley felt this true, in every bone of his body. He cleared his throat.

'No,' he said. 'I don't see that. No connection, if you ask me.' He wet his lips at the glass. 'No.' He breathed heavily. 'Were you thinking of leaving . . . her . . . your wife?'

'We'd talked about it.'

'The other, the other woman, is she free?'

'Yes, she is.'

'How old is she?'

'Thirty-nine, forty. She's never told me. Wouldn't say. I come out straight wi' my age. No use hiding that. She kept mum.'

'If anything happened to your wife, would you want to marry her?'

'D'you know, I'm not sure. Now. I'm not.'

He made to fill Riley's glass but was prevented; he topped his own up.

'Listen to me, Mr. O'Brien.' This seemed important. He leaned forward. Once again O'Brien jerked and tugged at his clothes to ward off judgement. 'Whatever's happened to your wife has nothing to do with what you've been up to elsewhere.'

'Mester Riley.'

'Your wife doesn't know. If she did, it's very unlikely it could have had the effects you describe. No. It's coincidence.' He cleared his throat. 'Moreover, the sooner you accept this, the better for all concerned.'

O'Brien made noises of disagreement, disgruntled fear, but did not commit himself to words. The visitor considered offering to visit hospital, decided against this, and left soon after, inadequate, ill-tempered. Joan Oxford, downstairs searching for a screwdriver, heard his story, comforted him. She sat so neatly, intervened and soothed, that soon he laughed at his own terrors. Before half an hour was out she'd convinced him he'd done his neighbour a power of good by listening to his tale of woe and mildly protesting against its superstitious conclusions.

After they had a cup of tea she said again that she'd soon be on her way back to her husband, and he felt a gap, an area of uncertainty, of exposure after just these few weeks. It frightened him, but at the same moment he knew what Oxford, what Frank, felt when she deserted them. All lacked rationality, sprang from pride perhaps, but spread powerfully, in desperation, in a cold tension.

'Don't go yet,' he said.

'They've had their lesson. I've had mine.' Poised, at ease.

'What about me?' Childish syllables.

'You can cope,' she said.

'You'll come round.' Now he almost shouted. 'Sometimes. We're lovers.'

'No, I shan't.'

'Doesn't it mean anything, then?'

'You know it does. But when I go, it'll be for good. That's that.'

He gathered his words like pebbles for a catapult.

'You'll resume relations with your husband?' he said. 'You'll sleep with him?'

'I expect so.'

She stretched a hand in tenderness in his direction and the movement conveyed her unconcern. Now she'd written him off; she'd used him for that little lacuna in her life and now it was filled. Love had nothing to do with softly spoken reasons, common sense, even kindness. Love flamed, blistered, scalded. He'd loved; she'd made use of him. Wondering if she'd any notion of the piling, hell-bent force of his anger, he walked to a mirror, saw the known face, its wrinkles gouged deeper by the poor light, something like a baked apple. He sat down in despair, again.

'I love you,' he said.

She nodded, mouth puckered, before she extracted a looking glass from her handbag. Perhaps his own doubts plagued her. No, she fingered her face, might start to make up.

'You've been kind to me,' she said. 'I'm grateful. I can't tell you how much. I don't know what I'd have done without you.'

'Don't go back to him.'

'I married him, Jack. I loved him then and I think something of him now. It's my place to go back.'

'Doesn't it mean anything? What's happened between us here?' She did not answer this time. 'I love you. You know it's true.'

'You'll miss me. *I* shall you. But you'll get over it.'

'He's got over it already.'

'I don't think so.' She shook her head, condemning him. 'I don't think so.'

That was right; he couldn't deny it. Somewhere back amongst the infinite numbers of events in the world, she and Idiot Oxford had walked down the aisle of St. Anne's Church, thinking God knows what. It seemed so trivial; neither knew what the bondage was, the commitment. For this minute Riley was consumed with jealousy that could neither be contained or rationally considered. His agony lifted him to his feet, thumped a cry from his chest before he ran for the door. The action, the run downstairs, the headlong steps into passage, through front door into the darkish square of front garden unoccupied by the ash tree steadied him. As a boy he'd run, talking to himself just so, up the street, going hard, down the next, five or six times. Breathless but steadier after twenty minutes' exercise he drank the coffee the waiting Mrs. Oxford had ready for his return.

He fingered her in his kitchen, masterfully marched her

to his bed where she stripped for him. As he lay spent, a spurt of mischievous jealousy, smallish now, almost contemptible in his body's content, made him quiz her.

'Do you think it's right to be here with me when you're going back to your husband?'

Her nakedness on his spread warm, while he touched and stroked her wedding-ring.

'It's what you wanted.'

'And I want you to stop here.'

'I know, but I shan't.'

'Doesn't this mean anything to you, then?'

'No. Not much. It's nice.'

'You'd do it with anybody?'

'You know I wouldn't. But it doesn't mean as much to me as it does to you.' She sat up, her breasts small, firm, but neutral now in the orange fancy light of the bedroom. 'You're like somebody possessed,' she said. 'As if everything you'd ever lived for led to,' she giggled, 'what we've done. Perhaps it did for you.'

'You're beautiful,' he said, face in her flank.

'Listen, Jack. I like it. I don't think I could do without it for ever, but it's pretty near that, now. It doesn't seem important.'

'That's because you don't love me.' He enjoyed the delicious perversion of announcing her lack of love naked to her nakedness.

'I wish I knew what love was.' She shrugged, straightened the bedclothes before she slipped down easily to lie flat. 'I can remember when I was young. It was a pain. I couldn't eat. Floods of weeping. Sex wasn't so good, then, but perhaps that made it better. When I just loved Ronald Oxford I could have kissed the paving-stones he walked on. I groaned for him, and ached. Inside me, like a madwoman. I'd lie in bed and cry, for him and others, until my pillow was saturated. I once ripped my sheet from top to bottom, frantic, and had to make some daft excuse for my mother.' The voice droned as if she deliberately sought to lose his interest. 'I can hardly understand it, now. My body's done, perhaps. I'm an old bag.'

He pulled her to him. She allowed it, disinterestedly.

'I don't feel that way now.' Serene and sad.

'You would if you fell in love.'

She blew breath out like a contented smoker through rounded lips to the ceiling. 'I doubt it. What's love now? A plate of faggots.' The conceit made her laugh, twist in the bed. 'A good fire. Comfort. Somewhere decent to sit down dry and warm. And not too much responsibility. It's all taped. They've learnt to put their shirts out for washing and make their own beds.'

'You left them.'

'I did. They wouldn't sit quiet. Frank's awkward. They came to fighting. Soon he'll be bringing his wife-to-be flouncing in. They'll want a room. I know what it'll be like. Not one meal on time. Dirty tights all over the landing. And Ronald, my husband, drinking and showing off to the girl.'

'That's what you're going back to.'

'I know. I didn't realise when I walked out that I was making for another man's bed.'

He laughed and in an explosion of high spirits kicked with his legs high and fierce into the air so that the loosened bedclothes were hauled off, leaving her naked and him lumpy in the pyjamas he'd pulled on.

'I'll get cold,' she called, energetic as he was.

15

At the factory Riley found himself in charge of another three machines which were fitted, with unnecessary hurry, in a spare wing of a warehouse further along the street. The haste of the installation brought no good; for a fortnight the engineers wrestled with perfectly sound machinery which somehow failed to function.

By the end of the two weeks the experts had finally read and followed printed instructions and the three new sizes of carton piled in perfection, though Riley, after the hours of frustration and oil, sweat and shredded hopes could barely believe what he saw. He heard again the loud voices of men shouting to convince themselves that they'd complied with every necessity and then would follow the clanking, the crumpled product, the burst of furious recrimination, sometimes even a frantic glance to him for some managerial anathema to shift the jinx. Now all clattered at efficient speed and for ten minutes Cooper presided over the rejoicing.

It had not been worth while.

They'd hired or bought this floor space, acquired the machines and now were whanging out boxes minimally different from those of the old place. It had seemed like a test, so organised that when he'd fled from the idiocy of inefficient underlings, Cooper, tight-lipped, tight-bottomed, would have stamped his cards 'Lacking Moral Fibre' and sent them to the labour exchange or the asylum.

Not until the crisis was over did Riley realise how he'd

tired himself. Fortunately Joan Oxford still seemed loth to move, even though she had announced her decision to her son and her husband. Now she seemed to hold Riley in mother-love and it suited his exhausted body; the two would sit watching television shows and sipping cups of tea or soup. Life was a picnic, but for old-age pensioners.

The cleaning-lad at the factory for the present was a university student called Woolley. He wore the uniform of his tribe, jeans, jungle-green vest, and crumpled semi-military jacket. His round, gold-rimmed spectacles, his fair beard, shoulder-length hair, long, dirty fingernails completed the caricature, but Riley liked him. He was nothing like as handsome as Frank Oxford, but he used words easily, 'the confluence of two roads', 'malice prepense', 'the practice of continual litotes', and the brown eyes smiled in the bush with a simpleton's charity. Riley used to talk to him, and retire defeated. It was not that he was beaten by Woolley's arguments or superior knowledge; only that this young scruff, with a brush in his hand, cleaning as if he meant it, could stop and talk with a diffidently expressed certainty that the older man envied. Of course, in a month's time the lad would swop his broom for a notebook, but the world owed him nothing and he did not mind.

'What d'you do at these pop festivals, then?' he asked.

'Listen to music.'

'Bloody noise.'

'I can see that.' He giggled at the ineptitude of his verb. 'Cools it off in the open air.' The candour of his eyes disarmed. 'We sit. We wait. We queue. For lavatories. For bread. For a wash.'

'Half of 'em strip off.' Riley exaggerated because the lad spoke so mildly.

'Half? You put a hundred thousand people together, or just a few score hundreds, and you'll throw up your nutters and your exhibitionists.'

'But you're supposed to be educated. You'll be a B.A. soon. And yet you lie there listening to blaring rubbish.'

'And intelligent conversation, and anecdotage abounding. Why, it's great. In your day you went to dance halls and listened to equivalent rubbish and, besides, you had to saturate yourself in alcohol to make it bearable.'

'What about your drugs, then?'

Woolley smiled, slowly so that Riley thought the lad would pat his cheeks like some Victorian parson with a parishioner's child.

'I should say that soft drugs do less damage than alcohol. Once you've ruined your liver, that's it. It's a one-way process.'

'Do you take drugs?'

'I don't. No.'

'Have you? Ever?'

'Yes. I've tried them. I'm busy, though. I can occupy myself. Besides, I'm not all that rich. I need reading matter. I like a shelf or two of books.'

Riley looked at the innocent hairy face. The appurtenances were those of some Victorian grandfather or a pioneer roughing it unshaven in the American west.

'When you've left university will you ever come back here? To see us?'

'I might want a job. You've read about graduate unemployment.'

'Are you frightened of that, then?'

'No.' Confident; merry; neither fearing God nor regarding man.

Riley rubbed his face, much puzzled. The lad reminded him of the voluble foreman of the painters in that both wrung more out of life than he did. They were younger; they enjoyed their words, but they did not seem circumscribed as he was by bread-and-butter worries. When one day he'd seen the foreman out with a young wife and two children in a pushchair, the man swaggered, in a blazer, still loquacious as if he saw his family, like his employers or underlings, in need of constant exhortation or explanations. He'd nodded to Riley, then nudged his wife; 'a gaffer speaks to me in the street' and that itself demanded a further, lively, bloodthirtsty commentary.

What was he missing?

The answer stood obvious: vigour. These young men set about living in a way that he'd never managed. But it involved, perhaps their personalities. Joan's boy, Frank, handsome as they come, had nothing like the dynamism of those two. He was nobody's fool, could stand up for himself and yet was an ordinary mortal, a wage-slave, a cardboard cutout compared with the polemical painter and the student with his smiling certainty.

Riley. 'Wry-neck', they'd called him at school.

He judged himself to be doing well on the edge of catastrophe. The factory's production leapt upwards; the girls yearned, as Cooper's advert put it, to earn. Mrs. Oxford showed no hurry to leave, had promised him she'd revisit him, and had joined her husband, who dropped in once or twice, in praising Riley as the saviour of her sanity. He was breathless, aghast at her hypocrisy. If only he could guarantee that each day was as this, without accident, with money, calm.

But next door O'Brien struggled his days in silence. They never met. The rent was pushed through the door in an envelope, and the book, signed and blotted, similarly returned. In the hospital Mrs. O'Brien lived or died while her husband clattered up the ward, slipped back in silence through his own front door. Riley ought to knock, or fetch the man in for a meal, or buy a few flowers to send, but he did not because lethargy spelt safety. As long as he stepped straight, neither right nor left, tomorrow would reflect the prosperity of today. Scotten juveniles bawled and thumped on the other side of the wall to indicate the world moved; inside his home Jack Riley polished and held his breath.

He met Frank Oxford in the street.

'Your mother's coming back, then?' he began.

'Ay, but she's in no hurry.'

'You'll be looking forward to it.'

141

'Why don't she come back?' The boy threw his aggressive words at the grey-gold of the sky. 'She's too well off where she is.'

'Do you think so?'

'She's only got herself to look after. Stands to reason.'

'If you were in her place you wouldn't come back?'

'I would not.'

'Are you at loggerheads with your dad again?'

'That'll be the time.'

The lad groused about his father's niggling, the unfair division of labour, arguments over money, girls, wasted opportunity. They had not struck at each other yet, though it seemed imminent. The basic trouble was that the old man was selfish, and idle, and saw good in nobody except himself. What was he? When you'd cut the trimmings out, and his exaggerations, he was a bloody factory-hand, a machine-minder and that was that.

'I've told him,' he said when Riley remonstrated. 'Wi' somebody like him it's no use mincing your words. And I also said, straight to his face, that my mam was better off where she was, and I'd go and tell her so.'

'What did he say to that?'

'What could he?'

'They're married, my lad. They exchanged solemn promises to each other.'

Frank bit his lip.

'He might have been all right when they got spliced. Now he's an idle bag of wind.'

'You'll regret saying that.'

Frank now considered.

'Perhaps I shall. He's a pain in the neck. All the time. He don't curb his tongue. And he'd put his fist in, if he dare. He's a failure.'

'That's hard.'

'I'm not much of a mucher. Twopenny-'apenny clerk. But he makes out he's a somebody, that he's done all this and that, when he hasn't. He's a factory-hand who expects me and my mother to slave for him. She wouldn't have it. Nor me. And when she comes home it'll be back to usual inside a fortnight. Where's my trousers? Have you ironed that striped shirt? Wouldn't have .drip-dry. Not him. Got to dress up, he has, to blue his bloody money in the pubs.'

'If I remember rightly it's not so long since you were begging me to get your mother to come back.'

'I don't say I'm not sorry for him. I can't help it.'

'Not much. I'm not shooting my mouth off.'

'Your wife's not left you.'

'She's spoilt him. All right. But he's not decrepit yet.'

'If he'd get something else in his head beside which shirt or what shoes I wouldn't mind.'

'I see.'

Both were silent in the street. Riley's anger seethed at the youth's self-righteousness, but he immediately recognised it as frustration, not only at Oxford's cocky inadequacy, but at the boy's own lack of success. He'd perhaps nothing to recommend him but his age; he saw himself in twenty years as a beer-swilling boasting nonentity inside a natty suit. It didn't do. Now Riley wished to put his hand on the boy's arm, convey some hope to the face that glassed his mother's, but again his own motivation dropped false. Riley felt a sentimental attachment to Joan Oxford which, when she was away, invited a scattering of benevolence on anybody who recalled her, however vaguely, even ridiculously. Paw a poor boy in the street for his mother's sake and what?

'We're none of us marvellous,' he said. He spouted words for five minutes so that it appeared almost as if his tongue had usurped the functions of his brain. When Frank had gone, Riley slouched up the road in a melancholy of argument. Human beings resembled those new machines that had not worked in spite of their shining, oiled appearance, the numerous adjustments, modifications, superstitious incantations and finger-crossings. On such and such a day they'd function to perfection, for no reason, and not before. He knew this to be sophistry, but the analogy pleased him because in the end those recalcitrant pieces of metal had moved, produced, continued.

'What's the drill?' he shouted to Woolley the student.

'It's a bastard.'

'Eh?'

Woolley jerked a finger towards one of the girls who bent with wooden-faced ruthlessness at her machine.

'Pat, there. Her husband's just up and left her. Last night.' He signalled Riley conspiratorially inside the annexe's cloakroom and loading bay. 'Just came in and said he wanted a divorce. First she knew about it. "I'm knocking off another bird," he says. Just like that. She's breaking her heart. I've told her to get a solicitor, and then give him nothing and squeeze the bugger till his pips squeak. But she says, "I love him." What can you say to that?'

'Nothing.'

'You're right. I just take over her machine while she goes and howls in the closet.'

'What a vulgar expression.'

Riley hated his facetiousness, felt the boy's anger whip him. He punched the lad in the arm, marched back, where he now saw the pallor of the woman's face, heard her fierce sniff, bit his lips over the holes in her tights.

'They all confide in you?' he asked Woolley.

'They've got to have somebody.'

'You're only a kid.'

Woolley's lips shaped a soundless whistle, sore as an obscenity, and then he shrugged, slapped his jeans, shook his mop-head of hair.

Riley stood rebuked.

16

As soon as Joan Oxford returned to her husband, Riley began to suffer.

He'd warned himself that in spite of her promises she would not come back, but he was not convinced. Now he walked the rooms where she'd lived, touched the furniture she'd used in hopeless idiocy. Suddenly, involuntarily, he'd find himself kneeling, his head smoothing the mahogony drawers of the dressing table for coolness, or the bed's end, while harsh grunts were mauled out of him. He'd pull himself up in embarrassment, but would be back, in a moment, in a welter of inconsolable nothing, a gaping chaos from which his eyes strained out to see what did not exist, could not be named.

He could not locate his grief.

Conscience and sense were appeased, but inside him some primitive hunger spread like a disease that killed without symptoms. Now he'd keel over, physically, as if his muscles had lost direction. This was envy, youth's incontinence.

Occasonally, as he watched his antics he concluded that such behaviour was necessary. As a man flung himself about ridiculously to avoid a murderous car or a stabbing knife, so he, in his agony, rescued himself by his posturings. As long as the therapy was private and recognised as such by him, that was what counted.

In the middle of his trouble Cooper's secretary phoned for him.

When he arrived at the agreed hour, Cooper had left.

Furious, because the secretary could have saved his time, he scoured his mind for mistakes. In the last few days he could easily have miscalculated, signed incorrect invoices, set in motion some money-wasting schedule; he could not remember. His work had kept him sane, but tension could easily have tricked him into an error and then closed his mind to it.

Cooper recalled him two days later.

'This won't be long,' he said. He waved Riley to a seat, lit a cigarette and glowered. It looked theatrical, this scowling podgy Napoleon. 'How did you get here?'

'I walked.'

'How long did that take you?'

'Not ten minutes.'

'You should have a car. Status symbol. Bet some of your employees have.'

'Yes. Their husbands bring 'em.'

'Husbands? Oh. Husbands.' Sour. Uncomfortable. 'Look here, Riley. What I'm going to say now is confidential. Is that understood? You don't speak of it to anybody. Anybody. Clear?' He was vulgar, Riley thought; likely to bounce into the washroom and pee down the sink. 'Things are moving in this firm. I don't want to particularise, but we're regrouping and expanding. We're buying big but fining down, if you follow me. We're negotiating for another concern, concerns you could say, but making certain that the new amalgamation's perfect, or near to it, economically speaking.' He was prodding the air with stiff fingers as if to shake these humdrum expressions out of himself, like numbers from a bingo-barrel. 'Getting rid of uneconomic ventures. Hiving off. You know what that entails?'

'Well, no, not exactly.' Riley grudged.

'Redundancies.' Cooper played that ace boorishly.

'Does that mean me?'

'Ah, then.' Smacking lips. 'Ah. We may sell your little place, if we get a good enough offer.'

'You've only just put new machines in, had it painted,

opened the annexe.' Riley sounded off his indignation.

'Chicken-feed, money-wise.' Cooper poked a finger up his nose, wiped it on his handkerchief. 'It's possible. You've done well up there. I'll say that. Otherwise I wouldn't send for you now.'

'We do a good job.'

'You say so. But by the time we've done buying we shall have a unit five times your size and with room for expansion doing exactly your job. It'll be part of the larger deal. You see. Thrown in. A perquisite. So we shall have to sell your . . .'

'When?'

'Six months, perhaps. I'm not . . .'

'You're sure it will happen?'

'No, I'm not. I shall be disappointed if it doesn't. It'll be a smack in the face for me, I'll tell you, but it's not a one million per cent certainty yet.'

'Why have you sent for me, then?'

'Good question, Riley. I like you, my friend. You jumped to it up there in Crocus Street. I tip you off in confidence. So that you can look round at your leisure.'

'Who'd give me a job at my age?'

'That's what you've got to find out. Test the market. At your level, I've no idea. There may be plenty of openings. You'll have to move.'

'From this town?' Riley's breath stuck short.

'Yes. That won't worry you, will it? You're an old army man. Posted all over the world.' Cooper began to laugh, perhaps at Riley's enforced odysseys. 'That's why I'm giving you time. And any day you're called up for interview, we pay your salary. You're a good employee, Riley. We'll support you with strong references. But this is the parting of the ways.'

'Does Major Erskine know about this?'

Cooper nibbled his thumb.

'You mustn't,' he began, 'get this wrong. Your Major Erskine, the simple soldier-man, the father of his troops, doesn't exist. He's a very rich operator and he's playing an important part in the consortium that's financing our expansion. He's in it for the money. He's sharp. He knows a thing or two, or his advisers do. No. Erskine's no more sentiment than I have about this. If he's slapping a quarter of a million down he wants some return.'

'All that? Is he worth . . . ?'

'He is. But he's only one. This is enormous.'

'And you've organised and planned all this?'

Cooper preened himself, seemed to swell, belly upwards, face widening, greasy with smiles.

'That's what they employed me for, isn't it? While I've been stepping production up here, and you'll admit I've done that, I've been chasing all the time, testing, filching information. I've had lucky breaks. It's worked out as if I'd planned the whole damn' thing. That's why it's happened so quickly. We could tie it up inside a month. Gone like a dream. I think big, Riley, but I wouldn't have believed this. No. Picking an old lady's plums.'

He moved expansively like a market huckster, fat palms flying. Riley felt a spasm of respect. This sweating man and his associates had collected millions together and had tricked or terrorised firms into their clutches. This man, this fourteen-stoner with his curling sidewhiskers, had done something as incredible to Riley as writing the Bible, or diving off the Eiffel Tower and living. Such men existed. When one watched the packed honeycombs, skyscrapers of office blocks, thumping up one must look to come chromium-barred desk somewhere for a Cooper, a man who'd planned, and grabbed, and dared, and inveighed, who started the project.

And he, Jack Riley, stood in a room with such a one, could have taken a step or two and then reached out and touched him. It would have been good if he had. It would have restored humanity. In this place, this carpet-bright office where Bowles, seen now as a rag-picker, had lorded it, Cooper kinged and godded. Not in London. Not with a title.

Not yet thirty-five. Riley shivered. Fright. Frost. He pulled his shoulders back.

'Do you mind if I see Major Erskine?'

Cooper frowned, momentarily troubled.

'What for?'

'I don't want to leave his employment.'

'You'll get yourself a job easily enough.'

'Do you mind if I see him?'

'No.' Vigorous thumbnail into nostril. 'See who you like.'

'You do mind, then, Mr. Cooper.'

For a few seconds the boss gaped as if his desk had addressed him, before he stuck out his legs, pushing his chair back, knuckling his great thighs.

'I don't give a monkey's, Riley. For all I know there might still be a place with us . . . new consortium. But you won't be a manager. You've about touched maximum, head of a small concern, twenty or thirty machine-hands. That's you. I thought you liked being your own boss. Plenty of openings, I guess, at that level. Don't know. Guesswork. Not much competition. Always telling me, "Can't get a manager." But the new thing won't run on small, uneconomic units. Very large. There, now. I've told you. Do as you like. But don't pass the word on. Clear? Is that clear?'

'I shall say nothing.'

'No.' That word menaced. Riley knew he'd made an enemy.

As he left the room he could not recollect what he'd said. Vaguely he remembered he'd made a fool of himself, but he could not say how, recall the exact inopportune words. He scuttled out, not calling for a word with Addison, and failing to notice Frank Oxford at his desk. The boy expected him to stop.

'It's better now my mam's back.'

What was he saying? Riley had no idea. The sentence concluded a paragraph.

'Uh, oh. Good.'

'Comfy like. We know where we are. She looks after us.'

'Yes.'

The boy drew back at the long-drawn-out syllable, sensing the lack of interest, the coldness, the apartness of the other man.

'She makes us run round a bit.' Frank recovered, tried to laugh.

'I expect so.'

Riley was walking away in the echoing corridor, leaving the lad flummoxed, wondering how he'd annoyed the other, embarking on breaking down on a sentence about how grateful they both were, him and his dad, for what . . .

Outside, the weather bloomed, St. Martin's summer, without wind under the pallor of blue sky, unseasonably warm while the horse-chestnut leaves yellowed and smirked, against the brilliance of afternoon light.

Riley, walking fast, knew terror.

He pushed hard to escape, as if his movements, his energy, would shift that incubus from his back. Shivering, he felt again childish horror, forgotten for years, of imminent punishment which blotted out all pleasure, past, present, to come, and which dried humanity out of his veins. Now, the world, like an angry father, would thrash him, and fear so mastered him that he could see nothing beyond the scorn of his elders, a flailing cane. He informed himself that there were chances of employment, that he might improve his position, but this infantile concentration on the rod, the disgrace, did not allow common sense or experience any word. A frightened atheist walked to execution.

Outside his own factory, four-square, white-neat in the afternoon's sun, he shuddered. He could go back in there to set about three little jobs which had to be completed that day. If he worked hard he could have them done by four-thirty, but what would be the point? He was out on his neck, a reject, redundant, a scarecrow without a bird to terrorise. One of the men from Despatch came leaping out from the main doors in his brown overall, laughing as he stumbled. Catching Riley's eye, he charged back in, announced his downfall to a roar of appreciative laughter. That was painful, to know that these young men howled with life, skylarking, punching, making faces at authority, while outside in the warmth of the street authority's symbol trembled, frog-cold inside his skin, frightened of his own breathing, scared by the swoop of a sparrow after crumbs.

As Riley went indoors he could see nothing of the despatch clerks. He did not acknowledge the girls who listened to the radio and shouted as they stood at their machines. They moved with grace, a sturdy, stocky fluidity, not ordinarily beautiful, but perfectly matched to the throb and drumming of the machines, the neat end-product. He noticed this, but did not stop, could not; they were not allowed to see him. Brusquely he refused the offer of a cup of coffee from Miss Rogers. Now he loafed, until with infinite loathing, against inertia, he pulled his wire in-tray towards him and began. What in hell? Did this matter? He was paid to do it. He read without understanding, tried again, made himself grasp. Within ten minutes he was at work, under a weight of dread, but occupied, carefully sorting out a routine problem. Inside an hour he'd completed the lot, had called in Miss Rogers for dictation, had ordered coffee and held himself steady.

Out in the lavatory he almost fell, as if his balance had been whipped from him momentarily. Again his will forced him to stand, walk, to order Miss Rogers to sit. As she delivered his cup, she brushed against him, held herself to his shoulder shortly, at his service, but he did not register this until she had stepped away, perched herself pad on knee.

Right, Mr. Riley.'

'Drink your coffee first.'

'It's four-thirty.'

'Won't take ten minutes, this. Have you got things to clear up?'

'No, sir. No more than usual.'

'Thank goodness for you,' he said. At the end of this ridiculous sentence he coughed, but she blushed on her cheekbones and patted her hair into place. All his compliments transposed themselves into sex. 'You do me well, Miss Rogers.'

She thanked him, little finger crooked by the coffee-cup. A lump choked his throat; he could blubber. Dully he dictated his letters, ordered her to type them for signature first thing in the morning, dismissed her. Slumped at his desk, he wasted ten minutes, straightened phone and blotter before he walked the factory floor. The machines were switched off; all lay peaceful as the women cleared up. While they worked filling waste-bins the lads from Despatch were placing the first piles of raw material from their trolley for the morning. Gaiety, though tired, subdued, was the order. The youths did not shout much and only two of the women spoke with anything like vigour, discussing arrangements for collecting a young daughter from infant school. Their voices rose and fell, partially dulled by the thud of cardboard or the scrape of metal. Riley, listening, knew that in four minutes Miss Rogers would touch the bell and they'd all be into the coats with a last shriek to desert the place. But for these last moments they continued, adept as ever, as if tomorrow's shift were important to them.

'I 'ad to tell the teacher I couldn't collect her. But she was very nice. She said Mandy could wait with her till Shirl come down from the big school. Stays behind doin' things. Real nice. When I told our Rog he laughed like 'ell. "What'd you say," he said, "if yo' 'ed to stop behind at your factory for another half-hour to clean your machine up, wi' no more pay, and then some cheeky bugger comes clagging baby-minding on you, an' all?" He laughed. "They different from us," I said. "Ay. Work a bleddy sight 'arder, for one thing. Can be put on, for another." '

The voice, strong, clear as a flute, was level, impersonal.

A harsh bell cracked on the wall. The women turned, left, becking to Riley if they had to pass him; cards were jammed into the clocking-machine and returned to the rack. The floor, empty, looked dusty, neglected. Miss Rogers, in her coat, waited for him by the stairs top.

'Would there be anything else, Mr. Riley?'

He shook his head. She wished him good night.

17

Riley slept badly, shouted short of temper, hated himself.

He, with care, could complete a day's work competently, but found no pleasure. At home he could dust, but not watch television. One evening, shopping on the way back from the factory, he saw Joan Oxford. She waved from the other side of the road, crossed, chatted trivially, then rushed away. In his misery he did not know whether he minded, but gaped after her retreating neat buttocks.

Determined, he wrote a note to Major Erskine. This occupied him for two hours, as he sat miserably sucking his pen, unable to fathom why his last attempt would not do. When he was satisfied he made a copy for himself and one to send to Cooper. At ten he took the two envelopes out for posting to prevent his tearing them open again. Back indoors certainty that he had misspelt or -phrased his plea plagued him.

He heard nothing for a week, when Erskine's secretary rang to say that the major would call the next afternoon. It was too late in the day to ask for any clearing-up operation.

Next morning he announced the impending arrival, asked for co-operation. They laughed behind his back, but tidied with a will in spare moments. The charge-hand issued clean overalls a day early, and the despatch clerks were so delighted with the spick-and-span appearance of their places that one, a quiet boy who'd never said a world, sloped arms with a broom and slapped out a butt-salute.

'Where'd you learn that?' Riley asked.

'Army cadets.'

'You present arms for an officer of field rank.'

Their faces sagged in incomprehension, but their department stood squared to perfection.

Erskine arrived at three-five, was met at the door, was brusquely gracious to the women. He wore tweeds, buckled brown shoes, carried gloves and an ash-stick with a shining gold ferrule. Upstairs he refused Miss Rogers' coffee, but sat at the visitors' side of the desk. Cooper, Riley knew, would have occupied the manager's seat.

'Now what's all this about, Riley?' he said.

The familiar phrase both sobered and frightened. Riley had heard it too often in the company office when the O.C., soldierly, without a notion what was on, flannelled or depended on his sergeant-major for explanation, for guidance, until he'd sufficient evidence to make up his mind, when he'd arbitrarily stop proceedings, announce his decision, which, as often as not, showed he'd neither understood the petitioner, the petition, the warrant officer's advice, nor even some recently announced, underlined, ruling of his own. Back in the mess, the sergeants laughed at 'Bonehead' Erskine, despaired of him, but liked him because he never objected if they altered his plan to something more sensible so long as higher authority did not kick back at him. They claimed he could never remember what he'd decided, but in reality they knew better. He left it to his experts while he acted his majority, looked the sort of man who could carry a crown on his shoulder and go on leave in a Rolls-Royce that made the general commanding whistle.

'What's all this now, Riley?' No use talking to him.

'I'm going to be made redundant.'

'Are you, b'God? Is it, er, Cooper? Did he tell you?'

'Under the new organisation you'll close this place or sell it off?'

'Won't you, uh, go with it? Part of a thriving concern?'

'Mr. Cooper didn't think so. He's advised me to look round for a new post.'

'I see. That seems sensible.'

The magnificent cuffs below tweed sleeves fascinated Riley, annoyed him. They symbolised the man's wealth, his inattention, his unconcern; he'd give a naked beggar the address of a good tailor. There was silence while Erskine tugged at his cuffs or studied the dazzle of his boots, and Riley flailed desperately round for the words to burst into this citadel of idiocy.

'I'd like to stay with the firm, sir.'

'Firm?'

'I'd like to stay with you, with the firm, sir.'

'Yes. I see. Yerrss.'

'I think, sir, I can claim to be a good employee. We've built this up into a really going business. Nobody's made a demand on me that I haven't been able to meet. Mr. Cooper's a driver: he doesn't hold his hand back, but we've kept up.' Riley moved, took, snatched Miss Rogers' production graph from the wall, thrust it into Erskine's hands. The major's eyes narrowed in incomprehension. 'That's a first-rate record, I think you'll agree, sir.'

'Yes. Yerss. Good. Good. Now, let's see, what is it you want?'

'To stay with the firm, sir.'

'Um.' Erskine scratching his hair vigorously did not disturb its iron-grey symmetry.

'Yes. You think . . . Well. Now. Yerss.'

'I shall be redundant when this place is sold off.'

The major rasped his moustache with a thumb.

'I realise that, Riley. Or so you think. I play little part in the day-to-day organisation of the firm. My part is finance. This country, if you want my view, is organised, and properly, to benefit financiers, like myself. Surprises you to hear me say that, doesn't it? You read the opposite in the papers? I'm grateful that both my mother and father had the foresight to leave me very large sums of money, very large, besides, the, er, the works. Even larger now. What was I saying?'

Riley waited.

'What was I saying, Riley?'

'I'd asked you, sir, if, when this factory is sold, there would be another position for me in the firm?'

'What's Cooper say?'

'He wouldn't commit himself, sir. Said there might be a chance. But he advised me to look about for another job.'

'I'll speak to him.'

That was it. The camera shutter had snapped shut, for better or worse. The little mind had made itself up. Erskine could storm if pressed, swore and bawled enough to turn his corporals pale. "You sh'd 'a 'eard Bonehead, effin' and blindin' at the sarn't-major." All that remained, now, was to make oneself pleasant.

'Thank you very much, sir. That's very kind of you.'

Erskine peered as if Riley had broken into Hebrew.

'Not at all. Not at all. Well, let's look round the place now we're here.'

They moved slowly, at Erskine's insistence on stopping to speak with the work-people. The women smiled, were impressed with his suit, his aristocratic smell, but answered him off-handedly, as if to match his tom-fool questions. He'd no idea that the place had been painted, that they'd acquired an annexe with new machines; Riley guessed that he'd be pushed to say what the factory produced. The manager plied him with information, figures, praised himself; it was all he could try, for one never knew what would latch on in the old man's brain. He'd be offered an unimportant snippet which he'd suddenly register as crucial, which would convince him how efficient you were, how necessary it was to promote you.

They paused by Woolley, the student, who was piling an order for despatch on a loading-trolley. As he moved, he hummed a Beethoven concerto. Erskine inquired his name; the boy flicked his mane back from his face, smiled, showing excellent teeth, to reply. In his jeans and black shirt, he'd removed his overall, he stood strikingly, like a bandit, a Che, a badman of the Westerns. Riley felt that the major, to equal this handsome wildness, should take a civilised gold monocle from his pocket to eye the young man.

'How long have you worked here?'

'Just this summer. It's a holiday job.' The plebeian voice mocked Erskine's incisiveness.

'You're at the university?

'Yes, sir.' Again the white smile under the black moustache.

'What are you reading?'

'Economic history.'

'Interesting?' A polite, formal nod, almost a bow, in reply. 'How do you like it here?'

'Pleasant.'

'What do you mean by that?' Riley recognised the parade voice, snapping at some squaddy who'd spoken out of turn.

'As a factory it's not too bad. The work's dull, but the conditions are quite good. It's not too big a unit, and not too noisy.'

'But not,' the major lifted his nose, 'like the university?'

'There's nobody to talk to. That's the difference. I enjoy a word with Mr. Riley when he comes round, but he's no time for conversation, let alone argument.'

'Mr. Riley's the best we can do for an intellectual?'

'Yes, sir. He's nobody's fool.'

The youth shook his hair; he seemed tenser now, suspicious that Erskine patronised him, but the major began to reminisce, recalling Riley in the army. Woolley stood distant, his face cold, moulded in wax.

When the visitor disappeared, Riley returned to the bay where the student still stacked his trolley.

'Quite a chat,' he said.

'Yes.' Woolley leaned on the handle, sweating. 'He asked me if I'd considered commerce as a career?'

'Have you?'

The boy shrugged.

'That man,' he said, 'couldn't earn his keep on the factory floor. Splats about in a suit the colour of vomit and asks me how I'll make my living.' Fierce, this.

'What's upset you?' Riley asked.

'Not him.'

'Me?'

'No. The whole bloody set-up. Sweep the floor for yellow-belly to walk round. Why should we?'

'It's not a bad thing to sweep the floor, though.'

'For ourselves, yes. Not for him. It degrades. He wouldn't notice anyway. He expects us to live up to the neck in shit. That's all we're used to or fit for.'

'Ay,' Riley said. 'I know how you feel. But let me ask you something. How often would you sweep up if you weren't made to?'

Woolley grinned, beautifully erect now, attractive, delicately amused.

'I'm a mucky sod,' he said. 'But you know what I mean.'

Riley made as if he knuckled him, and went, smiling briefly, upstairs. That evening as he left the factory he found Woolley on the street corner waiting for him.

'I'd got it on me today,' the boy said, disarmingly.

'Never mind.'

'No, I'm sorry. You'd enough on your plate with that cut-glass idiot poncing round, without my hysterics.'

'Very quiet hysterics.'

'Subdued. This is my day for the hospital. I go up once a month to see my grandfather.'

'What's wrong with him?' Riley asked. They seemed to be walking in harness.

'Senility.'

'How old is he, then?'

'Only just over seventy.'

'That's not old. What did he do? What work?'

'Bricklayer.'

'And your father?'

'He's a foreman brickie.'

'Do they live in Beechnall? I should know.' He did, in fact.

'Yes. Local boy. Wilton Crescent.'

'Where's that?'

'Leen Park Estate.'

Now they walked on and at the bus-stop Riley invited the lad home for a cup of tea.

'What's wrong with your grandad, then?'

Waiting, the boy described the old man sitting in an armchair by his hospital bed, looking down dully at the thumbs he twiddled, his single occupation.

'That's all he does. Move his thumbs. And he looks at you sometimes. As if he couldn't help it. It's no use talking or getting hold of his hand or anything. Even when the nurses, they're men, y'know, come round and shout things at him he takes no notice.'

'Does he like you to visit him?'

'I don't know. It makes no difference.'

'Why do you go then?'

'I keep asking myself that.' They mounted the bus, on to an upstairs front seat where they could talk free from eavesdroppers. Woolley's face set stern as he gnawed his lip. 'There he exists in a ward stinking of urine with another dozen like him, human vegetables. The nurses are very good. They jolly 'em along and cram food in. But I ask myself, "What use's this?" This is what we come to, sooner or later. This or dying. He worked hard all his life; he paid his way. My dad won't go to see him now.'

'But you do?'

'Once a month. My dad's more sensible than I am. He says it's useless, because the old chap doesn't recognise anybody. But you never know. Something, some crumb of comfort, might register, somewhere, down in his brain.'

Woolley spoke with such vehemence as if he'd melt the glass windscreens, but his voice whispered. Eyes protruded and his hands were clenched, as if he himself had grown mad. Perhaps a strain of instability showed already. Yet this was the boy who whistled, bustled at his work, stood up to Erskine, joked with the women, spoke with eager equality to his boss.

As soon as they left the bus Woolley described his grandfather's life, the allotment, the Labour Party, the arguments with his only and uncommitted son, the scorn for a boy who'd thrown up a scholarship at a high school to leave at fourteen for a building site. Then how his wife's death had left him stranded as soon as he'd retired, followed by the signs of eccentricity, the stopping of strangers in his street walks, a feeble old man's attack on a neighbour, the sudden loss of present memory, the mental chaos and subsequent fright and, finally, sadly, the internment and decline.

'When I was ten, he'd read to me. And speak. Beautifully. In balanced sentences. He'd the touch.' Riley busied himself with the tea-things, as Woolley talked on. Unlike young Oxford, this boy, though restless, said his say as his part of affairs, did not fuss with offers of assistance, merely altered the pace of the narrative to suit his listener's occupation. 'Sentences would roll out of him. If he heard a word he didn't know, down'd come the big dictionary. And he kept a notebook. He ought to have been a teacher. I wouldn't say he was good at logical argument, but he could excite me, move me, even as a child, so that I wanted to kick the bosses or pull their houses over. I know nowadays that there are actuaries who work out insurance risks, use all sorts of complicated mathematics to find out traffic density or travel demands, but these don't measure individuals. Inside the perfectly orthodox pattern we're all going our own ways. Only I can't believe it. There must be utterly limiting factors to our heresy. It may be ignorance, of course. When we understand our brain properly there may be mathematical rules of probability which will cover even that pretty precisely. Sounds like a TV serial.'

Riley, not seeing the connection, enjoyed himself tagging behind the youth's theories. In his last posting he'd been friendly with the 'schooley', the education officer, who'd sometimes talked to him in this way. Yet as much as he admired, he could not help despising, because in spite of their fluency these people were no better than he was when it came to choosing between one alternative and another. It was as if their gift of words, or ideas, only took fire with complicated, not easily verifiable topics, while discussion of such mundane matters as ordering and collecting rations for twelve men for two days, or filling in claim forms, or choosing ties and socks, or committing adultery was not to be attempted by similar methods. That was education, the power to hone the mind on superior, flinty problems. The 'schooley', a university graduate, a lieutenant, talked philosophy to Riley, and yet made a complete fool of himself over a corporal's wife. He'd take Riley on one side to discuss that, and when he did so his power of expression seemed to desert him; he stumbled, fumbled. That was not exactly so; merely the listener's gloss. Riley admitted the difficulty of 'philosophy', its abstract attraction, while the affair, the clandestine infrequent meetings, odd misspelt notes of appeal, fingers groping up her skirts, however described, were idiocy, invitations to disaster, because the young man was twenty-three while she was thirty-one, and a mother, and unreliable, and a dirty bag, whom Riley himself had screwed after a regimental dance while her husband was away on a course.

The two men ate their meal.

As soon as he'd finished his plateful, Woolley began again. This time he described a tour across Europe to Yugoslavia in a jalopy not fit to carry one to the corner shop. Again Riley was fascinated, and scornful. The tale of frequent breakdowns, of constant improvisation of engineering, of language, seemed foolish and yet endearing. It was as if these four young men had stuck knives into themselves and then made a song about blood. They wanted to sleep in barns and hedge bottoms, wash in streams, annoy autobahn travellers, misunderstand the police, wear the nerves to a frazzle and lose seven stone between them. Through the whole dazzling account the sombre burden 'We didn't get to Greece' sounded. Riley was amazed that they'd reached Leicester. He did not understand the motivation any more than he'd followed the logic of the harangue before the meal. The boy, like his grandfather, had the gift of rolling out sentences, each attractive, but all unconnected. Perhaps his own stupidity debarred him from grasping the underlying, implied structure, just as he could not follow the courting of constant breakdown, jeopardy, thirst, dirt and poverty as a form of enjoyment. Old Grandpa was serious; he fought for workers' rights. Or perhaps he looked on the end as unattainable, merely relishing the setbacks as exercises to release more rolling sentences.

After they'd cleared and washed up, the boy prepared himself to visit his grandfather. Now he smiled, seemed elated, as if he'd expiated guilt by a recital of his own shortcomings and foolishness.

'You should write a book about it,' Riley said.

'Nobody'd believe it. When I'm telling you it sounds absolutely far-fetched.'

'I don't know.'

'I don't think anything puts you out, Mr. Riley, does it?' A kind of compliment. As he set about his evening's chores, Riley questioned himself. Why did he invite these young men here? Did he prefer Frank Oxford sexually to his mother? Once he put it bluntly to himself he knew a plain answer. No. He needed company, distraction from his worry, and these were at hand. He'd invite Dyson if the old chap would come, but he'd a wife, a home, a club, a social pint or two, so the manager went round the highways and hedges compelling the poor, those at a loose end, to come in. He grinned to himself, and later when Mrs. Scotten called, to return a packet of tea borrowed a month before, he had his arms round her in no time. She protested that she was too tired, but she wore decent tights, and so he guessed she'd decided on an hour from home and had dressed for it. When they'd finished, inconclusively for both, he poured out glasses of sweet sherry, and they sat apart, proud of each other. She looked pale, with her lips thin, but there existed inside her a kind of life, liveliness, in abeyance now, but available, to him as to her, at some later more crucial time.

She raised the glass.

'Ah don't know,' she said.

He did not answer that; he'd more sense, and they both waited for the inevitable knock at the back door to call her to settle some domestic crisis. It came at nine-ten from her husband.

'Well, Ah'll go to Trent Bridge,' he said, eyeing the sherry glasses. He explained the snag, no night-gowns, clean or dirty, for the two youngest, and accepted a drink as his wife left cheerfully cursing.

'A good gel is Alma.'

'Are the pubs shut, then?'

Scotten stayed for half an hour before he made for 'The Robin Hood'. Riley liked the way the man toyed with this small glass, with an air, a straight back, as one certain of the social code. A sergeants' mess prepares one for the wide world.

That night he went to bed cheerfully, but the next week, on Wednesday, Dyson stopped him as he left the office. Keys still in hand, he'd locked the safe and the files, he walked back in, invited the man to sit.

'They're selling this place off,' Dyson said, growled. He stood, glum, hunched.

'Say that again.'

'They're going to sell this factory.'

'Who are?'

Dyson dragged his chair, crashed down on it.

'Don't tell me you don't know,' he said. 'And there'll be no security for us.'

'Us?'

'Me. The women. You'll be all right.'

Riley jangled his keys about the polished desk top.

'Let's start again,' he said. 'You say they're going to sell this place. Now, how do you know?'

'Common talk. The union.'

'I see.'

'It's right, in't it? They're getting rid of it. And we shall all be out on us necks.' Dyson's tone did not attack, mumbled sullenly.

'Are you saying this on your own?'

'Why shouldn't Ah?'

'This is not an unofficial feeler by the union?'

'They wouldn't send one. Not as they bother over much as it is. No. I've kept my ears open and I said to my wife, "I'll speak to Riley about it." Mester Riley. It's right, in't it?'

'I'm not on the board of directors.' Riley clasped his hands, knuckled his chin, abandoning his keys. 'They're no more likely to tell me than tell you. Less. They'll let you know through the union.'

'It in't true, then?'

'The firm is negotiating a big take-over. Where and what I don't know. It's possible that as part of the whole deal this factory may be disposed of. I don't know any more than you do. They may sell it, anyway, as a unit.'

'Unit?'

'A working entity.' Why did he spout? 'The machines and the personnel may be part of the . . .'

'Why would they get shut of it?'

'Presumably under the new set-up they'd either not want cartons of the sort we provide, which is unlikely, or else they can get 'em made more economically elsewhere.'

'If they can get 'em done cheaper, there's not much 'ope for us. Is there?'

'You never know. As a local concern. As opposed to national or continental.'

Why did he deceive the man with this jargon, and thus betray himself? He'd be at the labour exchange with the rest and smooth words wouldn't feed him. Lodgers. He'd fill his rooms with rip-roaring students and Pakistani bus-conductors. Depression fogged his head, but he forced himself to listen to Dyson's account of what he'd heard, what they were saying at the union office, what rumours spread. Now and then he made a note, driving himself to work, so that he wouldn't forget. Within ten minutes he realised that Dyson was embroidering, that no further information could be culled, but he let the man drone on, feeling, in a numbed way, sympathy for his predicament. In the end at twenty to six he made his own final statement, reiterating that he knew no more than his underling, but that now the matter had been raised he, the boss, could apply for enlightenment, whether he got it or not, from the managing director. He asked if Dyson had spoken to the work-people, but stopped the dribble of irrelevance with which he was answered, advising the man to keep his mouth shut for the present. He stood, took Dyson by the elbow, led him to the door, shook his arm, said:

'If this place closes, I'm out on my backside in the same way as little Handley.'

Dyson shook his head. He reminded Riley of a blind man he'd seen in the street learning to walk with a long stick he swept in an arc in front of him. Half-way down the steps, he sighed, said, 'Ah, we don't know what's 'ittin' us half the time,' and stumbled on.

Riley locked the office door from inside, sat rolling his head at his desk. Dyson had a union; he'd nothing, not even Erskine's goodwill. Dumb-sick, he dialled Cooper's office, and that was deserted. It was past six when he dragged himself up and home.

All that night he wrestled with himself and with the useless note he'd taken of Dyson's conversation. If only he could appear efficient to Cooper, on the ball, a spy who knew what he was about, there was perhaps an opening for him in the new firm. He didn't believe it. Most probably Cooper would see him as a blabber-mouth who'd let confidential information out to his employees, from stupidity, if not malice. Then he imagined Cooper in the maelstrom of re-organisation, a petty god felled by his own earthquake, unable to keep himself employed in the new richness of violence. This fantasy of argument banged about in his head, gouged through the fog of depression, the mild overwhelming pain of hopelessness. He was done. He knew it.

He waited until the next morning before he phoned Cooper. Below him he could hear and see the scurry of the factory floor. Slowly the obstacles to the managing director shifted themselves, and he was through after five minutes.

'What is it now?' Testy.

'I thought you ought to know, but Dyson, one of the employees here, came in last night and said he'd heard, down at his union office, that this factory was to be sold and everybody declared redundant.'

'Then he's heard more than I bloody have.'

'I thought you ought to know.'

'In the next weeks there'll be all sorts of rumours. Can't be otherwise. Just deny 'em.'

'I did.'

'Did? Did what?'

'I said,' Riley spoke slowly as one compelled to read his own death sentence aloud, 'that I knew nothing about the selling of the factory or redundancy.'

'Then you're a bloody liar, aren't you, Riley?' Cooper sounded jovial, bestial.

'I don't understand you, sir.' Breathlessly.

'You know about reorganisation. It's a pound to a pinch Carnell and Bloom'll go. I've told you to get yourself fixed up elsewhere.'

'So I should have told him the rumours were true?'

'Don't sod me about, Riley. Not this morning. I'm not up to it.' Cooper blew into the phone, the air. 'Use what sense you've got.'

'I did. And got called a liar for it.'

'Called what?'

'A liar. You called me a bloody liar.'

'Because you are a bloody liar, Riley. You're paid for it. What use is it creating havoc down at your home of rest by telling 'em they're all going to get the sack. What'd happen? Instead of cartons to enclose the product, we'd get slashed cardboard or sodden papier-mâché. They don't know. They hope. They may even be right. And they turn out what we pay 'em to turn out.'

'I see.'

'I don't suppose you do. These hands of yours are like you and me, only worse. Or better. They're in for what they can get out. They'll swan about if we let 'em. It's our job not to give 'em the chance.'

'What do I tell 'em then?'

'What the bloody hell you like.' Cooper stopped, as if choked on exasperation. 'You're being pretty stupid about this, Riley. We're in flux. That's the line.'

'Has anything been decided, Mr. Cooper?'

'Yes. But it's not tied up, and there'll be no public announcement inside a month.'

'Does what's tied up,' Riley persisted, 'involve the closing of Carnell and Bloom's?'

'God knows.' Resigned, now. 'Probably. Don't say I said so.'

'It affects something like thirty people here.'

'Does it? It affects a bloody sight more than that, if I know anything about it. But just you remember this, Riley. If a man loses his job, it's not the end of the world. And if it is, there's something wrong with him.'

'Ay, he's a human being.'

'What?' A nervous cough of a laugh. 'Uh. I see. Well. Yes. Uh. However, you know where you stand now. Say nothing. Keep your trap shut. A state of flux. That's the word. You can let me know how they react from time to time, but I don't want you ringing up every five minutes with tittle-tattle. Clear? Understood?'

'Yes, sir.'

'Oh, Riley. Did you see Erskine?'

'Yes.'

'What had he to say for himself?'

'He told me he'd speak to you. I don't know if he has.'

'Probably.' The word dropped like a gentle, insulting cuff. 'I don't see why you set such store by this place. There are others. Look about you.'

'You mean there's no job for me?'

'I don't mean anything. You've been in the army, Riley. You may have noticed that in a battle some men get killed. Often good men one wouldn't want to lose. But nobody's irreplaceable, and so the generals don't put off wars on that account.'

'It might be better if they did.'

'Might well. You've been in. I haven't. You may be right. Don't forget what I've told you. Flux. 'Bye, Riley.' Down went the phone. Below they concentrated still, but one of the women turned to speak to a despatch clerk. He clutched his heart, swayed, and they both laughed. Riley could not hear them above the clatter of the machines and through the glass partition, but their smiles seemed large, fixed, like toothpaste adverts. The boy passed her again, but this time hardly spoke.

At the end of the day Riley dodged out to avoid Dyson.

He was degraded, sullen. In the army, as an N.C.O., he'd found nothing wrong in translating an officer's quiet: 'That's not smart enough. Let's have it again, Sergeant' into 'Now, liven your bloody idle selves up and git some movement into it, you lazy-born, lead-swinging set o' paralysed square-bashers. On the command, "One" ' . . . That was the convention, acceptable, what they expected. It worked. No one took offence. Then men felt pride in the N.C.O.'s slight adjustments of traditional phraseology, of his gravelly voice, his own granite-faced explosion of invective. He'd once heard a woman, shopping bags on the pavement, watching the drill, say, 'Ought to be ashamed of himself.

Talking like that. If he spoke like that to a lad of mine, I'd kill 'im, I would.' But she might just as well complain about Frenchmen talking French.

Two days later he received from Cooper the address of an agency.

The envelope was addressed in the director's own handwriting, and scribbled across the printed card was: 'Get in touch here. Put Erskine and myself as refs. Don't leave this lying around.' Unsigned. Riley worried himself sick for twenty-four hours before he rang the place.

He filled in a detailed questionnaire, which he received next post, and three days later was summoned for interview. Mr. Aubrey Luke-Williams, consultant, his secretary so described him, perched in a huge, dark-panelled office, in front of a door which led to a strong room furnished only with heavy filing cabinets. Riley was invited to a brief glimpse, and told affably that a successful burglary there would cause some heart-searching in high places.

Coffee was introduced. Luke-Williams asked how Riley had learnt of his existence, nodded his thick wings of white hair at the mention of Cooper's name. For the next half-hour they combed through the complete questionnaire. Luke-Williams was sharp, leapt from the point made to six other questions. Riley felt exhilarated, as if at a massage. This man was out to know him, to probe, to reject if he found weakness. He seemed to recognise a boast, an exaggeration, at once, for what it was worth, and pounced, sarcastically. Perhaps the questions were so many, or switching direction so often, that the interviewer merely seemed fiercer on faults. Riley spoke up for himself, corrected the man twice about Carnell's administration, ticked him off once about a remark on army discipline. Luke-Williams was not abashed; he thanked, pressed on, scribbled.

In the end he paused.

'Our clients, Mr. Riley, are usually more advanced in the hierarchy of business men than you are, if you see what I mean.'

That was the first time he'd tried jargon.

'You can't do anything for me?'

'I'm not saying that.'

They breathed together, and Riley, staring, fiddled with his coffee-cup, at his leisure. The man named his terms . . . The initial fee was high, but Riley prepared to pay.

'We regard it as a challenge. So must you.' Still the same clipped syllables, the sense of urgency as Williams advised him to type his applications, if he could; to wear a plain, dark suit and army tie. 'We must suit the trappings to the personality. You're efficient, a keeper of the peace. Not a multi-millionnaire in the making. There's room for you.'

Riley rejoined the secretary, signed his cheque and application, and was given a thick folder of cyclostyled sheets, the top one of which read: 'How to use these notes.' The two men then shook hands, and Riley was escorted to the lift.

When he thought in the next few days about his office he felt lifted, as if he'd acquired a powerful ally. That such a place existed, without his knowledge, disturbed him. The foyer, the three typists with their machines, the secretary, the two waiting rooms, and the large sanctum where Williams sat on his judicial stool must cost a mint of money to maintain in that most convenient skyscraper. But it was Luke-Williams' interrogation which bred confidence: nobody interviewing him could be more thorough than that. As soon as the envelopes with lists of vacancies began to appear, Riley rang the secretary, typed his forms, took them in for vetting, re-typed them and listened to the secretary's advice. Mr. Luke-Williams was away.

He met Vaughan one Saturday morning in the Kardomah.

'Hello,' said the union man, 'reduced to coffee, now, are we?'

'Never drink before midday.'

'Or after, me.' He rubbed his belly, ordered tea and buns. 'Trouble at t'mill, then?'

'Come again.'

'They tell me you're closing down.'

'Your Dyson tells me so. Got it from the union office.'

'It's true enough, isn't it?' Vaughan tried to look pleasant.

'If it is, it's not known to me.'

'Look, Mr. Riley.' Vaughan leaned over the table, a pointing finger near Riley's cup. 'You won't do yourself any harm by trusting me. I don't blab. I'd like to know where I stand, of course. I'm not denying that.'

'I'll tell you what I know, then. After Dyson came in, I went to see Cooper. Big moves are afoot. No details to me, of course. Reorganisation. Flux. You know how he talks. "What about my place?" I asked him. "Carnell and Bloom's?" He wouldn't or couldn't say. Might go. Might be sold off. Possibility. Might just be disposed of as a working unit.'

'That's about it, is it?'

'You know as much as I do now.'

'He didn't advise you to look around for another post?'

'Not in so many words.'

'He did then?' Vaughan seemed friendlier, warmer, smiling at the waitress who brought his tray.

'No. But he said if I wanted to scout around, elsewhere, for other work, it wouldn't be held against me. He'd support any application I sent forward.'

'Looks bad,' Vaughan said, pouring, sugaring, stirring.

'D'you think so? You can perhaps advise me. I couldn't make out whether Cooper knew anything or not. He gabbled enough, but I couldn't . . .'

'If my experience is anything to go on, you'd better slap your applications in. He meant you'd be on your way out. And sharp. Have you started?'

'Not seriously.'

'Get a move on.'

'You sound confident.'

'Not me, brother. Not me.' He poured a second cup, the china dwarfed by his fingers. 'They're moving all right.

But they don't tell us. Not yet. They fix their own little acre and then we get a squint. After the feast we're led in to share the breadcrumbs.'

'In this big-money combine, do you, er, think, you know, Cooper is anybody?'

'Does he count, d'you mean? I wouldn't be surprised. He's a fly young man. You can't pin him down.'

'He's worse than Bowles?' Riley asked. Vaughan expanded his chest, smiled reminiscently.

'He was a tough nut, if you like, but he wanted settlements, basically. There was a sort of fairness about him. He was hard, but he knew men's livelihoods were involved. This bugger doesn't count like that. If every union official and member in this town was to be publicly executed on his say-so, he'd give the word if he thought he'd get anything out of it. I don't much care for him. He loves Cooper.'

'Can't you play on that?'

'No chance. If we withdrew labour on a large scale for a long time he'd convince his employers that it was our fault, that he'd done his best to placate us.'

'But,' said Riley, earnest now in the game, 'his employers wouldn't be pleased if they drew no dividends.'

'They've got eggs in more baskets than we have. And they know it. They've done well out of us. That's why they can employ a rough bastard like Cooper.' Vaughan grinned, clapped his paunch, looked delighted at his analysis, munched a pink cake.

'And what happens to me, then?' Riley.

'I'd think they'd give you a job if there's one going. You're efficient. But if you don't mind my saying so, it's in a small way. If there's something obvious, you'll get it, if they notice at the time or you shout loud enough. And they know we shan't kick up.'

'Not about our place?'

'No,' Vaughan said. 'Just think. Dozen union women. Few men. It's not worth it. In itself. If we did anything it would be for some other motive, not to save Carnell and

Bloom's. We're all bastards, Riley. Except you.'

'Thanks.'

'Oh, I like you ex-army men. You bellow a bit, but you're not frightened of work. You lick the boss's arse, but so does everybody. And you tend to keep 'em happy. I've been a squaddy myself.'

They talked, very friendly.

Riley was certain he gave nothing away, and he learned as little from Vaughan. The man spoke cynically, but it seemed a pose, a poor disguise, as if it didn't do to be earnest, to show principle. As he fingered cake-crumbs from his plate to his mouth, he huffed away, about his set-backs, his difficulties. The whole rotund, jovial tone suggested that the union was powerless, caught between the ruthlessness of employers and the indolence or apathy of the workers. He drank five cups of tea, always blowing heavily on the liquid before sipping; he patted his belly and thighs; he smiled. But Riley could imagine him at a mass-meeting breathing his words into the microphone until the surface of heads thrashed into turmoil and brandished fists supported the menace of his argument. Or perhaps at a W.E.A. table, considering Marx, not with his father's reverence, but with the sort of rough pragmatism that the lecturer couldn't match.

'Let me know,' Vaughan said as they parted. 'I don't suppose you will. I don't see why you should.'

'I'll back you hear before I do.'

Vaughan bit his thumb, hard, and sighed.

'Give me a bloody smallholding,' he said.

'What about it?'

'That's what I'd like. A few chicken. Pig or two. Cabbages. I'm moving anyway. Manchester. You know that.'

Riley shook his head, superior. He laughed as if the man had betrayed himself. He wouldn't manage the physical labour with that paunch, those lily-white hands. He shook his head largely. Now as he pushed, shouldering, among the Saturday crowd, face following face, half-sentences jabbed into his ears, anxieties or excitements momentarily pushed at him, he considered himself. Nobody's friend. Nobody raised a finger for him. Except Luke-Williams, the power he'd hired. Vaughan with his ladylike tea? Where would Cooper be this morning, then? In his dressing gown behind double-glazing. Or skimming down the outside lane of the motorway, stroking his lady-wife's thigh.

As soon as he'd reached home he was disturbed by a knocking at the back door. O'Brien waved his rent-book about.

'Sorry I didn't pay you last night.'

'Come in.'

They shuffled together. Slap of book and cash on the kitchen table.

'I can't stop,' O'Brien said. 'I've got the wife home.'

'For good?'

'No. She'll never be that. But they asked me if I'd just have her for the week-end. Come by ambulance. I've made a bed up downstairs.'

'Does she seem fairly well?' Riley signed and blotted the book. 'To say?'

O'Brien shrugged, shoulders exaggeratedly high.

'Will you come in and see her?' He seemed to wheedle. 'This afternoon? After I've fed her. Just for a few minutes. Will you?'

Riley agreed, grudgingly. The other slopped out.

Staring at the table, at the pound notes and silver, Riley widened his mouth, to a scream oval while he dug with a finger into a gap between teeth. His world crowded itself with ripples. Not long ago Joan Oxford would have been about, telling him what she'd bought for Sunday dinner. She'd made no bones about packing her traps when she saw fit. And O'Brien, with this corpse of a wife home for the week-end, stopping hanky-pank with his fancy-woman. The other side Alma Scotten who'd had sex with him as easily, as guiltless, as going to the pictures. The world lunged, loped into disarray. He fingered his nose, looked out of the window at two Scotten brats balancing on the garden

wall, arms outspread. Dyson, old grousing Dyson. He'd be
redundant. And there'd be nothing for him. He'd no qualifications but a few years' ham-handed experience which
would fit him for the dole, nothing more. The student's
grandfather, another zombie. Vaughan and his great strang-
ling hands round a doll's tea-set supping his brew. And, in
the middle, aching for standards he'd not keep, himself,
Jack Riley, ex-sergeant, nobody's lover, nobody's anybody.

He unwrapped his chops.

Not even a dog to lick the paper.

18

Within the next few weeks Riley was twice called up for interview.

Though he got neither job, he convinced himself that he'd shaped well. On both occasions he'd been shown round the place, made a fuss of, and closely quizzed. The secretary at the Luke-Williams Bureau, who retook him through the interviews with comment, reported later by phone that the employers, even when turning him down, had been impressed.

'You've got an aura,' Phillips, the secretary, said. 'It's the solid, dependable, no-flap, no-bull man. In both these cases they appointed university graduates and aren't sure they've done right. We'll fix you up, Mr. Riley. Don't you worry yourself.'

He saw nothing of Williams, but grew to like the underling, who, it appeared, groomed him almost out of personal ambition.

'You look the part, Mr. Riley, and like a good many old N.C.O.s you speak the Queen's English. You've a good prospect just so long as you don't over-extend yourself.' The man liked such phrases. 'Let us,' he'd say, stirring the air, 'consider and refine our approach.' Hand wagging for, 'We may encounter initial obstacles. They are part of the scheme of preparation.' Whether he'd learnt these from Luke-Williams himself or second-hand from a prospectus, he lipped them with relish. 'The pattern of our approach may appear to you to vary according to the quarters of the moon, though that's not altogether feasible. We must adopt the reasonably unorthodox.'

At the third attempt the secretary fetched Riley urgently in on a Saturday morning when other offices stood deserted, in order to work carefully through the typed letter of application, the curriculum vitae. He suggested an acceptable range of salary, but appeared shaken that Riley had no car.

'Can you drive?'

'Yes.'

'You'll need a car. They won't provide you with one, but they'll pay so much a mile, perhaps maintain it. You can get respectable hire-purchase terms, y'know.'

'I could buy one outright.'

'A new car, Mr. Riley? But what sort? A Cortina? A Zodiac? That's what you need, a biggish, newish job. You're not in the Jensen class.' Phillips laughed, but stopped, pursed his lips when his client claimed a new Ford was not beyond his means.

For the next hour he pressed Riley, made suggestions, handed over further reading matter. He had not quite the courtroom technique of Luke-Williams, but he spoke shrewdly enough for Riley to question him, in return.

'Don't you ever think of setting up on your own, Mr. Phillips?'

'No capital.' He smiled, not sadly. 'I've been with Mr. Luke-Williams four years now, and I know what it costs. I keep the office side tight, and now work's coming in apace, that's a matter of some importance, I can tell you. Occasionally I take a case or two of my own, like yours, for instance, and . . .'

'The less important ones?' Riley did not resist the dig.

'No, Mr. Riley. Oddly enough, no. If there's something that interests me. Mr. Luke-Williams is very astute. He must keep me informed, and eager. I work on bonus. It pays us both. I'm not starving, Mr. Riley.'

In the end, the pair stepped out together for a drink in the city's newest skyscraper hotel, where they stood at a long bar sipping whisky and water. Riley was quietly astounded at the large number of business men, all unknown to him, who had nothing to do this Saturday morning but swallow and shout here in the middle of the town, though he was not surprised when one or two greeted Phillips. He was delighted at the man's tact; for though his manner appeared diplomatic as ever, his language had become simpler, less rotund, a man speaking to men. They drank two doubles each, not quickly, and parted, shaking hands.

'Look into that matter of the car, and if you're called up for interview, be sure to ring me the day before you go.'

Riley followed his instructions and thus was disappointed.

The interview took place in a solicitor's office where the lawyer and two brothers, the Messrs. Furze, neat elderly men who owned the factory, crouched at one end of a polished table while Riley sat smartly to attention seven feet away at the other. The solicitor took him amicably enough through his application form before one of the brothers began a series of questions about the works. Riley, provided with information by Phillips, but oddly refused access to the place itself, answered fluently enough, but was forced to make inquiries for himself. This led to a disquisition on the history of the firm, present output, prospective changes, lasting something like ten minutes and which was interrupted by the lawyer to inquire what Riley knew of the technical processes of knit-wear, the product. This failed, since Riley admitted ignorance, and the solicitor began to demonstrate it so that the younger Furze intervened with a short informative piece. He seemed this time a different man as he spoke, so much so that Riley leaned forward.

'Excuse me, sir.' Sharp, but polite.

'Well?' The brother coughed, eyes startled.

'Why don't you manage the factory yourself?'

Nobody spoke until the solicitor tapped the table and consulted his papers.

'You must have some reason, Mr. Riley, for asking that question.' The brothers smirked thankful relief.

'Yes, sir, I have.' Parade-ground crisp. 'Mr. Furze, there, gave me a masterly summary of the technical processes. He clearly knows the work from A to Z. He's an energetic man to judge from appearances. You see, now, why I wonder you need a manager.'

The solicitor smiled, courteously signalling like a judge for a reply.

'I should know it. I started on one of those machines at thirteen. I'm sixty-two, Mr. Riley, and I've had enough. I shall be down interfering, if that's what you fear.'

They laughed. From then on the questioning was desultory, and not until Riley himself was asked for queries was liveliness restored. The elder brother hardly spoke, but sat stroking and fingernailing a white moustache. In the end the solicitors suggested that the Furzes should take Riley round the factory, although he pointed out that two other strong candidates would present themselves next day. He seemed to be warning the old men about precipitateness.

As they drove together, the elder brother, on the seat with Riley, whispered that he had been a regular soldier. All the short way, they exchanged experiences amiably, but warily, and soon bored each other. Furze droned about a jammed Lewis-gun on some exercise near Karachi, so that Riley was glad to step out.

The factory was larger than Carnell and Bloom's, built in the late nineteen-thirties with a post-war extension. The looms, oily neat, were housed in huge rows separately at the far end and were tended by men, while the smaller machines were handled by young women in blue, smart overalls. The atmosphere was not unpleasant, for the floor seemed warm and light, with plenty of space and not overmuch noise; no one appeared to exert herself. Perhaps it was unnecessary.

The brothers said little to their employees as they did the round, though the older nodded occasionally and rather shamefaced. They mounted to the office, which was enormous compared with Carnell's, sat on armchairs as the younger brother explained the running of the firm. Though Riley questioned once or twice, he let the streaming information flow over him. Nobody could take that in. He refused a whisky, and caught a bus which returned him to his own factory just before four o'clock. Both directors had shaken hands solemnly with him, standing, but neither had indicated his favour or otherwise.

When he'd signed his own letters he'd carefully cleared the trays the previous day, he rang the secretary at Luke-Williams' to report. Phillips seemed taciturn, or preoccupied, merely saying, 'Oh, we'll see, then. I thought they'd offer you the job this afternoon.' Perhaps he was disappointed in his protégé.

Suddenly when the factory closed at five Riley found himself nervously unoccupied.

He did not wish to go out for a meal; that wasted money. He ate a light tea, for the lager at the Furzes' lunch disagreed with him, and went to ask Mrs. Scotten if she'd accompany him to the cinema. Her house hung thick with steam from a clothes-horse which towered by the fire while children scuttered round the table where Alma, her husband and a child ate bread and jam over a newspaper. They listened in amused surprise to his request before she refused, saying that her husband had suffered a brain-storm and consequently was taking her down to 'The Prince of Wales' Feathers' once the brood were in bed. Scotten laughed as he buttered sliced bread from the packet. The noise from television, running feet, talk, and hammering upstairs left Riley edgy, but they insisted that he drank tea with them. Alma went to the kitchen to rinse a chipped mug.

He escaped into the coldness of the yard, and thence into the ordered quiet of his own kitchen.

The front-door bell immediately slapped its major third.

On the step with two carrier bags and a parcel Joan Oxford posed herself.

'Come on in,' he said, delighted.

'I've been shopping.' She downed her purchases. 'We shall soon have Christmas here.' They went into the kitchen, where he relieved her of her coat. 'What a weight!'

'I'll put the gas on in the parlour,' he said.

Flustered, he was glad to step out for a few moments to collect his wits. He patted cushions, picked up a book to lay it down elsewhere.

In ten minutes they were drinking tea together while she, playing havoc with the man, explained that the parcels had nearly cut her fingers through.

'Won't they be expecting you at home?'

'No. They're both out. I'm my own woman tonight.'

He made her Welsh rarebit, fetched out the congress tarts, enjoyed her licking polite fingers. She had settled in as if she owned the place, putting on airs, queening it almost laughably.

'I'd forgotten how nice this room was,' she said.

He cleared the dishes, sat by her on the settee.

'What have you got to tell me, then?'

'Nothing.' Her voice was small, sad, regretful. 'Nothing much.'

'Have you settled in?'

'Ron's better, if that's what you mean. And Frank. They try to be helpful.'

'But don't succeed.'

'Oh, I don't know.' Her glasses caught the light. She teased prettily. 'I don't expect perfection, not by a long chalk. I don't get it, anyhow.'

'Shall we have a glass of sherry?'

'Why not?'

They drank, talked, but Riley prowled about the room, unable to settle. It seemed he needed to make much of each second and that could be achieved only by movement. Once he kicked the ornamental coal-scuttle, startling himself.

'It's marvellous having you here,' he said.

'I should have been a lady. I like being waited on.'

She asked for television. When he refilled her glass, she giggled and said she'd be drunk. He turned off the light so that they now sat in the blue radiance watching a series of sequences from silent movies. Oddly, she did not laugh, knitted her brows slightly as if she weren't sure what was happening, held his hand. He kissed her, pushed her down. For a moment mouth sealed mouth before she struggled, strongly, even roughly, to sit up.

'I don't want that,' she said.

'Why?'

'It's not fair.'

'What isn't?'

She sat upright, bridling, proud of herself, until with a wail, a wheeze of sound, she began to cry, quite loudly, almost rhythmically. Now again she acted out a part, not so much a woman in tragedy as a crying-machine. If the ceiling had fallen, Riley would not have been more surprised.

'Drink up,' he said, patting her forearm. 'You'll be all right.'

He stood, straddling the rug, his back to the gas fire, peering down at her. She sat upright, chin to chest, small hand dabbing with smaller square of handkerchief the ruptured face. About her now, desperation revealed itself. Nobody in her right mind could sit so square to cry so blatantly. Her chirrups of sobs, hiccoughs, flopped into the room.

'What's wrong?' he asked.

The pattern of weeping did not change. She was a thing now, an object designed to annoy him. 'Here, Joan,' he said. No reply. Merely this noise, this occupation of space. He sat by her, took her hand. For all its effect he might have picked up an ornament, a cushion. In puzzlement, he rasped the bristles under his lower lip with his teeth and abandoned her, leaving the room, closing the door quietly behind him.

In the kitchen he snatched at a rose catalogue, skimmed a page or two, saw the ticks he'd made against the names of plants he'd ordered, but registered nothing. A picture, a whirling cloud of yellow roses, made no impact. With a groan, he let the book drop from his fingers, splay out on the floor.

He had run away.

His place was in there, listening to her sobs, making inquiries or sounds of comfort, however inadequate. That gulping woman at her wits' end needed him and he'd skipped. If only he smoked or had some means of occupying himself until he'd stumbled into an understanding of his obligations. Unwillingly he shuffled back.

Joan Oxford occupied the same position, but sniffled only.

Riley stood before her, awkwardly, while his mouth tightened with fear, lips pulled in rubber-hard on his teeth. He recalled her outbursts in the bedroom, her kick, the bursting slam of the door smashing his eardrums.

'What is it?' he said, not recognising the thin voice from the desiccated mouth.

She moved, in no hurry, as a worm unwinds, sucked in breath, then pulled off her glasses. When she had dabbed helplessly with her soaking handkerchief at the lenses, she felt the air, helplessly, touchingly.

Then Riley knew what to do.

He took the clean handkerchief from his pocket, reached, lifted the spectacles and set about them. She stared out, eyes large, blue, not blind but baffled, hurt. With a flourish he returned the glasses, which she replaced. That was human.

He sat by her side, remembering to hitch his trousers, put his feet together.

'Is it Ron?' he asked.

She wriggled, a freeing motion, a preparation.

'No.' Suddenly she jerked, galvanised by some flash of emotion. 'I'm exhausted,' she said. 'I feel exhausted.'

'What is it?' He'd the sense not to touch her.

'Oh, everything.' She shaped her face to smile, failed, primly put her hands on knees. 'I don't know. I don't seem to have energy for anything.'

'You're doing too much,' he said. She considered, smoothing the side of her nose.

'Frank's a worry,' she managed in the end. That was it. 'What's that young-feller-me-lad been up to?'

She disregarded his jocularity and, suddenly, again pity pinned him back, sucked her thumb.

'He wants to get married.'

'Well . . .'

'You don't know. It's no use your talking. It's no good anybody talking.'

'Who's the girl?'

'Some floozy.' He'd not heard the word. 'Brainless and senseless.'

'From the factory?'

'Off the streets, more like.'

He waited. He could do nothing. The woman tangled with herself.

'Do you know what happened? He came in the week before last from work, plonked himself down to his dinner and said, "Mam, I'm going to get married." Just like that. So I said, "And who to?" "She's called Rita Wisniewskaya." And I thought to myself, "One of them Polish girls. They're usually decent, know what hard work is. Bit of something about them." But, my God, when I seen her.'

Her solecisms underlined her distraction.

'Hair bleached and puffed like candy-floss. And a sallow face. Her mother's a slut; the father left them years ago; lives down the Meadows, the mother. No better than a harlot. And this flouncing miss with her blackheads and her dirty neck.' She shook her head. 'But when I said this to Ron, he just sat there, gulping. "What do you think of her, then?" I asked him. "She's not too bad," he said. Not too bad? Her? Skin like a batter-pudding. "Is that the one you'd pick for Frank's wife?" I said. I knew I was wrong as soon as I came out with it. "It's not us as is picking," he said. "It's him. He's old enough to make his own mind up." "Well, what do you think, then?" I said. "She's not too bad." And that's all the sense I can get out of him.'

He allowed her to sit, rocking herself, intent on the fire.

'Have you spoken to Frank?'

'Oh, he's as stupid. "I don't think much of your choice,

Frank," I said. But he won't agree. He humps himself up, and clears off. It makes me that mad. And then I'm sorry and I want to go and throw my arms round him. He's young for his age.'

'What's wrong with the girl?'

Joan Oxford levelled blue eyes at his with astonishment and hate.

'You can see what's up with her.'

'I can't. You tell me.'

'There's nothing about her. She's neither pretty, nor well mannered. Her clothes are nasty, her voice. And as to her mother . . .'

'She can't help that.'

'Perhaps she can't, but it makes no odds. Fingers black with cigarettes and nails chewed and sucked. Ugh.'

'Frank sees something in her.'

'He doesn't know better.'

'Oh, come on, Joan. I'm not having that. He's a fine big lad, handsome. He could have the pick of the girls. And he has, I bet.'

'You can't talk like that. You don't know. This Rita, if that's her name, had got a reputation amongst this brainless crew he knocks round with. She may be a marvellous dancer. Or something. They may admire her. And silly boy has to go and beat them all to get her. I could cry.'

'You have done.'

Why he said that he did not know. It was like a chalked slogan on a wall. I hate wogs. A mindless, unpalatable splutter of rancour.

She did not answer immediately, but when she did talk, it was as if to some third, better, maturer person who'd understand.

'I wish you'd never left Erskine's,' she said. 'He'd listen to you. He looked up to you. You could tell him things.'

Ashamed, flattered, Riley reorganised his expression.

'Do you want me to talk to him?' he coughed. 'For you?'

'It's past talk now.'

'Why did you say that? Is she pregnant?'

'She's five years older than he is. Five years. How he could act so stupid. He's a clever boy. He did well at the grammar school. He won a prize for art. A big book on lettering. We've still got it.'

'Can I do anything?'

'No, Jack. Nobody can do anything. I sometimes think God can't do anything. Frank'll do as she tells him until the day he lives to regret it.'

'And then what?'

'On that day he'll come bleddy cryin' to me.'

They were back in the back-street. Joan Oxford was reduced to the urchin, the slanger over the garden wall, the crude daub, a screaming voice in an entry. Touched Riley stood, waved the sherry bottle.

'Let's . . .'

'Oh, shut your fat mouth. You're as bad as they are. He's only nineteen, and that other one's had every mortal thing done for him since the day he was born by his mother and by me. But you're supposed to be a man. You've served in the army. You've had your wife die. You're in charge of men and damned women. But you're as wet-headed as they are. Let's have a glass of sherry. Let's sit down and talk. Let's make ourselves comfortable. You'd make me comfortable in the bloody gas oven.'

'Go on,' Riley said. 'I like to hear it.'

Her mouth sagged open, but she pulled her shoulders square. 'You're a nobody,' she said. 'No good.'

'I'm no bloody good to man nor beast,' he said, sang.

'Eh? What say?' She sniffed, screwing up her eyes. 'It wouldn't matter to you if I did myself in, would it?'

He considered. Probably she'd struck near the truth.

'What would you do if I killed myself?'

'You want to stop talking like that,' he answered.

The sober tone caused her to look up.

'I feel so depressed. I'm rotten as if my body's rotting. I've aches in every bone.'

'Have you been to the doctor?'

'It's my time of life. That's all he can say. Take these tablets.'

He sat down, his crossed legs at right-angles to hers.

'That's not bad advice,' he said. 'You take his tablets. And go on taking 'em. If you've got anything serious against Frank's girl, say it out to him, and then leave it.'

'Leave, leave. That's all you can do.'

As they talked she became calmer, her conversation less hysterical, more like an end of one day's grouse. She feared the quarrels at home; if she opposed anything, she found no support or satisfaction. She fought in a moral vacuum. After half an hour she'd declined more sherry but went herself to make tea. The little chore livened her. she complained now about her boss at work, her wages, some incident with a customer. By eight o'clock she gathered her parcels, kissed him and had gone home smiling.

Not ten minutes later Dyson presented himself, with his wife, at the door.

'We was just going to the club, and I said to Min here, we'll call on Mester Riley, damned if we don't.'

He ushered them into the warmed sitting room. Mrs. Dyson took it on herself to make appreciative noises as she allowed her eyes to dab object after object.

'We're not stopping long,' Dyson began. 'But we was on the way to . . .' Riley turned his mind on to the man's suède shoes, his wife's swollen ankles. They were more interesting. He simulated concern with small, humming noises. 'But I wanted to ask you about the factory.'

'What about it?'

'Are they closing down?'

'I don't know any more than I did when you asked me last time.'

Mrs. Dyson intervened. Compared with her husband, she hinted at social graces, a slight awareness that they trespassed on private time.

'Henry's been very worried,' she said, 'about redundancy.

Once you're past sixty you don't stand much chance of another job.'

Riley bowed his head.

'And he don't want to spend the last three years of his working life on the dole. On the scrap-heap.' Defiance, there. 'It's getting on his nerves, Mr. Riley.'

'In what way?'

'Can't sleep. Off his food. I don't like to see it. He's not the same man. He sits there. In front of the fire with the paper on his knee. Unread. I don't like it. I practically had to drag him out tonight.' Riley looked at Dyson, who now slumped in sheepish indifference as if his wife had dropped into a language he did not understand to deliver a message he knew only too well. ' "Have you asked Mester Riley?" I kep' saying.'

'I told her,' Dyson muttered.

'He puts things that roundabout.' She frowned. He disliked the puffy eyes, her rat-trap mouth, the aggressive self-assurance.

'No,' Riley said, voice gentle. 'No. He put it clearly to me, Mrs. Dyson. He asked me straight out what the directors were going to do with Carnell and Bloom's.'

She did not believe it.

'What did you tell him? That you didn't know?'

'Yes.'

'You don't know.' The sentence exploded mildly, a popping expostulation. 'You mean to tell me you don't know?'

'Yes.' Riley essayed a smile, stiffly.

'I can't believe that,' she said. Its effect was without rudeness. 'It's been common talk for a long time.'

'Mrs. Dyson.' Riley waved his hand, conjured silence. 'There are schemes. Carnell and Bloom's may change hands. It may be sold. But it may go as a working unit. That means it continues as before. The shareholders may be different, the board of directors, but we shall turn out cartons under a different name. But nobody knows yet. Our place isn't important in the negotiations. Therefore, I can't tell your husband whether he'll be holding his job down in six months' time or not.'

'What about you?' she asked.

'In what way?'

'Will you be holding your job?'

'I don't know the answer to that. I wish I did.'

'You mean they'll stand you off?'

'I do.'

'Mester Riley,' she said, 'I don't believe it. They wouldn't do it to you. Not the manager.' Her face soured, blackened its wrinkles. 'And if they'd do that to you, how would they treat our Henry?'

'How old is Mr. Dyson?' he asked brazenly, in front of the man.

'I can't afford to retire,' Dyson growled. 'We've got to live.'

The woman gestured with her right hand, fist clenching truth out of the air. 'It in't right,' she said, 'treating people like that. My husband's flesh and blood, not stone. To look at him, he's healthy enough for his age, but it in't so. It in't so, Mester Riley.' The voice was not strong, but struck out each word like a missile. 'He suffers from his nerves. He always has since he was a young man. They discharged him from the navy because of it. He's not strong. And they do this. Keep him in suspense. They don't care. Not for the likes of us.'

Her ugliness, in the putty-yellow face, the fat-veined hands, the swollen ankles, added to the words' impact. Her hair lay smooth, in waves, artificial shining troughs, under a pastel-shaded headscarf, like a wig above the deep-cut wrinkles, the pig's squinting eyes, the smear of bloody lipstick. Riley, ashamed, felt she'd no right to exist. If he were saddled with this hoarse sack of tripes . . . He turned towards Dyson, who, leaning towards the fire, poked a finger into his shoe. As he bent, the lines of his neck were cut deep and he seemed slighter, scraggier. When he stood up to you, Dyson appeared strong, a man of muscle and hard bone, but now his age, his vulnerability, his furtive dependence on his wife were apparent. As ugly, as mis-hewn as she was, he humped there in his best suit, a muffler pulled back from his throat.

'I see,' Riley said, wishing he did not.

'You don't seem a bad fellow from all I hear,' she continued, 'but I doubt if you know half as happens under your nose. Who keeps them larky young storemen under, eh? My husband. Is he paid for it? Is he even thanked for it? No, he's a nob'dy as nob'dy wants. No, Henry, I'm going to tell him. You won't oppen your mouth, so I will for you.'

'Go on, Mrs. Dyson.'

'He's a good workman. He don't skimp. And he's been there nearly twenty years now. He don't dodge, like some. You don't have to ask him twice to do this, that and th'other. That's so, in't it? You know it's right, don't you?'

Riley set his face.

'He's given value for his wages. And this is how you treat him. It's no wonder the unions kick up if that's your way. Gi'e 'im his cards. That's the reward.'

'Mrs. Dyson.'

'You don't care. Every man for himself, that's you. He's given service, his best years. He's a skilled man. And this is all you bother.'

His mild expostulations had no effect as she blasted on. Words tumbled sour, in a subfusc frenzy. And yet he suspected that the bile would have flowed as freely in another channel, on inflation, fashion, hospitals. Now she repeated herself while the two men sat silent until she noticed their silence, became uneasy, paused between sentences, among her words. She braced herself.

'You see how it is, Mester Riley. If he wain't speak up for himself, I s'll do it for 'im.' She embarked, but wrecked herself shortly. When she sat, uncomfortably massaging her knees, Riley said quietly:

'Perhaps you'd like to speak, Mr. Dyson.'

The rebuke passed unnoticed. Dyson, lifting his head like an old nag, said:

'Well, it's right, in't it? They don't gi'e a bogger for you. I'm a cipher to them.'

Riley allowed the man to tail off, invited by a look the wife to a second turn, before he lectured them quietly on management. It was no part of his job to annoy work-people; the more content the hands, the better their labour. He didn't always see eye to eye with Mr. Dyson, as they both knew, but he'd found him responsible, would write him a good testimonial at any time. But men and machines were controlled by financiers, who, when they didn't receive sufficient return, would transfer their wealth elsewhere. That was the system. They might dislike it. It might easily put them into the very dilemma they all feared. It probably would. But it was a fact of life.

As he talked, slowly, giving them chance to keep abreast, the word 'liar' branded itself in his head. Liar, liar, liar. He owed it to these people to confess he'd been job-hunting.

He owed them nothing. Dyson was a grousing nuisance.

'I'll tell you,' he said, 'that if a good job offered itself to me, I'd take it.'

'They are selling up then?' Mrs. Dyson.

'No. I don't know. It's the subject of negotiation.'

'They wain't be no good offers at Henry's age.' She began to blurt again, energy restored. Now Riley saw clearly that she considered him rich and secure in tenure, a boss.

'I've no union to fight my battles,' he said angrily.

'No, because you don't need none.'

When they'd gone, and the woman chafed, grumbled through the door, in the street, out of earshot, Riley threw himself into a chair. Fatigue savaged him; small teeth of pain mauled his limbs, his back.

He'd have hated himself, had he the strength.

19

Next morning Riley was summoned to Cooper's office.
Though he was kept waiting for half an hour, the
interview cracked brisk and efficient. How'd he got on?
What did he make of the Furze brothers? Did he think
highly of the set-up? Then the technical questions; Cooper
took advantage of the interview to find out about this tin-pot
firm, because he might crib an idea. He never commented,
merely jabbed for information.

After this, as expected, tagged the personal questions.
Had they made an offer? What salary? How much notice
could he give? With increasing impatience Riley noticed that
his boss took it for granted that the job was his. The surge
of pride gave place to fear, cold back, pins in the belly.
Cooper dismissed him curtly, was on his next chore before the other was through the door.

Addison was nowhere about, and again the personnel in
the main office seemed utterly changed. Mr. Addison had
gone down to the bank, a short-skirted miss informed him,
not bothering with more than a glance, hiding behind the
armful of files she carried. She wore a thick plain wedding-
ring wider than his mother's.

On the corridor he met Frank Oxford, who made as if to
walk past him, until blocked.

'Oh, hello, Mr. Riley.'

He stood on one leg shaking an ankle, hopping in embarrassment. Mr. Riley. This boy had gone to the older
man's home to punish his father, had arrived with that
father to plead for his mother's release, and now, presum-

ably, he wanted to forget the lot, to be allowed to get on with his unimportant work because it meant nothing more than Friday's pay.

'Are you all right?'

'Yes, thanks.' He shook his mane, more comfortable already.

'Mother and father well?'

'Ye'.'

'I saw your mother last night.'

The boy frowned, uncertain again, nobody's enemy.

'She was complaining, then?' Barely inquisitive.

'She said you wanted to get married.'

He screwed his lips, as if he'd bitten a green gooseberry, nodded.

'Ah, she's always on about that.'

'She's a sensible woman, I've found.' He'd done his best. 'Don't you think so?'

'In some things.'

'It's no job of mine to interfere with what's not my business, but you should listen to what she says. In the end, you'll have to make up your own mind, but she's an intelligent woman.'

'She's old-fashioned.'

'Nothing wrong with that.'

'She doesn't listen.' The boy stared away again, embarrassed, lacking conviction.

'You make sure you listen to her, then. I think experience is worth something.'

The boy nodded, swayed like an amateur boxer.

'I shall have to be going.'

'Ay. Don't let me stop you working. And remember what I've told you.'

Their footsteps clanked in the corridor.

Outside, mild for the time of year, with sunshine. Riley blinking considered what he'd done. He'd spoken so that he had an excuse to visit, to report to Joan Oxford, to creep back into her favour by spouting banalities at Frank.

But why? So that she, touched in her mother-love, flattered by his stated regard, would commit an act of casual adultery.

Riley looked round the bright cars in the yard.

If the Furzes took him on he'd need to buy a car quickly and make sure he could still drive without killing himself. It was fortunate he'd renewed his licence every year since he'd come out of the army.

But the brothers Furze were in no hurry.

In the end, desperate, Riley rang the Luke-Williams office, where Phillips soothed him down the phone. No, the position had not been filled.

'You must realise, Mr. Riley,' Phillips said, 'that they are old fogeys. They don't find it easy to make their minds up. I don't think I'd worry if I were you. No, there's not a thing you can do about it. We just have to wait for them to do three months late what they could do now. I'll speak to Mr. Luke-Williams to see if he can jolly 'em along. I don't know. More harm than good, maybe. Oh, yes. You're in the running all right.'

'But I can't be an obvious choice. They must think there's a chance of a better.'

'They'd always think that.' Phillips whistled tunelessly into the phone running tickles of semi-quavers. 'No, if you want my honest opinion, Mr. Riley, they're in two minds about retiring, in no sort of hurry to give the place up, and so they're hesitating.'

Riley despised himself for his dependence on Phillips' soft-soap, for while the voice lapped him round, he felt confident, befriended. There was something to be said for Phillips; he'd a touch of his master's charisma without the awe, the imposing presence, the guinea-a-syllable image. A man tempted in all forms like us men. A pal. Riley had no idea where he lived, whether he was married, with a family, and yet he knew that if he met that man casually in the street, they'd stop, shake hands like old codgers and he'd be, foolishly perhaps, heart-warmed.

At the beginning of December one of the women from the floor came up to ask if they could decorate the factory for Christmas and hold a little party. He agreed, made a solemn little speech about family feeling, shoved in a warning about not marking the new paint with sellotape and asked if he could contribute towards the garlands or the jollification. The woman, a Mrs. Smallwood, touched him gratefully on his forearm as a child might stroke an unexpectedly splendid toy and thanked him. Again she seemed afraid, as if he'd switch from his agreement to anger. Perhaps he looked grim.

'I'm delighted you're smartening us up,' he said.

'Some on us'll bring us Christmas cards in,' she said. 'They'll look better here, hung up together, than at home.'

'If we get any.'

She squinted at him, not an unattractive woman.

'I'll send you one,' she said. But it sounded nervously.

He nodded, and she retreated. They did not know him. Those few thousand memories of childhood, marriage, the services, which went to make up his life, were unknown to them as the details of Phillips' background were to him. But because Phillips flattered, spoke congenially, he was regarded as a friend, while Riley was judged a boss, a gaffer, heartless, uncaring.

The Christmas party was held a few days before the Day. Work finished as usual, on Friday, and then at seven-thirty all returned, to one of the spare storerooms where the packers had erected borrowed trestle-tables. Riley, tired by the week, arrived at eight when the sherry bottles stood opened, half-empty. In the factory itself, garlanded, belled, ballooned, a raucous speaker spewed alternately today's pop and Victor Sylvester. Couples, not convincingly, danced up and down the concrete floor alongside the machines.

Miss Rogers in an acre of green handed him sherry, a cigar-length glass, and made conversation. Already some of the youngsters were shouting as two lifted a girl, unknown to him, bouncing on to one of the trolleys, her diminutive skirt flicked up from her bottom. Mrs. Smallwood advanced, pushing her husband, a chinless, balding, scurf-flecked man in wide-bottomed trousers who made the right sort of remark about the weather and the difficulty of parking in town. Somebody flashed away with his camera, encouraging victims to link arms, circle waists, kiss, canoodle. To Riley, sipping dry sherry which pinched his lips, it seemed foolish, as if they'd tied ribbon-bows on the machines to make them attractive.

They suffered a song or two delivered with appalling noise through the amplifying gear from the daughter of one of the machinists, and then some keg-handed conjuring before one of the boys from Despatch sang of the few things he loved, stopping between each verse to treat them to obscene patter. At one stage Miss Rogers seemed to be showing a naked lady into Riley's office. That was the long and the short of it; without shape, reason or wit. Its only advantage seemed that Miss Rogers and her superior, those establishment figures, were placed verbally in conjunction with a nude dolly, and that the protagonists who showed no surprise in fiction were watched for results in reality. Riley grinned, especially at some woman screeching her approval, but was nettled by the peering eyes, the whispered judgements made, and later, doubtless, drunkly repeated. Miss Rogers eyed the floor as the youth burst into his next unintelligible verse; she carried it off perfectly. The lad's hands flew like ugly birds from his guitar. Gaffer Riley sent his secretary down, the saga continued, to the floor to borrow a pair of pants to cover the scandal upstairs. Not a single woman below wore any. Triumph. The screams of the traduced. A paper bell thrown at the joker's head. A fat woman's skirt lifted to show she had dressed decently.

Now they settled to carols.

Printed sheets were handed round, and an electronic organ wheeled in, connected to the deafening speakers. The singing rattled about the walls with some harmony, seconds and bass, as a crate of beer was dragged out. Hark the

'Erald Angels, Rudolf the Red-Nosed Reindeer, Noël, I'm Dreaming of a White Christmas. They were in full voice when at nine o'clock supper arrived, sausage and chips, in metal cases carted in by a man dressed improbably in a white, filthy overall and a chef's hat.

Riley, between Miss Rogers and a simpering girl he'd not seen before, ate in the grace of shouted insults, the quiet of the trough, the call for beer. Men proposed toasts to the firm, to Riley, to the union, the Premier, Val Doonican, the local football teams, Riley again, coupled with the name of Miss Rogers. Innuendo. Plates were carted away; apple pie and cream were slapped down during the drinking of healths. Towards ten, a contingent of youngsters moved off to the pub, leaving a score of the more staid who turned the record-player down and congratulated each other on the quality of the entertainment. Riley, fighting indigestion, listened with half an ear to Dyson's grumbling, was kissed by one or two of the women under a sprig of mistletoe and left miserably. As he'd served beer to the men on Christmas Day, so now he'd done his duty, but without pleasure, grudgingly, unable to understand let alone join in the high spirits.

A poor soul.

He called in next morning and, as he'd expected, found they hadn't cleared up. He was sweeping litter when two of the women arrived to do the job. They were as down in the mouth as he when they saw him. Ten minutes later Miss Rogers, looking tense, pushed in with Mrs. Smallwood. Inside half an hour, the place spick and span, they all sat in his office drinking coffee, recalling the party, blackguarding Dyson for not appearing. Riley took his bottle of sherry from the cupboard, but found there were not enough glasses; whatever he did now, he'd made a bad impression by turning up unwanted.

Back home he could not bother himself to prepare lunch. O'Brien called in with the rent, in need of conversation. Usually if he couldn't get his landlord to the door he pushed an envelope through, but this morning he sat on the edge of a chair bellyaching.

His wife was no better, never would be, and yet the authorities expected him to have her home over Christmas. This meant a bed downstairs, constant cleaning up, spooning baby-food into her. 'May'll come in to help,' he said. 'Though that's expecting a bit much.'

'May?'

'My . . .' O'Brien lost his tongue. 'Woman. May Bright. Good as gold. She lugs her about and wipes her. I don't know.'

'Is she married?'

'May? No. Never has been. Looked after her parents. Invalids. Not much of a life. She's got a job now. First time sin' she were twenty.'

'And how old is she now?'

'Thirty-six. She's told me.' Victory.

O'Brien talked. Just as he'd flashed his photographs around, Riley thought, so he'd describe his sex with May, but the man was crudely tactful. His wife was going to die; there wasn't any doubt. 'They don't hang on to 'em in hospital for the sake of it, y'know. Best thing, an' all.' He wanted May to move in with him, but she had refused.

'I've told her she could call herself my housekeeper. But she wain't. Not her. Got her good name to consider. I told her you'd had a married woman lodging wi' you and no-body'd said a word. D'you know what she said? "That's different. Lodging's different. Beside, that Mester Riley's got a position to keep up. He wouldn't be tempted into no indiscretions."' The ugly face creased uglier at the word. What Miss Bright could see in this lizard-skin was not apparent to the other.

When the man had gone, Riley mended his stove, lit the gas fire in his parlour and wrapped a blanket across his knees. He moved restlessly in his chair, so he switched on the radio, to be troubled by a series of punching voices, leaping excited over the prospect of the afternoon's football matches. Easing a cushion higher to support his head, he tucked his legs under the blanket and fell asleep.

Now, again, hours, seconds, later, he woke terrified.

He'd been in the cellar, with the machines, the dead, Macmillan, and yet not. Arms and legs thrashed to burst open the congestion, the constriction of his nose, his mouth. All he grasped was terror, mad suffocation, the final flicker of agonised drowning before death. But he choked not on the sweet whiteness of water, but in earth, friable tumbling tons of sand and loam clogging his nostrils and windpipe until his ears and eyeballs shrieked for release, for a gasp. He seemed to be digging a tunnel, a mere yard or two, with his fingers, wildly, in desperation, knowing in certainty that both ends of the prison were blocked and that his activity scraped down the thick tumbling of the earth-ceiling and the soft rising of the sand-thick floor. His lungs burst with dull heaviness so that his squeals stifled inside him, and in, marsh-clogged, the dropping mould.

It took some time for him to realise he sat in a chair, breathing free.

His terror seemed not in his brain only, but suffused or running electric through his whole body, so that his diaphragm was an instrument as sensitive for recording fear as his head. The limbs and trunk revolted against the plain idea that he lived, was safe, in a warm room on a Saturday lunch-time. He thrust the blanket aside; nothing amiss, no cramps, constrictions. He could walk upright, breathe, be a manager, though, still tingling with the echo of fear, he remembered his animal whimpers, trapped beastliness, of a minute or two back.

At the window he heard children shouting, and noticed, at the other side of the street, an unidentified hand at a skylight hanging a Christmas garland. The world continued. The mundane justified itself. While his dreams strangled him. Half-heartedly he searched in the pantry for a packet of soap.

The women at the factory prolonged festivities right up

to the last day. Every morning they'd bring more cards, or a paper bell, in one instance a picture of Father Christmas. This tempted one of the despatch boys to bring a female Santa Claus, bare-breasted and simpering, but the girls wouldn't stand for it, appeared shocked not so much, he gathered, at the sexuality as at the blasphemy. They shouted their objections in strong language, but their lurid words meant nothing in themselves, would have been similar if the youth had brought in the wrong packet of wrapped fish and chips on a Friday. He suspected that some drinking went on in out-of-of-the-way corners in the dinner-break, and when work was slack the women opened packages to boast or complain about the price or quality of a present.

Riley felt himself remote from this.

He'd sent off half a dozen Christmas cards to surviving relatives from whom he'd get no answer. Two days before the holiday he'd called Mrs. Scotten in and presented her with a bottle of gin and a bottle of whisky, and a five-pound note in an envelope for the children. Her reaction impressed him. She'd nothing to say. As embarrassed as he was in the giving, she'd tried to pump up suitable words and failed. It was kind, very nice; she didn't expect; well, she didn't, and on, on in nothing. As she left, she turned, said:

'You're a good sort.'

That was the judgement passed on him in the factory because he'd calmly received his ribbing about the nude in his office. Good sort. Can take a joke. They didn't exactly make the announcement to him, but they did not exert themselves to keep their voices down, and they'd prompted Miss Rogers to pass a similar message on. Jack Riley wasn't above a bit of smut. Who rogers Rogers? they'd asked, cracker-style. It is, Riley (really). He'd bought her a Christmas present, any road. A handbag. They'd seen it. And she'd bought him a lovely biro set, in a presentation case. 'What's she put in her handbag?' they asked lewdly. The festive season glowed with sex for them, a saturnalia of drink and dirty talk. He could imagine them, reeling-happy, shrieking outside the pubs, over their piled fires, cracking nuts and crudities.

On Christmas Eve Joan Oxford and her husband appeared in Stoney Street.

He'd sent them a card, received one in return and now they were here with a neatly wrapped bottle of after-shave lotion. He lit the gas fire, marshalled them into the front-room armchairs and slopped whisky and sherry into glasses he had first to rinse. Raising their drinks, they exchanged seasonal greetings, talked of the past, began to know the right reeling spirit.

First the Oxfords invited him over for Christmas dinner, for Frank had announced that he wouldn't be at home. Riley, ruefully, sorry for himself, accepted, thinking of the small frozen chicken he'd laid in. Joan Oxford showed her delight, smiling, dress hem back on her shapely thigh as she sat, making a speech delivered in small formal lengths to declare their joint gratitude to him for his care of her, his concern for Frank, called Francis, his advice to her husband. Nothing was said of the blow, or of adultery. Ron himself tumbled out words in a slow slurring deliberation so that Riley guessed both had been drinking before they set out. Half-happy, he filled glasses.

Frank, they announced, had given up his slut, but this won him no regard from his parents. They flung about an antiphony of abuse and criticism; he'd not improve if he lived to ninety. Whatever the boy did he'd rile his parents, that was certain, but then combined vilification seemed artificial, formal, the resultant of alcohol and excitement.

Suddenly, Ron Oxford jerked to his feet, demanded a lavatory with grimaces, then said he must call at the cut-price stores for a bottle of brandy. He reprimanded his wife for not reminding him on the way down, claimed the place would be sold out if he didn't hurry. Again drink rather than reason dictated behaviour.

'I'm having some'at stronger than custard on my Christmas pudding,' he shouted. The loud voice, the flushed cheek, his gait, sketched him pleasanter, as if one of the unemployed had been transformed into Santa Claus. He left humming 'While Shepherds Watched', conducting low down with a gloved, stiff left hand.

Joan refused more sherry.

'I'm dizzy already.'

Riley kissed her and she hugged him. They toppled to the sofa, where unchidden he stroked her legs, her breasts.

'I love you,' he said, believing it.

'You don't, you know.' The blue eyes enlarged by her spectacles opened wide, seemed to examine his claim steadily. 'We're drunk.'

'You speak for yourself.'

She refused his love beyond intimate caressing, and as she lay on him, or he on her, he in his half-stupor, lolled content, her mouth heavy on his, his hand on slow exploration up her skirts.

'Did you lock the doors?'

'Don't know.'

'Go on. Ron might catch us.' He made the move shouldering the passage wall.

'What would he say?' he asked, returning. She shook her head, dizzily. Now she sat upright, frock pulled down to knees. 'What would you say?' They cackled dully, enjoying the thought of their spooning observed by a drunken, outraged husband. Even as he lounged, her head on his shoulder, her bright hair stopping his mouth, brittly perfuming his face, he felt the coarseness of her fantasy, her lack of regard. Like a strip-club dancer she made her gesture for herself, for some sort of payment, if not in money then in retaliation. If she cared for him at this moment, it was because she loved herself, and this cheapened them both. When they'd made love in his bed, they'd clung to each other in a shared distress, a partnership, a communion of infidelity. Now both stroked and mouthed, making fun of the brandy-buying drunk in the cold streets and claiming nothing for themselves but a thin, unsatisfactory warmth, a pale gruel of pleasure as of two groping juvenile delinquents.

In the end one lay against the other, in a fug of idle relaxation, waiting for the thumping on the door, the husband's shouts. When Ron arrived, his brandy wrapped in tissue paper, he seemed soberer, less hearty, saddened. The air was raw, he claimed, and the money some people had to chuck about they wouldn't believe. 'Don't tell me this is a poor district,' he said. 'Crates they was buying. Crates.' He refused another drink, perhaps because he could not match the observed affluence and so refused to compete. They left swiftly not saying much, affected by a blight.

'Come soon after one o'clock,' she said. 'Lunch is about half-past.'

'An' at twelve if you're joining me in the pub.'

Both invitations sounded sluggish, devoid of warmth as typing exercises.

Riley settled to the television set, locking his drinks away.

Not a carol singer cheeped. He thought that the Scotten clan might risk a verse or two in the yard, but adults had warned that his generosity had been sufficiently lavish already. He noticed them only once, in a minatory shriek from Alma. From the other side not a sound; presumably Mrs. O'Brien had been bundled home that afternoon but he heard nothing of it.

Comedians cackled, groups assaulted, hen-faced girls rocked as they devoured hand-mike lollipops, all pre-recorded to fill the ears and houses of those who'd nothing to say for themselves or nobody to say it to. Not switching off, Riley struggled out of the back-door, knocked at the O'Briens'. Mild, cloudy, the night was full of awkward aerials on chimneys, twigged shrubs and the lighted cracks in window curtains while over in the distance cars grumbled along the main road.

O'Brien opened the door.

Surprisingly he was in his shirt-sleeves and wore a clay-brown rubber apron such as dentists wrapped round one thirty years back.

'I've come to see if there's anything I can do for you.'
He'd prepared that.

O'Brien waited, blocking the door, uncertain what to think in this contingency. When finally he moved back, invited the other in, he glanced suspiciously, as if he'd take to his heels.

'Just washing up,' he said. He'd cleaned a full dinner-service, piles of plates, a gravy-boat with a china spoon, soup tureens, a dish nearly the size of the draining board. 'Got to be ready for tomorrow.'

'Missus home?' Riley asked.

'Ah.' He sighed, drying his hands on the roller towel. 'Come in.'

At the living-room table a woman sat cleaning silver. She was thin, lean-legged, with hair dyed black. At once she smiled and apologised that she could not shake hands.

'I should be wearing gloves by rights,' she said, in a voice emaciated as her limbs. 'We're smartening up for Christmas.'

O'Brien did not introduce them; both were in the know. The trio edged towards the front room.

'D'you think she's asleep?'

'She wasn't,' May asserted, 'a few minutes back.'

'A coal fire burnt in the grate, but the place smelt slightly damp, its air unbreathed. Mrs. O'Brien lay, hands on sheet, with her eyes almost closed, breathing heavily.

'Don't wake her up,' Riley said, willing to slip out.

'Are you there, Bet? A visitor. You've got a visitor.' No banker could have matched the heartiness. Her eyelids flickered mechanically, without volition.

'Riley. It's Mester Riley.'

'Look who's come to see you, dear.' May spoke in a genteel treble, but roughly pulled the woman higher in bed. For a moment the eyes widened, in a spasm of fear, it seemed, as if some recognition of situation or individuals had terrified the numbed brain. Immediately her head dropped and she dozed.

'Don't know you. Don't know me,' her husband grumbled.

May fussed at the bed, revealing her chapped, red elbows, before the three left to drink glasses of sherry. Every house now bragged Yule bottles on its sideboard. Once the three had exchanged civilities and trivialities, they'd nothing left. O'Brien looked at his glass as he held it to the light, perhaps expecting chemical change. May Bright sat, knees together, ugly green shoes together, by the fire, in the chair of honour, the newest, smiling, like a pitiful mouse, intent for the moment but already half-poised to scurry off, to disappear into some darkness of safety. Riley thanked them and shook hands as if he were making a presentation.

Nobody wanted him.

His failure to land the position at the Furze brothers mauled. He'd not hear now, over the holiday, and that ought to release him. It did not because he was convinced he'd never hear, that they'd decided against him, and rightly. What had he to show for himself? He could act as pay clerk or sweep the floors efficiently or perhaps after some weeks' training handle one of the looms, but as the man in charge they could drag in the next baker's roundsman or window-cleaner who came down the street and provide an equal satisfaction for themselves. The Furzes, or that grease-haired solicitor, or perhaps, treasonably, Luke-Williams had seen through his pretensions and thumbed him down. And not without cause. He offered nothing, had nothing about him. Now he could not hope.

Christmas dinner with the Oxfords dejected him.

Ron had left for the pub when he arrived, and Mrs. Oxford seemed preoccupied, edgy, rushing from this rattling saucepan lid to that falling Christmas card or scatter of biscuit crumbs, nut-shells. When her husband returned late, she did not hide her anger, scathingly brushed aside his inebriated tenderness. The meal was excellent, but the hosts resented his company, Riley decided, or perhaps chafed that so much preparation or anticipation amounted to so little. These did not want him; the woman's best dinner-service, skill, thought had been exhibited so that he could chew silently and mumble through bald compliments, while the man, worse for drink, rejected one who'd failed to join him in approproate celebration. Brandy flames flickered and when he'd helped his hostess with the greasy dishes, Oxford was already asleep, Riley kissed her feebly in the kitchen and went home. Though she seemed near tears, she did not attempt to stop him. Neither thought it worth while to rouse Ron.

Back in Stoney Street, he went to bed, slept fitfully and came down to nurse his indigestion with cups of weak tea and the pre-recorded clatter of television. Nothing for him there. He watched the legs of girls, of circus beasts, made no sense of the cheerful signals and by eight o'clock was out traipsing the raw streets. Some few curtains were undrawn so that he could see the garlands, the fairy-lighted tree, the family crowding settee and chairs to watch the box, but mostly there was silence, cold drizzle, some old dear walking her dog. No cars moved, and the bright pubs made no noise. Grateful to his gas fire, he made a pot of coffee, laced it and settled to universal entertainment.

Early to bed he slept badly, the pillow under his neck like a twist of rock. At one-thirty the slam of a car door woke him thoroughly, and the hot repetitive words of his troubles thumped in his head. Furze did not want. He was too old. He lacked qualifications. If he were appointed, he'd fail. One look at him. Unemployed. Redundant. Too old at. Solicitor. Phillips laughing behind his broken back. His nightmare did not trouble, only the fierce sense that he was snarled up in reality, pinpricked by his own puffy vanity.

Over breakfast he decided against cooking his lunch, determined to go out. He wished he were at work or had a hangover to contend with. The clouds dropped low, sooty; chimney smoke hung in the bleak damp; mist blotted distant roofs. Colder. He'd be a fool to venture out. He opened a tin of corned beef, made sandwiches.

Again he walked empty streets, eyeing the occasional

child straddling a new bicycle with father's help, and once an Indian bus conductor wearing an open navy topcoat over his uniform. Riley made for the high ground, the ridge above the town, stepping all the time between silent houses, drawn curtains at ten-thirty in the morning. Up on Hilltop Road a garage showed one bulb and the shop windows decorated for Christmas looked insecure, dusty, transiently promising the spurious to the undeserving. Mist thickened here, wet cloud dumped untidily round dull brickwork.

He quickened his pace.

Even when he began to leave the town the road stretched as cheerless. In the gardens of Victorian villas maisonettes had been thrown up, and once behind a farm square to the road a brand-new terrace of ted-tiled boxes struggled into a sodden field. The boles of trees shone sallowly, as if coated with grease. Hawthorn hedges jutted black, moist.

He turned now to the right, pleased with himself, warm with arm-swinging. He saw little of the countryside, for the few farms he passed seemed inhospitably built with blank outhouse buiildings backing on to the road. Presumably they had work to do, though he did not know. A mound of vegetables at the edge of a field he could not put a name to: turnips, swedes, mangold-wurzels? He passed a motorists' pub, gaily lighted inside and out, but as yet its car park bare. At noon, and dark, a grey, gleam-less chill in the thin, un-shifting fog.

When he paused, at a field-gate, to eat sandwiches and drink his coffee, Riley felt the cold immediately, in his feet, across his face. Great white precarious drops of moisture hung on the branches, hedgerows, cross-bars. Why had he come so far out? While he'd been walking, light bag bang-ing on his shoulder, he'd been content, unthinking, a man with a chore, a charge. Now he stood a fool. In depression, miles from the world, out in the cold.

Soon he left the road, this time at the direction of a sign-post, 'Public Footpath to Woodborough, 2 mls.' The track, such as it was, the unploughed edge of a field, sloped downwards sharply, but was lost in the valley mist. One could see, dimly across perhaps two wide fields, grass or turned clay, but beyond, over hedges or pinched single oaks, the vapour oozed, reflected the chill. Each step he took carefully, for the clay under his feet was treacherous, and once when he tried to run he skidded so that he was lucky to end clinging to a length of fence. Air touched colder as the damp penetrated his boots which were soled now with great clods of mud.

The path swung right, joining an unused pebbled lane by a gateless gap in the hedge. Fifty yards across the field he could make out a house, a farm, outbuildings, heaps of rubble, though no road led to it, not even a foot-wide trail through the sodden grass. No sounds, not the bark of a dog.

The roof and the end wall this side were down, exposing a small staircase, some cramped bedrooms. He rounded the building, finding the front intact, though the door was gone and the stone step dragged some yards off. A Victorian farm with a shallow roof in grey slate, bricks dark as a scowl, windows still glazed, it appeared to him, peering in, as bleakly desolate. Stairs leading to the principal upstairs room faced him, while on his left lay a big pleasant lounge without floorboards, a shoddy paper still hanging down from the wall. He turned right, into another smaller dining room, and then further into the spacious kitchen with its built-in cupboards strong and outside pantries roofless, grass-wrecked. The beams in the ceiling stood exposed, pasted over first with newspaper and then with scraps of whitish flowered covering. He scrabbled above to pull the paper down, hoping for a date. November 1959. Twelve years ago people living here spruced the place up, made it fit to cook in. Above a door black fuse boxes were fastened as good as new.

He pushed on to the outhouses. The doors on the cowsheds swung easily on their hinges; the stalls were firmly partitioned; dry hay rustled scattered on the floor. Perhaps the present owner used these. Further along, a building had been flattened so that only a concrete floor remained, while beyond another barn had been stripped on one side of its pantiles, the beams and grey laths broken. Piles of bricks were dumped, wire, a rotting stove, a kettle, a heap of sacks. All round the house in the valley mist hovered, icily indifferent.

Clambering over mounds, he reached the stream, cut deep in its channel, and consulted his map. Stoop Hill Farm. He walked some yards, slithering in a morass, clay ruts puddled, until he stopped again under a twisted tree. He picked about at the khaki leaves. Oak. The stream made no noise.

For some minutes he considered himself, his depression nagging for precedence over his physical weariness. He'd brought himself to starve out here, clog his boots clay-thick, poke round other people's leavings because he'd neither the energy to occupy himself at home nor sit socialising in a pub. The man without occupation. He'd have to scrape his soles tomorrow, and brush the mud-streaks from his trousers. He turned about and slogged up the hill, but this time on the grass by the side of the pebbled lane, wondering when that, the only ingress he could see to the deserted farmhouse, had last been used. Recently, perhaps. Because a home, a family disappears, fields remain, yield, must be reached. Now he breathed heavily, face red, but he was warm.

On the road he tore a handful of grass to daub at his boots, then snatched up a length of branch, which snapped, a flat stone. As he banged his feet on the tarmac he felt comforted, a man with an aim.

By the time he reached the town the afternoon had darkened and as he marched downwards from Hilltop the fog thinned so that the lights of the next main road shone almost masterfully. Cars skimmed now; an ear-splitting motorbike; a whole family, on the way out or home, cheerfully across the pavement, the skipping children in bobble-hats. He envied their energy.

Back at home he considered cooking his chicken to occupy

himself, but rejected the scheme, lolled about in his arm-chair, uncomfortable, grotesquely on holiday. Half-reluctant, he dragged himself next door to invite O'Brien and his May in for a drink. They refused, claiming they could not leave the invalid. In his rancour, Riley saw them lying across a bed together without thought of dying wife or suffocating neighbour. He clumped round to the Scottens' where he could hear racket galore. Dressed to kill, the parents could not manage it; they had to take Alma's mam to the club. Could they drop in for a minute, sup the first of the evening with him? They exchanged glances and were sorry. They'd promised; he knew how it was.

He knew.

Collapsing into his chair he fingered his slippers on. At ten he went to bed. Outside the streets glistened and the Scottens' shrieks were diminished. Through the O'Briens' back bedroom window light glowed. He looked again into the front. Nobody in the street, though cars now lined both sides.

Glad to consider work, he wound his alarm.

20

At Carnell and Bloom's people moved soberly, as if afraid to impinge on a neighbour's hangover. They'd had, they claimed in answer to Riley's politeness, a quiet Christmas. Whatever the truth, they were quiet enough now, and he did not disturb them. They provided the excuse for his being there, with bits of paper to play with, one or two soluble problems to sit out and he was therefore grateful. If they didn't fulfil today's quota, then he'd defend them, argue with Cooper who, in any case, would be combating a similar slackness at his own place, and from more accomplished scrimshankers. He looked down with affection.

Miss Rogers brought coffee and a biscuit, and he kept her talking.

She'd nothing to say, except to boast, in a raw excited way, that she'd had just a little drop too much last night. The vaunt annoyed him, mildly. She'd no call to get drunk, with her big breasts and her anxious, wooden face. The powder was laid on thick this morning; he imagined her flushed and sweating, laughing high-pitched, holding her glass out as she refused another gin. Who she'd been swilling with he didn't know. Presumably her father couldn't leave the house, so that the rest of the boozers must have come in to her, relatives, cronies of the dad's, some other old maid.

'Got a headache?' he asked.

'Yes.' She tried to smile. 'Serves me right.' He shook two aspirins from a bottle.

'Take these with your coffee.'

She stared at the tablets on the palm of her hand as if mesmerised, mesmerising.

'Have them with your coffee,' he said.

All at once she groaned, a loud sound, ample as her hips.

'You should take more water with it,' he said, and realised that she'd no idea she'd made any noise. He peeped at her through the partition and watched her dissolve his aspirin in water, which she drank violently before she sat to sip her coffee.

As he shuffled papers, the office clock ticked loudly and he pulled the necessary faces, drumming with his fingers. No sooner had he managed to absorb himself than the phone disturbed him.

'Call for you, Mr. Riley,' said Miss Rogers. 'Mr. Phillips. Right, sir, you're through now.'

' 'Morning, Mr. Riley.'

' 'Morning.'

'Phillips here. We've some good news for you. You know what that means. Good news. I don't want to say anything further on the phone. Could you come round at lunch-time?'

They fixed a time, and Phillips reiterated the phrase 'good news' as if he understood the chasm of unbelief that Riley crossed. This is what he wished to hear, but because this man refused to say, 'The Furzes have offered you the job,' Riley refused to accept the implication. Inside him he recognised the stirrings of joy, frozen deliberately, and knew that was what Luke-Williams & Co. would want. He'd now have an hour or two to acquaint himself with the principle, and thus would be readier to hear advice about final negotiations of salary. By one o'clock he would have convinced himself that he was a manager and would have regained equilibrium.

Phillips knew little when Riley called. Luke-Williams, in his office, did not emerge for congratulations. A salary six hundred a year above his present one had been suggested, but Williams, apparently, was for squeezing them. They wished him to start as soon as he could leave Carnell's.

When Riley suggested to Phillips that they should celebrate with a drink, the offer was courteously refused. 'I know how you feel, Mr. Riley. And I thank you. You've got no more than you deserve, I'll say that, and I'm pleased for you. We'll let it rest there. I've nothing against congratulatory cups. Don't get me wrong. This is a job to me, Mr. Riley, my business. I'm not saying I don't enjoy a twinge of euphoria when this sort of thing is brought off . . .' He allowed his voice to fade, like a holy man in some corner of a cathedral whose tone is whisked away from him into the dizzying spaces of high vaulting, but whose meditation solidified into God in comparison with whom this spectacular edifice of stone was no more than the flash of a bird's reflection in the shifting face of the sea.

Phillips had become business-like, suggesting Riley rang Cooper with the news from this office so that Miss Rogers wouldn't know too soon, spill it round the floor. They failed, and agreed that Phillips should pass the message.

Riley ate no lunch, did no work.

With the afternoon tea came Cooper's call.

'Can you come up? I've just heard. You've not told anybody down there, have you? Well, don't.' Cooper spoke shortly, as though the news had roused his envy. 'Don't suppose you're doing much, now. Down tools, then. You've set me some snags up there, mister.'

Riley, smiling sourly, wondered what Miss Rogers made of this, and then, in his pleasure, rebuked himself for the suspicion.

'Have to see Mr. Cooper,' he said, donning trilby and raincoat. 'Are you feeling any better?'

His superior, as usual, made him wait, showed no pleasure at his entry and immediately demanded when he'd want to leave. When Riley suggested a month, Cooper blew his cheeks out, kneaded his incipient paunch, but did not demur, sat humming to himself. Finally he asked about salary, heard the suggested alternatives, yanked on his waist-coat and said:

'You're bloody lucky to get it, Riley. That's all I can say.'

Anger. A small cold spasm of dislike.

'You don't think I'm any good, then?'

'I didn't say that.'

'Not in so many words.'

'You've done a respectable job for us,' Cooper said. 'I'll grant you that. Kept production up and your women happy. But that's about your lot, y'know.'

'What's wrong with it?'

'Nothing, nothing. More than some manage. But it's expansion, reorganisation, redeployment that count today. It's no use getting a hundred per cent efficiency out of plant that should have been scrapped in nineteen-forty-five. Modern establishments running at half-cock'll wipe the floor with you. That's no fairy-tale, either. Seen too much of it.'

'What do I do, then?'

'You're out of date like the machine. A modern manager's the sort of man who looks about, spots the changes, and starts collecting the capital. My predecessor here now. Bowles. He was your type, writ large. If one of his bits of ironmongery broke down, he'd mend it himself. He knew the unions and the least they'd dare accept. He prodded Erskine, up to a point. He could put a name to the kids of all the women on his benches. If I believe the stories they tell, he fathered half of 'em. But if it came to big money, real finance, reorganisation of anything like size, he was lost, innocent as you are.'

'Then, why . . . ?'

Cooper waved him down.

'I'm not so sure that it's not the Bowleses and Rileys who've ruined the British manufacturing industry, between you. You're just efficient enough to keep reality, new plant and new ideas out.'

'Why've Furzes offered me the job?'

'They're living in the nineteenth century.'

'You mean we'll be put out of business.'

'No, I don't. It's a family firm. They'll produce a decent article. But they won't get the return on their capital that the really big operators want.'

'Such as you?'

'Such as me.' Cooper tucked his double chin into his flowered shirt. 'I know you don't like me, Riley. Don't blame you. Put me fist in his silly shitty face, you think. I'm not going to die a pauper. Furzes don't want money. They've got plenty, comparatively speaking; they've done well, they think, and an occupation to go with it, and they don't honestly want more. Erskine's a different kettle of fish. Now I like Erskine. He's as thick as two planks, but, by God, he's greedy. He wants his money to breed.'

'He could lose it.'

'Theoretically. Not likely. He could lose some, I'll grant you. But if you don't get off your arse and take a risk, you'll end where you started. Erskine'll die a millionaire. And yet I often wonder if he could hold down a clerk's job in one of his own factories.'

Cooper laughed, now, an ugly-fat young man in a beautiful suit, his nails pared down, his hair beginning to thin. Riley, invited to sit late in the interview, began to understand, as he listened, the drive, the neurotic energy of the man, the ambition that nailed him to unease, that ripped him loose to chase and fret after every glint of opportunity. The man acted a ferret, biting down the dark rat-holes of money. A stinking beast. A firework jumping-jack, which would end in a blackened stub of shredded cardboard.

Suddenly Riley sat straight, interrupted his master.

'Why are you telling me all this, Mr. Cooper?'

The sentence fell impudently, claimed superiority. Cooper smiled, Buddha-wide.

'Good question. I'm talking to myself. Don't suppose you cotton on, do you? Money, the chase after money. Occupies me. Obsesses. That's the word. Do you know how many hours I put in a day? Something like sixteen-seventeen. None of your nine to five touch for me.'

'Why don't you live in London?'

Cooper nodded, with respect.

'I should like to. The real contacts are there. But I'm learning my way round. When I started, it was all one-way traffic, me to them, cap in hand. Now they're beginning to come to me.'

'This reorganisation's all due to you, would you say?'

Again Cooper eyed Riley. Shrewd.

'To some extent. I've acted for Erskine and two others concerned. And for a friend of mine who puts money in my way. But there's one big operator, at least, I mean really big, in on this.'

'You've watched him?'

'Of course. And I don't mind telling you, Riley, I'm not too impressed. He's smart enough, and really well advised, but it's the amount of his capital that talks. That's what life's about up there.'

Cooper talked on, quietly, spitting his words and though he qualified his admiration of the big capitalists, he could not disguise his reverence. Riley, taken aback by the fluency, did not interrupt, but questioned himself how far the man would progress. Country estate? House of Lords? He'd no idea what the top prizes were. He listened, slightly flattered that this tycoon took him aside into his confidence like this. In the army, comrades had spilt their privacies to him, and though that had shocked him from time to time he'd seen their exposures as between equal and equal. The sexual difficulties, the perversions, the shortage of money or understanding, the failures of nerve or organs were exhibited as troubles that might as easily have buffeted him. But this incisive, monotonous flow, this insight into meetings that changed the face of the earth, or polluted it, meant nothing. He could not rid his mind of the idea that Cooper was an outsider, a little man, judged on his performance and rewarded accordingly, but no more than the office-boy, the commissionaire, the janitor. Perhaps his own suspicious nature suggested this, for Cooper complimented himself as a prime mover in these concerns.

'Do you know Lord Sawbury?' he asked Riley.

'No.'

'Earl of Sawbury? Metals man? Frank Sawbury?' As if the listener needed prodding to recall a nonentity. 'He said to me, and he's shrewd, I'd say, at a conference, private affair, y'know . . .' Again, sour Sgt. Riley didn't see much in the anecdote except milord's name.

Cooper rang for coffee.

A surprised, curious secretary brought cups at once, smiling at the visitor. A drink meant approbation. Cooper played with his spoon, scooping and stirring, as he talked on to Riley who grew apprehensive. This lasted overlong. When, half an hour later, Cooper snatched his cup, gulped the cold coffee away and dismissed him, he was glad.

'Can I announce it?' Riley asked.

'Please yourself.'

No friendliness there. The thick, hooding eyelids were down and his finger pressed a machine for fresh service. Walking back, Riley blew angry at the selfishness of the man, his absorption in himself. It was almost ridiculous except for its strength. Determined to prosper, Cooper concentrated only on success, until it seemed a mania, sane enough externally, average even, but revealed by the hour-long monologue. What was Mrs. Cooper like? Weren't wives supposed to be important?

He broke his news first to Miss Rogers, who parked herself down and began to cry, loudly. This was so far from his idea of her character that he'd no inkling of what to do. He sat; he made calming sounds; then he moved across and stroked one shoulder, much, he thought, as one might test a length of cloth. This succeeded no better.

Now she stood, wiped her eyes, spoke normally, first apologising, then offering him her congratulations. He filled in two minutes with an account of the Furze place before he asked her when he should make the announcement. She suggested at the end of the lunch-break and went off to manage arrangements.

At one-twenty-five he came down his steps, followed by Miss Rogers, clacked the length of the floor where his people had grouped themselves. There was no noise; they'd obviously discussed the nature of the meeting, and feared.

He stopped. Miss Rogers edged to one side. She was not carrying her notebook but seemed to set a standard of propriety and attention for the rest to imitate. He cleared his throat. Uncertain, legs weak, he faced those thirty-odd eyes, those clamped mouths.

'I've something to tell you all,' he said. He shifted slightly; they copied. 'I've been appointed production manager of the Furze Brothers factory at Bastow.' They moved more freely, sniffed. 'I shall take the post up in a matter of a month's time.'

The work-people were lost until Dyson lunged forward.

'Is that because this place is closing down?'

'No, Mr. Dyson, it isn't. I've not kept it from you that there's reorganisation in the wind, that there might be big changes. I made that plain to Mr. Dyson some time back and to one or two of you, when you asked, at the Christmas party. What form that reorganisation will take I do not know. I wish I did.'

'Why are you going, then?' Dyson.

'A better job was advertised. I applied, was interviewed and accepted. But for all I know this factory will be kept as a working unit. I'm not promising. I don't know. It is a possibility. And you'll keep your jobs under a new establishment. I spent an hour this morning with the managing director, Mr. Cooper, and he could still tell me nothing.' The lie flummoxed him for a moment, it had appeared so pat, without need, so that he stumbled, had to hide his hesitation with a cough. 'Nobody yet knows. You may be lucky, if that's the word.'

He stopped to scrutinise his staff. Their eyes seemed

round so that he was reminded of a group of infants in a school-yard standing alert to watch the teacher mop up an accident. Aghast at blood, but afraid to miss it. They stared helplessly at him, wanting something, dreading some tail-piece of a sentence that would condemn them to another stint to the Labour Exchange and the adverts in the evening paper. He must lob his crumb of comfort.

'I want to thank you all for the help you've given me. I was new to the job, but you made me welcome. We've got a good team, and if the directors were of my mind they'd keep it together.'

'Who shall we get in your place?' He'd no idea who'd asked. A man.

'That I don't know, either. Mr. Cooper didn't mention it.'

'Will the fact that you're going affect the, them, well, closing us down, y'know?'

'I shouldn't think so.'

He answered a few more questions, never at length, not trusting himself, afraid to swerve from truth for the devil of it. In the end he thanked them again, gravely, and sig-nalled Miss Rogers to lead him out. Inside her office, she said:

'Won't be the same, with you gone.'

'I haven't been here long.'

'No, you haven't. But you looked right in there. With Mr. Morley I couldn't care much, because he was a withered old stick. I was frightened what you'd be like, but as soon as I got to know you, you were right.'

He'd no answer for that.

'I'll always associate this place with you. It's like people and houses, isn't it? A family three doors from us flitted this week; they'd lived there years, and I thought, "That's their house; they've brought children up in those rooms, and done the garden and papered the walls and now they're gone." It's Whalleys' house to me, though. Still. It always will be.'

Riley guessed something of the rage of feeling under this genteel chatter. The woman grudged his going.

'Mr. Morley, now,' she said, 'he was a nobody. He was all right, mind you. Bit of a fusser, but he was like an old spider, scuttling in the corners. God knows what he was doing. I couldn't make it out. But you ran the place. You were the manager.'

Pleased, he shook her hand, held it, retreated to his own desk.

The next week or so stretched dull.

The firm allowed him time off to visit Furzes', where the elder brother seemed put out by the directness, or perhaps stupidity, of Riley's questions, but the new man did not allow himself to be rebuffed, pursued information, unravelled it, until he was satisfied. This might not impress Furze, but Riley determined not to remain ignorant. He was reminded of a sharp Scot in the army, a drill sergeant, who with different parents would have been a war-house general, whose favourite cynicism was 'Ask 'em the most obvious questions you can think of. It frightens 'em, first, because they're damned pushed to answer and secondly they think you're up to something. As you bloody well should be.' 'They', of course, were the officer caste. So Riley prodded, and insisted, and failed to apologise when he demanded a second and a third time.

By the end of the afternoon of the first visit, Mr. Furze sprawled exhausted, as if he'd been harried by a hostile examiner.

'There's plenty of time, Mr. Riley,' he said. 'I shall be with you for a month or two. I can explain procedure then.'

'There's plenty to learn.'

Furze looked at the round face, unsmiling, the bald head, the hairs oiled across the pate, the broad shoulders, the not-too-smart suit, the splashes of mud on the highly polished toe-caps, showing the man had walked from the bus, and was slightly dismayed. He'd caught a Tartar, he decided; a persistent, quiet, dangerous peasant.

Riley enjoyed his ordeal. Having no real confidence in himself, he was delighted to get hold of the right end of the stick, and showed his pleasure by questing for one fact more. If he'd a new weapon to learn in the army he'd take the manual back to married quarters and pick through it, word by word, if need be, until he'd mastered the description. His wife laughed at him, but listened uncomprehending, as he repeated the words of the book she had to hold away from him. Then he'd go down to the weapon-training school to fiddle with the parts; he could deal with machinery, strip it down, clean it, clap it back into working order. It was the words he feared. So he'd do it the hard way, until the printed marks on paper began to make sense even without the metal and the oil.

Management consisted of words. Or figures. Nobody asked him to make or mend anything, merely to arrange for others to do so. Thus, with his notebook and pencil he recorded Furze's descriptions, compelled him to expand his shorthand code, so that he could sit at home that night and pore until he'd acquired this by head, to spill it out fluently, either to an inspecting big-wig or, better, thick-witted rookie.

He came back as a man justified, even stole time from Carnell's to study the word.

One afternoon coming out from work he met Francis Oxford. Again the boy would have walked past.

'You're out of your way here, aren't you?' Riley said, stopping him.

'Calling round to see my mate.'

'I see.'

'We're studying Spanish together. From a record course.'

'At this time?'

'No.' Frank spat amusement. 'I'm just calling to warn him I shall be late tonight. We're going to the Costa Brava for a holiday.'

'All well at home?' He did not enjoy the lad's superior delivery.

'With me, yes. Since, y'know . . . since I gave Reet up. Not with them, though. Get on your tits.'

'What's the trouble?'

'Don't ask me. Don't get on. That's all.'

Frank stood there, lips slightly parted, long hair curling over a velvet collar. This, Riley ordered himself to understand, was the boy he'd taken in. How he'd ventured that he could not fathom. They'd seemed to be workmates, then, in a welter of small trouble together, equal, ready to give or receive help. Now he'd taken a commission, cut his own umbilical cord, hacked roots out, died, as that drunken padre used to bawl, unto sin once.

'I'm sorry,' he said.

The boy pulled the expected solemn face. He was very handsome. 'I'm leaving here,' Riley said, thumbing back towards the painted letters on the double gate: 'Carnell and Bloom, Carton Manufacturers'.

'I've heard.'

'Does Mr. Addison know?'

'Should think so. He said they were putting some man in from down south in your place.'

The boy nodded, made up his mind, walked away not quickly but firmly, almost like a middle-aged man, hair flapping. His coat-sleeves were too long, as if he shrivelled inside them.

21

When Riley set off for work on Tuesdays and Thursdays it was still darkish.

He enjoyed the lighted bus, always sat downstairs, and wore his brown trilby, as he carried a briefcase, a symbol of status amongst the coughing cloth caps. Conductors indulged in no back-chat with him. He unlocked his office soon after seven, in complete quiet, set his electric fire tingling and a vacuum flask of coffee on the desk. He'd started this way on Mondays, but the machinists disliked it, though they'd no objections to the other two mornings. The early arrival wasn't necessary now; he could do the job on his head between nine and five, so that sometimes he brought in a radio or a newspaper to occupy himself, but he liked to stand in the warmth upstairs looking at the chequer-board of light thrown by his fluorescent bar across the factory floor below. He'd glance at his watch, and know that in less than an hour the machines would whirr up, the voices call, the lamps shine, but he'd remember the quietness, the dark shapes, the morning brightening outside the windows, the society of himself, bricks and mortar.

Towards the end of January he stepped from his bus into the cold streets where he marched smartly along, briefcase militarily square under his arm. Usually the streets were deserted on his early mornings, though now the sky had become bright. As he slapped along, he was aware, vaguely, of movements, subdued shouts, bustle, things astir. A newspaperboy, bag empty, dashing along the pavement, stopped in front of Riley, mouth agape and said:

'There's a factory a-fire.'

'Where?'

'Crocus Street.'

Riley was toppled. Carnell and Bloom's. The boy had gone careering off, his footsteps clanging between the bare warehouse walls. Fire. He clutched his case, as if thieves gathered, and walked, not ran, towards the factory. As he turned into the street, it seemed full of people, small standing figures round the two fire-engines. The air blackened with smoke so that he noticed, taken aback, that he'd smelt it already without putting a name to it. The whole area now was warmed by the blazing factory; from yards away a summery heat attacked, dissipated the frost. As he quickened his pace, a great leaping tongue of fire burst from an upper storey, twisting in a wild explosion straight, then skywards, only to disappear.

The racket sprang from the fire, not the people. They stood quiet, cowed, black-coated, as at a prayer-meeting in the roar, the eating, hoarse ferocity of burning. He'd done twenty yards along the street before he realised that it was not his factory that was alight, but the small builder's next door which presented a blank wall to his place. A cry broke from his mouth, and he heard it with amazement, a breath of relief, of deliverance, of selfish comfort.

He joined the crowd, three or four deep, and realised, in fact, that they were talking, curious half-sentences of commentary and longer paragraphs about the fire's discovery, the alarm, the arrival of the engines. Heat-reddened faces, a blast wiping the crowd, scorching their excitement.

For some moments he said nothing, observed the smart firemen with their tangle of hose, their air of detachment, of disenchantment even, as if the blaze didn't test them savagely enough, the leap of flames, the heavy bundling of smoke, like great flexible carved tree-trunks pushed from the windows. The whole operation seemed haphazard, as though the brigade had little idea what its opposition was, or how to smother it, but presumably this was not so. From a man next to him Riley learnt there was at least one other engine in the next street, and that the alarm had been given an hour or so back.

'Didn't seem so bad, they reckon, when the first engine came. Smoke, y'know. But not flames. Well, there must ha' been. By God, look at that.'

A ball of fiery smoke coughed from the windows into the air like some dulled enormous bauble.

'Gas,' the man said. 'Bleddy gas.'

The crowd chattered at the sight. A mother arriving to drag her children back for breakfast wavered for a moment, mouth gaping.

Riley, face stiff with heat, moved over to some person in authority, a small moustached man, shoulder to shoulder with a police inspector.

'Excuse me.' They both looked balefully in his direction. 'I'm the manager at Carnell and Bloom's, the place next door. Is there any danger there, do you know?'

'No, sir.' The voice twanged local in certainty.

'Shall we be able to open up?'

'Can't promise you that. What time d'you start? Eight. No. I don't think you'd better go in then. No.' He signalled to two of his men, sighed, rubbed his moustache.

'It won't spread there?'

'You make cardboard boxes, don't you? Go up like tinder. No, sir. Yo'll be all right. It's under control. Don't think you need worry.'

The man marched some yards away, was joined by underlings to whom he issued a series of orders, emphasised by pointings and gesturing, as if his few words with Riley had brought matters to a crisis or precipitated a new line of action. The firemen chased off and the officer disappeared smartly.

'A scientific business nowadays,' the police inspector said to Riley. 'Not like pre-war, at all. Fire-fighting's been organised.'

Riley, affably, scared, asked questions, was treated to a

lecture. Either he was too preoccupied or failed to hear in the hubbub, but he made little of the fluent, brusque delivery. The man talked, shook his gloves about, used both hands at points of special importance, but he did not realise that he might have been spouting Dutch for all the sense his listener made. Riley nodded, looked serious.

'My people will be turning up soon,' he said. 'I suppose I'd better get 'em together.'

'Where?'

'There's a little yard on the farthest side.' Riley pointed.

'Yes, sir. Right. But keep a watch. Fires are unpredictable as mad dogs. But I should think that's sensible.' They parted.

Riley, by the main factory gate, which he noticed had been broken open, saw the arrival of Dyson, rather late.

'What d'you think o' this, then?' Dyson said. 'Beats cockfightin'.'

Riley issued his instructions. Dyson was to stand at the gate to direct the rest towards the small yard. But the man seemed incapable of listening, braying out his barrage of questions: When did it start? How? Who called? Did anybody? Riley, annoyed, answered shortly, and repeated his orders. This time understanding printed itself with a hurt hangdog expression across the man's face. He'd do it. The manager imagined it. 'O'd Bundook's round the dustbin yard. You've got to report to him.'

No flames now? Perhaps the smoke ball had signalled the last of the conflagration's mastery. Smoke rolled, flowered, stemmed wide into the morning sky, a broad column, streaming up, and congealing in the still air before spreading like soft grey paint.

Riley collected his people, spoke brifly to them and asked them to wait in the annexe. They, he noticed, were apprehensive, as though he'd blame them or dismiss them. It seemed they hated the unusual, especially when it was announced by the manager. The fire officer approached, again said he saw no reason why they shouldn't go into the factory in an hour's time. He'd have a look himself before that, and they'd have to be careful.

'Fires have funny effects. Electricity, machinery, your sort of thing, are vulnerable to heat, y'know.'

Riley unlocked, had his premises inspected, ushered in his people who were warned by firemen of possible emergencies. Cowed, they began work; Miss Rogers tiptoed as if the floor would crash under he feet and removed the typewriter cover as though the metal underneath were red-hot.

Cooper was informed, said he'd come up.

His Daimler was much admired by the knot of people still watching the one fire-engine, and the manager put in a jovially aristocratic question or two to the firemen. He then clacked into Carnell's, looked at nobody, thrust himself straight upstairs to Riley's office, doffing lordly gloves.

He showed no pleasure at the report of absence of damage.

'Wonder how it started,' he said. Riley offered non-sentences, but Cooper had begun on vandalism, incendiarism, industrial sabotage. Riley listened carefully, sure he could learn from the man, but after a matter of minutes was convinced the boss had lost his reason. In Cooper's mind they lived in a country of savage anarchy, with groups blowing up, burning down factories, plant, transport. The motive, he claimed, was political, to disrupt and destroy so that international communism could pounce and occupy. The voice clicked in monotony, but the fabric or argument stretched unlikely. Riley, who voted Conservative, wanted to pick a ledger up and bang some sense into the idiot head. If all the Trotskyites or Chinese or their agents could manage to burn down in the whole city one workshop belonging to a small jobbing builder they weren't very adept at arson yet. He didn't tell Cooper, but politely produced biscuits with the managing director's coffee.

'You don't believe a word of this, do you, Riley?'
'No, sir.'

'You're an arrogant sod. Since you landed that tin-pot Furze job you're cocking your leg up more than's wise.'

'Yes, sir.'

'Yes, sir. Yes, sir. What the bloody hell does that mean?'

'Nothing.'

'Nothing? Your factory's damned nearly burnt down and you say it's nothing. Where's your sense? Thousands of pounds' worth of machinery are put at risk and you say it's nothing.'

'I shouldn't raise my voice if I was you, Mr. Cooper.'

Cooper's eyes bulged; the veins at his temple swelled ugly. He panted, without words at the quiet impertinence.

'What did you say?' The words edged, squeezed out so quietly that his body seemed to bounce in a St. Vitus's dance of fury round them.

'Don't raise your voice.'

'Riley,' Cooper said, angrier, calmer now, 'I don't like you.'

Riley folded his arms, insolently, and looked the director in the eye. In the army he stood to attention, answering an officer's rocket with a series of smart, impudent 'Sah. Yes, sah. Sah.' He knew the burst of temper was traceable to too much whisky in the mess, or bridge losses, or bad news, or a wife turning over from her drunken husband, and recognised that the system encouraged the superior rank to insult the lower with impunity, and this he did not mind. He could stand still enough, and listen to Erskine or his like swear sour guts out, and realise that behind the thin partition the lance-corporal clerks were taking in every word, and not care. That was military discipline. To allow one man to abuse another, orally, with rank as the only excuse for the outburst. The officer, it was acknowledged, mustn't indulge himself too often, and must make up with passes or blind eyes or a pint or two when he was invited into the sergeants' mess, and then fair enough. Senior N.C.O.s were made for field officers to swear at. Occasionally.

Occasionally.

In civvy street there were no such conventions. Riley waited.

'You're an ugly, jumped-up turd of a sergeant-major,' Cooper said.

'Sergeant,' Riley said.

'Eh?'

'Sergeant.'

'Sergeant, sergeant-major, all the bloody same. All piss and wind. All mouth and no head. You're not fit to sweep the floor.'

'Are you going to keep your voice down?' Riley said, amicably.

'I shall talk as I bloody well like.'

Riley walked over to his own desk where Cooper sprawled, circled it, and stood at the younger man's side. Very gently he put his hand on Cooper's lapel, quite flat, but pressing, hinting at weight. The other looked up, startled now, uncertain, seeing or understanding perhaps for the first time the breadth of shoulder under that nondescript suit, the girth of wrist, the full bone of the clenched, poised left.

'Take your hands off me,' he said, betraying himself in the squeak.

Riley lifted his palm to take the lapel delicately between the thumb and middle finger and then massage it, up and shortly, easily down. He was not the man to think out a tactical position rapidly; how he stood came slowly to him, late, painfully, but he realised now that he held advantage because he'd frightened his opponent. He did not hurry himself, therefore, stared at Cooper, who shifted slightly, not chancing his luck.

Riley let go the lapel, stepped back.

'You called me a turd,' he said.

'That's what you are.'

'If I lay one on you, you'll go right through that cupboard.'

'I shall sack you, Riley.'

'Try it.'

'There's no try about it. You've got your notice. And Furzes won't touch you. Don't forget that.'

'For what?'

'Incompetence.'

'Have you heard of wrongful dismissal?'

'Often,' Cooper said, smirking. 'You can try suing. Expensive. Won't stick, Mr. Sergeant.'

He rose, began to pull on his gloves.

'Sit down,' Riley said.

'Eh?'

'Sit down.'

'I'm on my way.'

Riley was on him, jerked him down by his coat. The man was heavy, inert, like a big concrete block, but the other exerted himself, worked, let his muscles rip so that Cooper sat, went, collapsed hurriedly, bang into the wooden chair, jarring, crack on to his spine, scraping the hams. The fat face was expressionless, flabbergasted with fright, yellowly pale.

'What do you want?' he said, in the end, unable to hold the silence.

'Sense.'

This time Cooper did not speak but made sounds, gasps, to demand elucidation.

'I want to know why you're on at me like this.'

Nothing. Perhaps he could not follow words.

'I've done nothing to harm you. Why do you call me a turd?'

Cooper fingered the polished desk, almost smiled.

'One thing and another,' he said. 'Piling up. And then the fire. I thought it was this bloody place burnt down.'

'So did I.'

'I took it out on you. I've nothing against you, man. You've done us pretty well here. But you stood there with a sneer a yard wide across your face and I couldn't stomach any more. Things haven't gone my way this last week, and then this, to top it all. The insurance companies and all the time-wasting and form-filling and interviews with assessors and unions up my nose. And I thought, "Christ, why can't Riley look after the place without bothering me? It bloody near runs itself." I was seething when I got here, worrying myself sick and everything's peaceful as a grave.'

That was apology enough.

'I know how you felt. When I turned into this street and thought we were on fire, I'd have murdered anybody for fourpence.'

Cooper smiled again.

'Forget what I said, Riley. I'll not balls you up. That's a thing to remember when you get to Furze's. There's no harm in playing fair. Hard on the buggers, but fair.'

'Will you have another cup of coffee?'

'No, I ought to be off. The stuff I've got tangling round my neck up there.'

'You need one, then. Sit down, sir.'

Cooper smiled, ballooned his stomach, while Riley rushed for Miss Rogers who'd boiled the kettle in readiness. She'd heard nothing, to guess from her demeanour. The two men sipped, had nothing to say, though Cooper now named Riley's replacement and promised he'd be able to say something definite about the factory's future inside the next month. But the atmosphere was amicable, without grudge. When he left, the managing director slapped his subordinate on the back at the door in full view of the machinists, and ordered him to keep in touch. He waved again from the Daimler.

Riley did not trust the man, but felt he'd done himself no harm. His whole ethic warned him against that assumption because he'd come up against some grotesque superiors in his army days and had been slapped down flat when he'd seemed safest. But that hot coffee and the figure learning to wave symbolised his security, even his manliness. He'd fought and won, and best managed it without hard feelings. God. He'd not enjoyed that and could still be out on his neck at the Labour Exchange.

Though he slept badly for a night or two, sweated nightmares, dozed on terror's edge in that callous cellar, his boss did nothing vindictive. Twice a week he summoned Riley and treated him to a homily on managerial responsibility, and once came down to Carnell's to announce from the floor that it now appeared as if the factory would be sold as a working unit and that they'd very likely keep their jobs. He did this ponderously well, so that there was a spontaneous round of applause and delighted chatter for the rest of the afternoon. Dyson swaddled his suspicion and Vaughan, contacted at the break from the street kiosk, phoned to say he believed Cooper told the truth. That day Riley first overheard discussion about his farewell party.

At home he was undecided about moving. There was a bungalow in the factory grounds which the Furzes offered him, but he turned that down and ordered a car. The brothers viewed the decision, he thought, with respect, and advanced sophisticated reasons why he was right not to live on the job.

He visited the O'Briens each week-end where he found Miss May installed as housekeeper. On the delivery of his Zodiac, which stood grandly in the street until he'd negotiated the purchase of a lock-up garage, he drove them gingerly up to the hospital to visit the wife who lay there now near-dead, after two unexpected heart-attacks. She'd die soon, in a week, a fortnight, O'Brien reported, with the sorrowful decorum of a husband, not the anticipation of one who'd chosen his next mate. Riley liked him for the hypocrisy, and the two men talked, over bottled beer in the spotless kitchen of Number 10, Stoney Street. Both were about to better themselves; both tried to avoid the appearance of liking the prospect.

'There's something about you,' O'Brien claimed. 'Don't know why you live in a street like this. Full of gas-men and thicks. No Pakis yet, though. If I were in your position, I'd set up in Woodthorpe.'

'What should I use for money?'

'You didn't buy that car of yours with shirt-buttons.'

May Bright spoke with a servant's deference, as if he'd kick her, or perhaps, he decided, from a sense of degradation. Her eyes, wide and black, under the scared hair seemed ready to glance to door or window. He could not joke with her, because she'd squeal into tears. Watching her red fingers clitter-clattering the tea-cups into saucers, he wondered what O'Brien had done with his naked photographs, whether they were wrapped still in the cupboard waiting for May, spring-cleaning, to pull them out, goggle or wrap them away and clap her lips shut.

On the other side the Scottens neglected him. They raised hands promptly, talked amicable trivialities, but showed no relish for his company. They seemed in no sense offended, but acted rather as if they'd found a new life-style, which did not include him.

'You never come in to see me, now,' he said to Alma.

'Don't have time, duck.'

'You had time before.'

'Now his mam's livin' with us, she can baby-sit while I go out at night wi' 'im. But I have to get on, make time up.'

'I see.'

'Do you miss me, then?'

He did not know what to answer, nodded glumly enough.

'When I used to come in,' she said, 'I always thought I was interrupting you. You looked that busy. Or you'd just straightened up and didn't want me spoilin' it.'

'I didn't think that.'

'Well, you looked it, then. When I come in to see your wife, she'd be glad. I liked her. It didn't seem fair she died.'

'No.'

'You were lost. You were. But your face didn't change. Nor show nothing. I said to our Arthur only the other day, "You know, I've talked to Mester Riley, and been to the pictures wi' him, but I don't seem to know 'im." And he said the same.' She delivered naïvely, not considering him.

234

'Well, s'll 'ev to goo. I c'n 'ear th'band startin' up.'

She rushed indoors, laughing, perhaps at herself.

Riley considered.

He'd made progress this last year so that when he joined Furze Brothers he'd practically double the salary he'd been drawing twelve months back. Moreover, he wasn't frightened of the job because he'd learnt to work things out, make his mind up, act fairly and not let his subordinates see how much he worried. Yet, and he admitted it, he'd not got on because of his deserts, or his ambition for that matter. If he'd been left on his own he'd still be pushing a pen under Addison's eye at the old place. Erskine had given him a lift and, at Cooper's insistence, Luke-Williams. He'd soon account for the money, or the new car would. In the army he'd had dizzy rises which had disappeared on nothing. But he was a manager, and, better, so regarded by his underlings. They didn't dislike him; his nickname showed that, but they stood aloof from old Bundook, treated him with care. When he was a boy, a man in his street had been promoted inspector on the buses, and though they'd all been glad to be spoken to by him, they'd eyed the officer's pockets and braided peak with awe. He was different; the man recognised it himself and moved to a house with a front garden.

Riley considered.

Now he'd made his grade, and would worry for his money, lie awake for it. He remembered one of Cooper's cynical fooleries: 'In business, Riley, in this country they'll promote a man if he shows he's got something about him, and if he shapes at his new level, they'll shift him up again, and up, and up, until he reaches a job at which he's no bloody good and there he'll stick. That's why we've got so many pricks in the senior ranges of management.' Perhaps that was true.

This was his home town. Here his father, an engine-driver, had hated his boy's signing-on in the army. In this place he'd been to school, boxing-club, paddled in the rivers,

kissed the girls in the cinemas and entries, swanked along
the streets on Sunday promenades. It seemed long enough
ago, his youth, and though he could sketch it in words it
was tenuous enough to elude him. In the mirror he held his
shoulders back, square, and he knew he could step it out still.
Sgt. Riley. Old Bandúq. The manager. His father, a snob,
would have been delighted and his mother obsequiously so.
No brothers, no sisters, no parents now, no children, he'd
a good job, a bit of property, health, an appearance as
smart as his false teeth.

Jean Oxford rang the doorbell.

She had dressed in blue, which suited her hair, now re-
styled, but not tinted out of its attractive grey.

'Frank told me last night about your new job.' Her congratulations were high-spirited, but forced. Praise pleased
him and when she listed his deserts he stuck his chest out.
She felt, she claimed, that she must come to speak to him
about his promotion.'

'Some weeks,' he said gruffly. 'My time's nearly up at
Carnell's.'

'I don't see much of Frank. I'm not living at home.'

'He's not?' he asked, mishearing.

'I've left,' she said. 'It's a fortnight now.'

This was why she'd appeared.

'How's that?' he asked. 'Why didn't you come back
here?'

'I've fallen in love.' She spoke prettily, with her shop-
floor accent, as if she'd chosen that sentence and kept it
ready to fling in his teeth. He sat down bewildered. What
did promotion mean in the face of this? How did he
counter?

'Tell me,' he managed, unsteady.

'It's my boss. Mr. Stainforth, who owns the two shops.
One I work in, one in Radford.'

'Is he married?'

'No. He's a widower.'

'Old, is he?'

'In his fifties. He's very nice. You'd like him.' The child-ish voice nettled. She'd lisp next. 'He lives out at Bearstead, in a bungalow.'

'You with him?'

'Yes. I do.' She smiled, candour of blue eyes. 'Well, it seems only honest.'

'How long have you been there?'

'Just over two weeks. We were rowing at home again, even when Frank gave that Rita up. I couldn't do noth-ing, anything, right for Ron. It got worse. He wouldn't give a hand. Then he kept his money.'

'Had you told him about this Stainforth man?' Riley asked.

'I did in the end. He didn't seem to care at first. Acted like a mardy kid, flouncing round the house, banging things down. But then one night he hit me. He'd been threatening he would. Told me to clear out.'

'And you did?'

'In the end. Not that night. I'd nowhere to go to. But I told Mr. Stainforth. He knew I'd been crying.'

'What had he to say for himself?'

'He put his arms round me.'

She talked on, rather low, but as if deliberately, to make him hear, to drag his attention down to her, about furniture, visits to a solicitor. She did nothing to shape the story, re-traced its contours, dodging as if to learn the lines.

'How long have you been in love with this chap?'

'I thought he was nice for a long time. Even when I was here with you.'

He hung his head. While she'd sheltered here, lain in his arms naked, she'd made a set at her boss.

'How old did you say he was?'

She hesitated, shamefaced.

'Well, he's sixty-two really. He doesn't look it. You wouldn't think he was that. He's very active.'

Riley made his mind up to cling to his scattered wits. This bitch thought nothing of him, dandled her love before him, did not notice his distress. He'd win, beat her. As he examined his condition, he seemed adolescent again, uncontrolled, thrashed by neglect, casual behaviour, selfishness.

'Ron knows you're out there?' She nodded. 'What does he say?'

'Nothing.'

'He's got somebody else?'

'I don't know.' She appeared shamefaced for a minute. 'You'll marry this Stainforth?'

'He'll marry me when I get a divorce.'

'Will you get that?'

'I've seen a solicitor.'

This burst of crude questioning settled him, so that now in spite of his puzzled unease he thought he might recover. He knew now he could hang on. That cellar with its puppets, endless horror, its annihilation of humanity, had disappeared; this hurt burnt sore, but he'd be himself again, a somebody, Bandúq, the gaffer. In the recognition of his safety he found no pleasure. He'd face this battering, this hiding, but in a week or two, or months perhaps, he'd stand up and count the scars, over it.

'Why do you tell me all this?' he asked her.

'I thought I owed it you.'

'Uh?'

'Well, when we lived here, we . . .' She blushed, stroked her hands, felt the tights about her knees.

'You're getting rid of two husbands? In fact.'

She didn't mind that, brazened it out, asked in her whisper if he loved her. Angry, he kept her waiting for the answer.

Riley could remember, in words, the fierce cold of his Christmas walk, the mist, the clay and sodden grass, that ghost of a farmhouse, ugly and deserted, a pinch of civilisation crumbling back into yokel earth, but the memory was warmly pleasant, accomplished, not to be missed. So with this shallow woman. In his present pain he'd have liked to cuff her, clout the expectant expression off her face, but he refrained, promising himself he'd one day be glad to be rid of the rammel.

'I don't know what love is,' he said, lying.

'I don't think you do.' She'd not got from him whatever it was she wanted, fawning, tears. 'You didn't really care for me.'

'Not like Stainforth?'

'No.' Explosion, strong as a bottle-cork. 'You only know about yourself and what you want and what's good for you.'

'Ay. Perhaps you're right.' Spring was on the way.

'Our Frank didn't like you. "There's something funny about him," he said.' She sounded quietly furious now, bubbling with an acid fervour of dislike. 'Nor Ron.'

'I'm sure you'd follow their advice.'

She broke off at that, and as she twisted her face, she managed, and dabbed away, a few tears. He watched the performance, sourly convinced he'd done well.

'Have you come in specially to see me?' he asked in the end.

'No. I had a little dressmaker's bill to pay. And Henry's called in on his brother. I'll meet him at eight.'

'Does he know you're here?'

'No.'

He was glad of that petty victory. Love was O'Brien next door at it with his bony miss while the wife he'd stripped died in a hospital's antiseptic stink. Or Alma Scotten's holey tights on his hearthrug. Or this woman shedding a tear in bed and then getting out to check with the mirror that her hair hadn't been spoiled. He'd learnt. Not much, not overmuch.

In the next few weeks he listened at presentation ceremonies to the inanities of colleagues and underlings. He knew how little they meant, even though the work-girls hadn't begrudged the bob or two collection. Miss Rogers, who'd brought him a fountain pen, couldn't conceal now that she concentrated on his successor, made herself ready to take each new word as her law. Bandúq is dead. He'd been

239

somebody; he'd be somebody, perhaps bigger, elsewhere, but at the moment, he, Jack Riley, was a nobody, a body. The position made the man. Neither love nor respect seemed in evidence, but he knew when he looked back he'd forge them, conjure them from nowhere, write them on himself. An old R.S.M. coming back to the mess was shaken by the hand and patronised even by his old toadies while the new men looked on in bafflement.

Jack Riley, man made of smoke.

'I ought to be going,' she said.

'Yes.'

'Will you forgive me?' What visit to the pictures accounted for that?

'Nothing to forgive.'

They shook hands, she kissed him and left.

He looked round, at the banging of the door, searching to find himself.